TRIP THROUGH YOUR WIRES

TRIP THROUGH YOUR WIRES

A NOVEL

SARAH
LAYDEN

Sarah Layden

EB
Engine Books
Indianapolis

Engine Books
PO Box 44167
Indianapolis, IN 46244
enginebooks.org

Also available in Hardcover and eBook formats from Engine Books.

Printed in the United States of America

10   9   8   7   6   5   4   3   2   1

ISBN: 978-1-938126-17-8

Library of Congress Control Number: 2015930801

For Tom

It stung like a violent wind
that our memories depend
on a faulty camera in our minds.
—*"What Sarah Said," Death Cab for Cutie*

But don't behave so childishly in [the] future,
or be so anxious to see the world;
for an honest maid and a broken leg are best at home,
a woman and a hen are soon lost by gadding,
and the girl who's anxious to see also longs to be seen.
—*Sancho Panza in* Don Quixote

PROLOGUE

SHE HAD SO FEW photographs from that year in Mexico, she sometimes wondered if it had happened at all. More than once, she'd been careless and exposed an entire roll of film to the light. She could just buy more, she reasoned, though she never did. The snapshots that did develop captured blurred subjects in unflattering shadows. And then there was Ben, insisting that she ought to live the experience, not photograph it like a tourist. After the first few months, she barely used her camera.

She told herself that she'd always remember the winding streets of medieval Guanajuato, the mountain range casting shade, creating places to hide. That she would remember Ben, backlit by the sun, leading the way down an alley, Mike trailing close behind. She was there, just outside the frame. She was supposed to stay a full year, but couldn't in the end. Her mind's film flapped at the end of the reel, blank and sputtering.

She thought that memory was hardened and permanent, something you could touch. An object as fixed as a photograph. But even pictures went missing. Mexico ought to have been embedded in her mind, but no.

•

Carey, usually cautious, had managed to get herself to Mexico, to Ben, who hadn't even known her. She'd labored over her study abroad application, almost certain she was applying to his program. There he was in glossy color: Ben and Mike pictured with others in a brochure for Intercambio, standing in front of a frighteningly beautiful cathedral. She'd seen another version of the photo on the wall at Prisanti's, the Oakview Mall pizza shop where Ben tossed dough. He posed alone in that snapshot. Carey didn't even have a job, didn't need one, her parents insisted. Not like Ben, who could reliably be found behind Prisanti's glass counter. She knew he'd graduated from Trinity Academy in Indianapolis and then moved on to University of Wisconsin. Reconnaissance via t-shirts and baseball hats. And then he was gone in late July, well before Wisconsin's first day—she had called the university. It was several weeks before Carey finally screwed up the courage to ask at Prisanti's about Ben, whom she had never spoken to but once had followed home, secretly. The young man working the register shrugged, pointed to the picture, and said, Back to Mexico.

Early in the fall semester, the brochure had been tacked on the bulletin board in the Languages building on campus. If this wasn't his program, she told herself, it would still be an adventure. Her parents were surprised, reluctant, and Carey found herself swallowing her own anxiety to build a case: what a good use of her Spanish minor, a worthwhile cultural experience, *life-changing*.

At that point Carey hadn't even known his name. Benjamin Curtis Williamson, read the obituary a few months later, and the headstone she'd never seen. Ben's disappearance, his actual vanishing act, would happen on a night when he was supposed to be with Carey. She'd expected Ben to come loping across the Jardín Unión to meet her. *I want to see you again*, he'd emailed. *Just you.* Long-legged stride, ducking under low-hanging tree branches. Curly hair a purposeful mess, maybe tied back with a red bandana.

She waited on a wrought-iron bench that welted the back of her favorite skirt, her runner's thighs. Her legs were tan, even in late February. The day was clear, high seventies; she'd run five miles, matching her high school cross-country pace. She was semi-attempting to read *Don Quixote* in Spanish, which she could barely parse. She kept it open on her lap for show. Then Mike emerged from the newsstand. Mike Gibley, Gibs, holding *Wired* magazine and a glass bottle of Coke. She waved him over. Oh, hey, he'd said, so casually, and she wondered if he knew Ben wasn't coming.

Andrea Cunningham, the director of their exchange program, would knock on Mike's dorm room door the next morning and barely register surprise that Carey was there. Carey looked at her flimsy purple skirt waiting in a polite circle on the dark tile floor. She was thinking about O.J. the rooster crowing from a nearby rooftop. He crowed at dawn. He crowed at dusk. He crowed repeatedly in the middle of the night. Carey had asked, Who keeps a rooster in the city? Mike snorted. It's Mexico.

She didn't live in the dorms. She lived in a walled-in house on the western hill; the Alarcóns were her host family. Carey hadn't bothered to let them know she wouldn't be home. They must have called Andrea, who was at the door in her baggy sweats and a blue oversized sweatshirt stamped with *Guanajuato* in peeling, glittery script. Lupe would have been polite but urgent. Lupe's son, Bartolo, four years older than Carey, might've sat on the roof in the cool night air, keeping watch. Andrea had seemed so much older than them, wiser, though she was only in her late twenties.

Andrea was at the door with tears in her eyes, and Carey was thinking about her own smeared makeup, her clothes, her alibi. But it wasn't about her. Ben was missing. His wallet had been found. And Carey rationalized the wallet away until Andrea told them, "They also found a shoe."

Carey felt a sickening burn at her throat and behind her eyes, and nothing could be done.

No. She wasn't remembering that right, either. What could have been done should have been done before.

Her synapses fired without her consent, a mind's movie projector replaying images she didn't want to see. She could push back these memories if she tried hard enough, if she made herself believe that she had control, like pressing a button on a laptop or VCR. Rewind again. Once more. Now pause here. There was Ben, her boyfriend, looming on the edge of the whitewashed rooftop, late afternoon sun haloing his hair. This rooftop wasn't theirs but they had claimed it, they could be alone, this was the third visit in a week. A small triumph. This time, to take pictures. Ben raised his camera to one expert eye.

"Wait," he said. As usual, she did.

He crossed the distance between them to brush a few stray strands of hair off her forehead, tucking them slowly behind one ear. His hand moved as it wanted, resting on the nape of her neck. She could make herself shiver, even now, remembering his hand on her skin.

"Better," he said. His own hair had a life of its own, curls out of control, more auburn that day than brown. She had to laugh at this image of him with a halo: St. Ben. No such person. Saints kept their word, kept their stories straight.

He returned to the roof's edge, balancing on the railing for a better angle. Seven years later and she cringed to remember it, but this wasn't how she'd lose him. Not that day and not like this. His feet turned out on the narrow railing like a dancer's, and he settled there, focusing his attention on her. Finally.

Carey wanted to create a lasting image. She clasped her hands in front, then let them hang at her sides. She retucked the hair that had already come loose in the mountain breeze. With his eyes on her, it took great concentration not to fidget.

"I don't know how you want me," she said.

Ben's expression softened. He smiled a two-dimpled smile for her, his real smile, and winked, his eye like a shutter.

"Just look at the camera," he said. "Just look at me."

An easy assignment. Carey had never told him that she'd been looking at him for some time, that she knew him from Indianapolis, that it was not random chance that had placed the two of them in Central Mexico, in the mountains, with American college students from across the country. She felt that she knew him. Back home, she had watched him walk across the mall food court to where a boy of about ten groped for spare change beneath the pop machines. Ben reached over the kid and fed quarters into the slot, then walked away without a word. Following his shift at Prisanti's, she had watched Ben flip through CDs at Oliver's Music, using slow but sure sign language to chat with a deaf customer. Or once, when she was running along 56th Street, he was driving a red sedan filled with little kids in soccer jerseys. She swore later to her best friend, Nicole, that they had made eye contact, even at forty-five miles per hour. She'd never tried to learn his name. Meeting him was not the point. Nor was stalking—she didn't consider her behavior that dire.

Just look at me.

He aimed and shot and nothing happened. He made a clicking sound with his mouth and turned the camera around to examine it, trying to advance the film. Ben's camera was his only concession to materialism. He wore the hefty, long-lensed model on a strap around his neck, bouncing against his white t-shirt. Walking the streets of Guanajuato, strangers would wave and smile and ask him to take their picture. Sometimes he would. This was his second year in the program. He was no tourist.

Ben's green backpack slouched along the wall, and he jumped down to retrieve it, ancient soccer shoes kicking up a tiny cloud of dust. He pulled out the Swiss army knife he'd bought from Bartolo's shop and traced the knife around the shutter button. He'd loaned the camera to someone, he said, and it hadn't been the same since. Crusty, he said. Ben buffed the lens with a special chamois and stuffed his tools into the backpack, on top of his journal. Ben always had the leather-bound book with him, always in his green backpack, and sometimes she or Mike would ask what he was writing about.

"The cost of bananas in Costa Rica."

"A manifesto on how to marry rich and live long."

"A list of my favorite breakfast foods."

He climbed back on the railing and applied gentle force to his prized possession—six months of pizza shop money, he once told Carey and Mike. Finally it clicked as he stared into the lens, capturing his self-portrait. For a split-second, he wobbled. The building was five stories high, narrow stone steps they climbed together, single-file. A place they'd been using lately for privacy, though they never discussed Mike's exclusion. Now Ben's arms splayed, the camera gripped in one hand. She cried out, and he made eye contact as he wavered. He had to have seen the terror on Carey's face. This was one odd comfort: that he understood how his absence would devastate her.

Ben fell forward to the roof instead of backward to the street. He went down on one knee to keep his camera from taking the hit, head bowed as if praying. She wasn't Catholic but had seen Ben genuflect at the Basilica, where she'd attended Mass with her host family. After a beat he raised his head, eyes guarded, and smiled a one-dimpled smile to reassure her. He stood, white pebbles lodged in his bloody knee, and limped forward. "Necesito curitas," he said, though he usually spoke English with her. She had no bandages, hadn't even carried a purse. They headed to the stairs, Ben limping with his knee straight.

They forgot about her portrait, the one he'd promised to shoot, documenting her first time abroad, and the rooftop, that plainest and most significant of landmarks. Ben forgot.

Even without a picture, she remembered. They were there. They were together. Without the record, the physical artifact, she could only imagine what was real and what had changed. Of course, this photo shoot wasn't just about him taking her picture. It would be a souvenir better than the stamp on her passport, placing her on his scene.

Her only proof lived in her memory. They were there together, she reminded herself. It was all she had. A few weeks after that, he'd be gone, erased from this world, as fast and easy as hitting the delete key. She could see her own finger hovering there above the button.

CHAPTER 1

THERE IS LITTLE PROTOCOL or fanfare for the replacement of a temporary employee by the person *she* replaced, but in Carey Halpern's case, it meant a goodbye lunch at a newly-opened Mexican restaurant, because it was nearby and her temporary boss had a coupon.

She wasn't being fired, no no no. She would be compensated appropriately, depending on the temp agency's policy for these sorts of things. It was just that her assignment turned out to be more temporary than originally expected, *see?*

She did.

She was alone, driving from the improperly quotationed Westside "Office" Building where she'd worked for the last four months with an option to renew, option now denied.

You can take off the rest of the day, too, Senior Vice President Dave Appel had said, *Paid, of course. So if you want to drive your car?*

She did.

The Westside Indianapolis landscape scrolled by, empty big box stores at the anemic mall, burger joints, strip clubs, Burritos as Big as Your Head, and the faded springtime detritus ground into the roadside: McDonald's cups and Coke cans and cigarette packs, windshield flyers and the occasional disintegrating diaper. This new Earth. This trash landscape.

Her boss had given directions: It's called Casa Colmo—you like

Mexican, right? Go about a mile past Don's Guns. She was passing the big signboard now, with the owner's properly-quoted slogan, "I don't want to make any money, folks, I just love to sell guns," which he'd recited on TV throughout Carey's childhood. The sign depicted a brown cartoon handgun.

Now that her precarious temp status had been revoked, there remained the question of paying her parents back. She pulled into the parking lot beside Dave Appel's Taurus and forced herself not to ding it. Not even as a fake accident. Progress.

She didn't have to go out to a free lunch. She debated leaving, but where would she go? Home to her parents, with whom she'd been living since she ran out of money and options in Chicago? She'd stranded Nicole without a roommate and the rent was too steep to manage alone. Nicole, back in Indy, had refused Carey's calls for months. Now she screened and sometimes called back.

The restaurant's door was etched glass, an image from another time. Carey touched the hood of her car with her fingertips, as if for support. A Mexican church: one she recognized. One she had been to. The Westside was becoming repopulated in a way that felt like a memory of a dream. One bodega displayed in its window five different flavors of Jumex in colorful cans. The Kroger stocked its shelves with novena candles. "Now Hiring" signs at auto body shops and drive-thrus also read "Se Emplea." And now this restaurant, showing her a place she'd once been.

Dave Appel was holding open the door for her, blocking the etching with his stocky body and gray London Fog raincoat. Light perspiration beaded his forehead.

"There's our favorite temp!" he said. "Hey. Lunch is on me." A fact he'd already noted before they left the "Office" building. Where she used to "work."

Bob and Sue from accounts were already settled into a booth and crunching complimentary chips. Free on top of free. They were here for the meal, for the camaraderie Dave Appel attempted to cultivate in his team; Carey had worked with them in brief and insignificant ways during her assignment. Collating, faxing, copying. The pair sat in the booth's interior, against windows where starched café curtains hung, the red, white and green mirroring Mexico's flag. The thin carpet bore outlines of a manual sweeper. The air was thick with frying tortillas and the overpowering chemical scent of the new carpet.

"Nice," Carey said.

It was 12:06 p.m. They were the only customers.

"Great news about Felicia," Bob said around a mouthful of chips, as if Carey weren't even there. Sue elbowed him. "Sorry," he said.

Carey had filled in while Felicia had undergone chemotherapy for breast cancer. Now she was in remission and ready to reclaim her rolling desk chair and plain-paper fax machine. She would wear a headscarf, Dave Appel had told Carey while essentially firing her. The occasional hat. What could Carey say to that?

"No, it *is* great news," Carey said. "I mean, how fantastic that she's better now. Really awesome."

Dave Appel, a man Carey scarcely knew, eyed her. In the months of working as his office assistant (the term "secretary," he'd told her, was demeaning), she hadn't learned how to read his gaze: there was hunger there, or longing, or maybe he needed new glasses. Perhaps he was searching for Felicia in her face and gestures and expressions and wardrobe, and always coming up short. Carey instinctively knew "really awesome" was not a phrase Felicia would have uttered, and Carey's skirt, a wool blend that both looked and felt lumpy, was not an item Felicia would have worn. She stuck to "tailored business casual," Dave Appel once confided, miming air quotes, and was a "real team player." The phrases stuck in her mind. The lumpy skirt had been a mistake. But since she'd spent the money, she made herself wear it. "Not the most flattering," her mother had said. "But once you get a job you actually care about, maybe you'll start caring about your appearance."

The hostess, a young woman with dark hair hanging loose down her back, brought menus to the table. "Gracias," Carey said by rote, her accent perfect. The woman smiled and bowed, then gave the workers standing around the bar—all men—a look that said Get to Work. They moved into various nonessential tasks: rearranging salt and pepper shakers, re-wiping spotless surfaces, straightening a chair.

"Muy bueno," Dave Appel said to Carey. "Mucho talent. You'll get a new job-o in no time."

Bob snickered, but Dave Appel wasn't making fun. He was making an effort. "Trabajo," Carey murmured. "Job is *trabajo.*"

Their waiter stood before them with a pad of paper and a pen, grinning broadly. His ears stuck out like butterfly wings. His features identified him as the hostess's kin.

"Ready?" was all he said. *Ray-deee?*

They ordered specials by number, and their burritos and tamales and plates of tacos appeared in ten minutes. The waiter brought the items on a large tray, and another waiter carried pitchers of water and pop to refill their empty glasses. His floppy dark hair fell over his dark eyes, drawing attention to them.

"Gracias," Carey said, trying for eye contact. Both men only nodded and smiled and walked back to the bar to join the rest of the underworked staff. The one with the hair glanced back at Carey, but only for a moment.

Sue took a bite of refried beans and moaned. "I'm not on a diet today. It's settled."

"You should think about our company Wellness Plan," Dave Appel said. "Never diet again!"

On two televisions fixed above the bar, the local newscast played, the volume low. The Pacers were in the playoffs. Something menacing about manure lagoons. The murder rate was lower than last year at this time. And speaking of murder, the male anchor said, handing the story over to Maria Cortez, who was broadcasting live in front of the justice building downtown.

You knew it was serious because Maria Cortez, known for her bubbly on-air persona, wore a suit and a frown. She still exuded her usual nonthreatening aura that lured American and Latino viewers in equal numbers.

In her manicured hands was a blue U.S. passport. Her tomato-red nails raked the pages. The hostess who had seated them lifted the remote control and raised the volume. She swung her blue-black hair over one shoulder, standing straighter.

"I think you would have enjoyed working with Felicia," Dave Appel said. "She's very motherly, very kind."

"Shh," Carey said, rude enough for her whole table to quiet and follow her eyes to the TV, where Maria Cortez held court.

"Fifteen U.S. passports were found inside an abandoned suitcase in the Phoenix airport," she intoned. "But Indianapolis authorities weren't prepared to discover one belonging to an area man."

The news anchor opened the passport cover, revealing Ben's full name in all caps. BENJAMIN CURTIS WILLIAMSON. Carey's pulse and adrenaline surged, and she believed for just an instant that this had all been a mix-up. There was Ben's passport, there was his name. The document proved his life.

She'd never seen his grave or headstone, but she knew they existed, his name there likely in all-caps, too. Every reminder of Ben's life brought a reminder of his death.

Maria Cortez was here to remind her, too. "I'm holding the passport of a man whose senseless killing seven years ago remains a mystery to this day," she said, eyes gone sad.

Her fingers, previously covering the passport photo, moved gracefully away. The photo showed a Mexican man with a thin face and rictus grin, perched atop Ben's name. So clearly not Ben that Carey could see little else.

But Maria Cortez wasn't done. Illegal, she spoke, and immigration, and murder, and Guanajuato, and unsolved, and 1996. She worked one sharp red nail beneath the photo, making eye contact with the camera. A sheriff's deputy hovered at her shoulder, ready to grab the evidence she probably shouldn't have been holding anyway. Maria Cortez turned her shoulder slightly to block the deputy from the shot.

She gave a solemn nod, lifted the small square photograph, and beneath was a picture of Ben, with short hair and a serious expression and something of a smirk in his eyes.

Next to her in the booth, Sue, mother of three teenage boys, crossed herself. The gesture reminded Carey of Lupe, her host mother, who was in near-constant conversation with God. "That boy's poor mother," Sue said. Carey gave her a withering glance. What about her?

Carey Halpern, whose heart was stuck in her throat like a flapping bird, whose ears thrummed with pumping blood. The low din of the restaurant workers cut through her brain static.

"Yo lo conozco," they whispered. "Es el fotografo." The young woman told them all to shut up, and the bartender grabbed the remote control from her and clicked. Carey envied the ease with which he shut it off.

Dave Appel telegraphed an expression of concern, which Carey ignored.

"Change it back," Carey said, once in English. And then again, in Spanish.

Nobody did.

She veered onto the exit ramp near the auction house, the I-65 stretch named after famous son Kenneth "Babyface" Edmonds, the musician. All of Indianapolis was in quotes, as if it could not decide what it was or wanted to be. It was not so hard to declare her old building an office, or herself an employee. Either one was or one wasn't. The highway, "The Babyface," ought to have had a bit more dignity.

She was not panicking. This was not hyperventilation.

It began raining; the April sky dropped low. Bad news on a clear, sunny day makes less sense. Almost two years ago, that September morning when the planes were launched into buildings like bombs, the blue sky was spotless, stretched tall as a movie backdrop. That had been a tragedy. And this? She did not know how to categorize what she'd learned at the restaurant.

She drove down College Avenue, where two Hispanic men loaded a brown plaid couch onto a pickup truck. She knew, instinctively, that they were Mexican. Most of the city's new immigrants were. Four more men filed out of the row house with the cushions on their heads, like a line of ants with bits of leaves.

Her goodbye to Dave Appel, Sue and Bob was awkward, flailing, un-Felicia-esque. There was a form she was supposed to sign for her last paycheck and she had not signed it, did not want it. She'd barely eaten her enchiladas. The waiter asked if something was wrong with the food. She shook her head, trying to find answers in his eyes.

Driving the wobbly ring of I-465 could waste an hour or more, but she was low on fuel. The Circle City, they called it, for the brick road around downtown's Soldiers and Sailors Monument. She had lived here all her life, not counting her abbreviated year in Mexico, or her Chicago experiment with Nicole. Here in the Circle City: a place that repeated itself. A car scene in a low-budget film, endlessly looping the same increasingly obvious background.

Driving distracted her. The glaring neon signs and the boom box of the Dancing Man at 38th and College, the jangle of his purple velvet Crown Royal tip bag. She locked her doors.

The radio played an old song, something by The Doors. She remembered all the words. She loved The Doors, so much that she could not listen to them. She pushed a button and a new song played.

Eventually she was heading north, the car pointing home. North always led to home. The guiding light of the north star. *El Norte*, the film about horrifying border crossings to the U.S. She had been so sure, all those years ago, that traveling south would lead her somewhere. Her compass was off.

Home. More specifically, Brian and Gwen Halpern's home. Carey's father planted himself in his study each night, legal briefs cluttering the desk, "catching up." But Carey could see the computer screen reflected in the window behind him, the colorful pixilated cards of a solitaire game. Her mother frequently was out, as if "out" were a named location.

Many nights, most nights, Carey lurked in online chat rooms. Occasionally someone would see her screen name, "La mujer," and try to start a conversation. Usually in Spanish. Her language had rusted over, clunking through her head. She watched the scrolling text of flirtations.

Benson689: Mujer, you there?
La mujer: Yep.
Benson689: How you feeling tonight?

In a matter of minutes, maybe two back-and-forths, she'd be propositioned, asked to join a private conversation. The Internet had rooms and rooms, dark corridors she could barely picture. Sometimes she went, knowing better. Sometimes she logged off, left them hanging in the middle of their fantasies.

Benson689: I'm in Tucson. So what do you do there in Indy?
La mujer: Office temp. For now. Not very exciting. You?
Benson689: Tell you what I'd like to do. Lick you raw til you scr—

A clean break, easy as clicking a button.

She anticipated as she arrived that her parents would be enmeshed in their private, individual cocoons, and she could retreat to her bedroom with a bag of chips. She rolled into the garage's third bay, beside her mother's Jetta and father's Cherokee. She entered the house and walked into a steamy gust of air: broth and wine and chicken and herbs. On the rare occasions Gwen Halpern cooked, she cooked with wine.

Gwen and Brian sat across from each other at the table, chewing silently, politely. Her father, in jeans and a sweatshirt, must have gone running before dinner. Flushed cheeks, his mussed blond hair darkened by sweat, the slight gray prominent as tinsel. Her mother still wore work clothes: a long, flowing skirt of iridescent purple, a fitted black sweater, and looping silver chains from her store, Finer Things. Despite never exercising, Gwen Halpern remained naturally slim. Carey had gained a few pounds in the years since she stopped running. She had competed for years at cross country and track, and in college she ran almost every day. Even in Mexico. But she gave it up, after. Her runner's body was hard to remember. She'd hidden the bathroom scale in the linen closet. She self-consciously tugged her sweater away from her stomach.

A place was set for Carey at one end, her usual seat on the rare occasions the family ate together.

"Am I late?" Carey asked. "I didn't know you were making dinner."

Gwen acted surprised. "Really? Guess I should feed my family more regularly," she said, glancing at Carey's skirt.

"Bet you had a busy day," Brian said. "Usually I can set my watch by you."

Something folded within her. Dismissed from her clockwork job: unsprung. She worked on establishing a neutral face, the kind of mask her mother had been wearing for years.

"I was pulled in to help on a big project," she lied. "Sorry I didn't call."

Her parents exchanged a look. "You're an adult," her mother said. "No need to call. It's helpful in the sense that keeping dinner hot is helpful. But that's what microwaves are for. Convenience. I wouldn't want to inconvenience you."

Her mother smiled with exaggerated patience. "The chicken's probably a little dry."

Carey smoothed her skirt with both hands and sat down at the end of the table.

"Forget all that," her father said. "You're a go-getter, kiddo, getting the hang of the working world. That calls for a toast."

Gwen snorted into her glass of pinot grigio. Brian ignored her, filling Carey's empty glass. Her mother held out her own goblet for a refill; she drank, made a face, then took another sip.

"To Carey," her father said. "Our little girl is all grown up."

"She's twenty-eight," her mother said. "So, yes, she is, isn't she?"

Carey barely listened. Her mind circled back to her lack of job, to the restaurant, to Ben's passport, to Ben, to herself in Mexico, to Mike. Where was he now? Had he seen the news? She rose slightly from her seat, as if to call him, though of course she didn't have his phone number. She had told him, years ago, to stop calling. Her parents mistook the gesture and lifted their wine glasses. Carey followed suit.

"Cheers," she said, clinking glasses. "And thanks. You've helped me a lot."

Gwen's gaze softened. "We're glad about your job, honey. Really."

Carey sat down and launched into a too-detailed story about the project she'd allegedly been working on as Dave Appel's assistant. Databases, spreadsheets, coding, line items. Her mother's expression glazed over, probably running mental inventory of her stock at Finer Things, and her father nodded at each description, reaching for seconds of chicken. Carey said she'd most likely be home late all week, so they shouldn't wait on her for dinner.

"You can help us celebrate tonight, then," her mother said.

"Oh?" Brian asked. "What are we celebrating?" His wife's eyes registered hurt, disbelief, and seconds later she slipped on the invisible mask.

"Would you believe I forgot the vegetables," she said. "Excuse me." Her tone indicated that this was the social gaffe of the season. She carried her nearly full plate to the kitchen. The lid of the stainless steel garbage can clanked open and shut.

Carey took in the tablecloth, the white tapers lit and gleaming in silver candlesticks. Cloth napkins instead of paper. Usually they dined separately, in shifts on the stools surrounding the kitchen island. If they ate together, the meal came from boxes and bags: pizza, rotisserie chicken, sandwiches in butcher paper. Gwen, an excellent cook, had catered to her husband and only child for many years. Once the gift shop took off, she rarely touched a pan. In junior high, Carey mastered the art of microwave cooking. Microwaved scrambled eggs for dinner were her specialty.

Now Carey chewed the chicken, which was in fact dry from reheating. She drank more wine to wash it down. Her father was doing the same.

"Mom's in a good mood," Carey said.

Usually sarcasm made her father laugh, but he didn't answer. His eyes were on the kitchen door, awaiting his wife's return. His face drooped like a basset hound's whenever he was tired or upset. It looked that way often, she'd noticed since moving home.

"Brian?" Carey stage-whispered. She often called her parents by their first names and had for years. "Are you in the dog house, or am I?"

He tousled his own hair for a long moment. "That's a good question," he said.

Gwen's high heels drummed on the polished hardwood floor, and she swept into the room wearing her beige trench coat with the oversized black leather belt. She carried a Tuscan-style bowl filled with fingerling potatoes and fresh green beans. Out of season in April. A product of—where? Mexico? She set the bowl in front of Carey.

"I have lost my appetite," she said. "But no sense in letting perfectly good food go to waste."

Carey attempted and failed to catch her father's eye; he was staring after his wife's retreating form as if willing her to turn around. But he said nothing, and returned to his meal with studied interest. The kitchen door slammed, and the garage door rumbled upward.

"Potatoes?" he asked Carey, offering the bowl.

She shook her head, waiting him out.

"I seem to have forgotten an anniversary," he finally said. "That's the only thing I can think of." Their anniversary was four months ago, in December. Carey was still in Chicago then, failing to convince Nicole, her oldest friend, that she'd find a way to make rent.

"I'd be mad, too. You're four months late, and the woman can hold a grudge. Believe me."

"I got her a card," he said, waving his hand. "This is the anniversary of when we met. No, wait. Not today, yesterday."

"Then she forgot, too," Carey said.

Brian forked more potatoes into his mouth than was polite. He chewed and chewed as the Jetta's engine revved, the noise fading in the distance. He swallowed his food and took a long sip of water, not wine. Finally he looked at his daughter as the house's silence covered them both like a layer of dust.

"And then she remembered," he said.

Carey wasn't hungry but brought a bag of potato chips to her room, anyway. She logged on to her usual chat room, where Benson689 and three other users were idle. She searched for the ad she'd noticed a few days before. TheOldSchool.com, a high school reunion website, offered a free trial for chat room users. Carey clicked "yes" to the offer, "yes" to the terms of agreement. Yes, yes, whatever you say. Next screen.

She went to the University of Wisconsin reunion page and scrolled to Ben's year and name. She searched these types of sites for him occasionally, as if to confirm that he actually was dead. Like his murder had been a mistake, it had never really been him, and here he was listing his likes and dislikes and current career and family if applicable.

His name was listed with a parenthetical shushing: (Deceased.)

Carey exhaled hard and fast, like she'd been punched in the gut. What did she expect? That his email would be linked, that he'd want to get in touch with classmates and talk about the old times? God. She was as bad as people who earnestly used Ouija boards.

She moused up the alphabet. Since she was here, she rationalized. Since the chat room was quiet. Since she had to, she did not acknowledge, not fully.

There was Mike Gibley. His name was highlighted, hyperlinked, an active user. Mike was Ben's classmate, roommate, best friend. After Mexico, Mike continued to email her, though she'd stopped answering. He'd kept calling until she told him not to.

His profile said he lived in Chicago. Business degree, cum laude, minor in computer science. He liked artisan pizza, whatever that was, and craft beer, ditto. The band Counting Crows was high on the list of favorites. He was single.

SEND MIKE GIBLEY A MESSAGE? She clicked the button. Before contacting him, she had to create an account. Under Profile Name, she opted for her chat room moniker: La Mujer. She filled in Indianapolis, IN for location and added nothing else.

In the blank message box, she typed:

Mike,

I hope you remember me, though Mexico was a long time ago. I need to talk to you. Ben was in the news today—they found his passport. Maybe you heard about it, or saw the photo stuck on top of Ben's. This is totally surreal.

Write me.
Carey

Soon, she thought. Now. She clicked around the site for a few minutes, learning Nicole had completed her profile with very sincere, paragraph-length responses, and included a glamour-shot picture of herself dancing in a black leotard and flimsy skirt. She left Nicole's page and hit refresh multiple times but there was no reply. She switched off the computer and pushed the warm laptop to the other side of the bed.

She slept, dreaming of nothing. Or dreaming of Ben, who cradled her head in his hands, gazing down at her. Her sleeping mind, more present than waking life. The dreams happened like real time. Her arms moved as if underwater. Her hair blew like a fashion model's in front of a fan. He stood there with a camera, wearing a once-white T-shirt coated in what looked like blood, but he reassured her: No, it's only ketchup. Taste. She leaned forward. Licked.

The next morning, a smattering of her own blood speckled the pillow and crusted beneath her fingernails, the back of her head a small mess of scrapes. This happened every few months. Her scalp stung under the hot water of the shower. Eventually the water rinsed clear. Seven years of these dreams: often enough that they felt routine. Each time, she tried to remember the plot of her sleeping stories, made hazy and polluted by her waking mind, but she couldn't. Wouldn't.

After throwing on jeans and an old track t-shirt, she meandered downstairs and stepped on the nail sticking out of the loose floorboard at the bottom of the stairs, which made a small red dent in her insole but didn't break the skin. The coffee percolated, frozen waffles sprung from the toaster. Out the kitchen window, small buds populated the forsythia; a robin perched, placid, on the empty feeder. She'd lost her job, but she didn't have to pay rent. She had a window to look out of. An empty, quiet house, now hers for eight hours.

The Halperns' house had been built in the late sixties, and the neighborhood abutted the marshy area near Eagle Creek, in the suburbs on the city's far Northwestside. Despite weekly visits from a cleaning woman, a damp, moldering smell remained. The décor was impeccable. Even the old items in her parents' house appeared new, a catalog home. Things to be admired but not touched, as she'd been admonished her entire life. She twined her bare feet on the stool's rungs, glancing over the newspaper's comics, her horoscope. "Taurus: No matter how intense the mood between you and a loved one, courageously communicate your feelings."

Carey had taken the phone off the hook in case the temp agency called before her parents left for work. Daytime TV shocked her with its dullness; the suspense of game shows displayed only the guilelessness of the contestants. The second Iraq war, now one month in, had not hampered Americans' right to compete for valuable prizes on national television. Solitaire on her father's computer lasted an hour, his high scores unbeatable. She took the want ads to her room. Rather than read them, she spread the newsprint on the carpet and painted her neglected toenails a deep crimson. Still no reply from Mike Gibley, and though it had been less than twenty-four hours, she resented his silence, assigning it meaning and weight.

In the early evening, to keep up the ruse of gainful employment, she changed into work clothes: black pants, a cream mohair sweater, and nylon trouser socks. Her toenail polish had not fully set and the socks kept sticking. No family dinner that night, just the low rumblings of her parents' voices, a quiet fight in her father's office. She made a sandwich with leftover chicken, spooning globs of mayonnaise to counter the dryness. She waited for someone to bear witness to her office apparel. The sweater shed its fur. Her lap was covered in a fine coat of cream fuzz; she'd have to borrow a lint roller.

The house was silent. A parental impasse. She grew tired of waiting. At the foot of the stairs, she snagged her sock on the loose nail in the floorboard. Carey lifted her foot to check for a wound, and tore a gaping hole through the thin material.

In her room she lifted the laptop lid for the thirty-seventh time that day and refreshed TheOldSchool.com's website.

Carey,

Do I *remember* you? Jesus H. Christ. I actually looked you up but didn't realize I needed a secret code. La Mujer, then. OK. Yes. Sure. Anyway, Carey (or cruel joke-playing person), I'm coming down to Indy this weekend to visit Ben's parents. We'll talk then. No excuses, mujer. Pretty please.

I want to see you.

Gibs

He left three different phone numbers where he could be reached. Carey's heart thudded in her ears. Through the computer, Mike Gibley appeared in her room, floating in the air, in her memory. She'd found him. He'd returned.

All that we long to suppress does.

CHAPTER 2

IT WAS LATE WHEN they finally arrived at the exchange school that interminably hot August. The bus ride took more than five hours from the Mexico City airport. In the capital the traffic oozed like lava, allowing Carey plenty of time to translate the billboards for ice cream and sex shops and telenovelas. A Plexiglass case housed a bullet-proof statue of an indistinguishable saint, perched on the high stone wall of a bodega. Green Volkswagen bug taxis swarmed the streets. For sale on the sidewalk: reclining, reconditioned automobile seats. Nearly forty minutes after entering the Capital, the bus emerged from the Districto Federal's perpetual smog cloud, and Andrea Cunningham, the American program director, pointed out they were heading the wrong way.

Cesár had driven south to Cuernavaca before turning west. Outside of the city, he explained, the day was shaping up to be clear and they'd have a good view of the volcanoes. You couldn't count on that happening again, he told Andrea, who'd been checking her watch. The bus's broken door hinge squeaked and the door swung open when Cesár rounded a corner. Pairs of American eyes followed the door's movement.

"Ees OK," the bus driver told Andrea. She frowned briefly then tried a chipper expression, murmuring about locking the door. Cesár just shook his head. Held his palms up and shrugged.

Later, while the other students were dozing or plugged into music, Carey paid attention when Cesár spoke.

"La mujer," he said.

Carey looked up and caught his eye in the rearview mirror. He pointed out the window at the mountains while driving one-handed on the curving road. "La mujer dormida."

The sleeping woman, Carey translated. A rolling stretch of mountain, purple in the dusk against a darkening sky, curved like a woman asleep on her side. An unbreakable, impenetrable mold of breast, a hint of hip, feet. A sleep carved from rock hundreds of thousands of years ago. The Sleeping Woman was the oldest, most constant thing Carey had ever seen.

She did not yet know that the woman had a name, Ixtaccihuatl, or the myth that she was a princess who died from sorrow, falsely believing her lover had died in battle. Carey would learn that when the warrior returned and found the princess dead, he built her a pyramid, watching over her from the twin peak nearby. In the winter, glaciers formed on her breasts. Beneath, buried deep in her core, the molten life of a volcano bided time.

Carey wished for her camera, packed in her luggage below, though she knew the motion of the bus and the lighting and the film speed would blur any attempt to capture something as beautiful as the Sleeping Woman.

A pair of students began singing in Spanish; Carey understood only half the words. When she next looked out the window, the shape in the mountains had disappeared.

Carey's head ached from altitude changes as the bus bumped and curved up the mountain road. The landscape was worth a little pain. A few students chatted or slept, but Carey sat alone, gaping out the window at the donkey alongside the highway with a man in a cowboy hat, and the eucalyptus brush and alternating green and brown hills. Isolated, crumbling houses dotted scrubby pastures. She'd lived in Indiana since birth, yet she'd never seen anything so rural and remote. The information packet had detailed that students would have email access for the first time in the exchange program's history. In a place where people still used donkeys as transportation.

Outside the bus window, roadside stands glowed against the darkening sky. Racks of candy and bottled drinks flashed by. A shantytown of tarpapered plywood shacks clung to a patchy hillside. Hovels like she'd seen on evening news programs after war or natural disaster. Third World. Yellow sheets printed with the name "Bardahl" were pasted over some of the structures, the same motor oil logo emblazoned on race cars at the Indy 500. She glimpsed an orange fire with shadowed figures huddled around it between shacks. Nearby, a clothesline held what looked like dirty rags.

Pictures she'd seen of Guanajuato had featured colorful, crowded adobe houses, medieval architecture, churches with gilt altarpieces. Among this rubble and these huts, something close to terror clutched her.

Then they were pulling into town, through the subterranean highway, emerging into the winding, cobbled streets. The students unloaded their bags at Intercambio and shivered in the cool August night. Weak yellow lights in wire cages cast dim shadows on the side of the bus, the suitcases and duffels piled in a small mountain on the curbside. Inside the building, host families waited to claim their students. Teachers looked over the straggly, wilted crop of newcomers. Andrea Cunningham alternately hugged the staff and checked off names on her clipboard.

Conversation in Spanish, glances in Spanish, laughter and body language in Spanish. The building spoke Spanish, with its glowing fire safety signs: "Salida," "Entrada." Spain was in the building's regal stucco and brick façade, in the moss that clung to shady stone.

In the parking lot, other American students shrieked a non-accented "Hola!" to their new Mexican parents and siblings. The noise bounced off the tile floor and brick walls. Host families held up signs, American names black-markered on flat pieces of cardboard.

Carey's underarms began to perspire. She wasn't ready to be claimed. She'd been on the plane and the bus for hours, almost a day, suspended in travel, barely thinking about the year to come. She hadn't missed her parents. Not for the first leg of her journey, at least. Now she needed to be alone. She wasn't going to cry, and if she was, no one would see her. There were, she knew from experience, many ways to hide. She stepped to the other side of the bus, blocking herself from the loud scene at the school.

Ben was there. She didn't know his name yet. But she knew him. The curly brown hair, the green eyes that crinkled at the corners, the long arms that stretched skyward to catch pizza dough. She took a step backwards. She'd engineered this meeting, but hadn't let herself believe it would actually occur. She and Nicole had made up nicknames. Pizza Guy, then The HPC, which stood for Hot Preppy Catholic, after spotting him in a Trinity Academy soccer sweatshirt. Here he stood, in the parking lot of her Mexican school, without pizza dough, without Trinity gear, fiddling with the metallic flashlight he'd unclipped from his belt. He belonged in the States, in her city. Months later, in her lowest moments, she would wish that he'd stayed there. She could not imagine Mexico without Ben. After, she had to recreate Indianapolis without him.

They'd never spoken. She'd imagined a thousand conversations and even acted out lines alone in the car, but never worked up the nerve. Now she straightened her black T-shirt and her spine and smiled.

"You don't smoke, do you?" he asked. He stuffed the clip-on flashlight into his pocket and pulled a pop bottle from his green backpack.

"No," she said. "Why?"

"You're hiding. That's a smoker kind of thing to do."

She bristled, happily. He had tried to guess her. "You wanted to bum a cigarette, didn't you?" she asked. This forwardness was a surprise. She tended to gravitate to a room's corners.

"I don't smoke," he said.

"And I wasn't hiding," she said.

They both smiled. He nodded towards the school building and raised his thick eyebrows. "You getting a host family?"

Surely she would have spotted him if he had been on the bus. Did he recognize her? He spoke familiarly, watched her with interest, but that meant nothing. Everything.

"Of course I am," she said, cartoon-character fast.

He uncapped the Coke and took a swig. Amused, he idly wiped his mouth.

"Hey," she said, "can I have some of that?"

He passed the bottle without hesitation. She drank, silencing herself. They stood face to face, closer than they'd ever been. Sweat trickled into her bra. She had an urge to touch his hair. She wanted to mess it up.

But she didn't. She wouldn't have. Instead, the sugar rushed straight to her head, and she bent over quickly at the waist as the familiar black danced across her eyes. Sometimes she'd get a head rush after finishing a long run, six or seven miles. Her high school cross country coach claimed she'd get a cramp in her side from doubling over so soon after running. She never listened. She knew her body and what it needed.

When she leaned over, her head struck Ben's forearm. Their first contact. Blood rushed to her cheeks, her forehead.

"It's the altitude," he said. "Happens to everybody. You okay?"

She assured him she was fine. She breathed for a moment before slowly rising, waiting for the black spots to fade. She heard the shuffling of footsteps before she connected them to a person. Mike Gibley, standing before her for the first time, wearing a tight t-shirt that showed off his muscles. Carey remembered her first impression: cocky, unimpressed with her. But she'd been wrong. He was like a bird, feathers puffed out to twice its size, preening. A different creature lived underneath, delicate-boned.

"Who's she?"

Mike's first words, both to her and about her. Ben and Mike had been inseparable for three years, when they were paired as roommates in their freshman dorm at Wisconsin. If Ben was singular, unmistakable, Mike was the opposite. He stood out in Mexico: blond hair, pasty mixed-European skin turned ruddy in the sun. A uniform of a T-shirt and khaki shorts, a ball cap. Back in the States, he would've been at home in a frat house, at a Dave Matthews concert, driving a used Chevy with the windows rolled down. Too common to notice. After Carey was shipped back to Indianapolis, she saw his plain, indistinguishable features in men on the street, at the store. The clear, close-set blue eyes; a straight nose with a pushed-in end; the small mouth, a thin little line, the slightly fuller lower lip. She searched instead for Ben, someone she could never find. Even when he stood directly in front of her, with Mike asking, *Who's she?*

"Some girl," Ben said. "She stole my Coke."

Ben said *some girl* like a compliment. An event had happened, a ping, as if Ben were a violin and a string had snapped loose. Mike crossed his thick arms over his chest. *I know Ben better than anyone*, he would tell Carey months later, staking claim. He and Ben had studied at Intercambio the year before. At Wisconsin, they spent years sitting across from each other in the dining hall and the Lucky Pub, where the waitress would bring two tall mugs of beer before their coats were off.

The caffeine went to Carey's head. She smiled at both men: Ben, a familiar stranger, his flicker of interest like a permission slip. Stocky, hesitant Mike, always waiting for her next move. For the first time, she could do what she wanted. Going away to Millerton College in Dayton was not independence, as it turned out, but disguised responsibility. A dorm, followed by a perpetually dirty apartment. Comfortable, safe, boring. But the plane and bus had somehow delivered her not to a destination, but to another version of herself.

Adrenaline signaled in her hair follicles. A light sweat beaded on the small of her back. In her memory of this moment, Ben and Mike were frozen like characters on a screen. As if she'd hit the pause button on a movie, lingering over them, comparing them.

Her control over the situation was illusory. There was no movie on pause, no remote control. Ben never stuck in one place, and Mike moved behind the scenes in ways she could not see.

Still. She'd made a choice. The green backpack dangled from Ben's shoulder, and Carey reached to unzip the front pouch. He let her. She put the half-drunk bottle back into his bag and zipped it closed.

"Now I'm unstealing it," Carey said.

Ben smiled widely. A dimple pierced each cheek. Mike reached out a hand as if to ask, *Where's mine?* Ben ignored him and patted the pocket where he'd stashed the flashlight. He stretched and yawned, bored, and the mood quickly changed. Carey's damp shirt chilled her.

They could hear but not see the throng of people on the other side of the bus. Ben waved dismissively in the direction of the noise. "A host family, that's good for your first year," he said. "After that, you need freedom. Me and Mike live in the dorms."

He spoke as casually as if it were summer camp. She'd rarely heard his voice before—Thanks, can I get change—and never directed to her. She studied up close the clarity and darkness of his green eyes, a half-smile underneath a slightly crooked nose, muscle and sinew visible beneath a white cotton T-shirt. A couple blackheads on the side of his nose. His expression bordered on a smirk. He wasn't mocking her. She thrilled at the possibility that he might recognize her. Still. She wanted to be new.

She'd ordered pizza slices from Prisanti's before, and he was always in the back, behind the glass, tossing. Showing off. His hands twisting a beige blob of flour and yeast into long ropes. Flattening a ball of dough into a circle and flinging it into the air. He had behind-the-back moves like a basketball player, though he only played soccer ("A cardinal sin in Indiana," he told her later, "especially if you're six-two.") Despite his skills, at times he stretched the pizza dough so thin that a hole would tear. He might wad the circle into a ball and start over, but usually, he'd launch the torn dough upwards to the ceiling, where it stuck for a few minutes, then fell. Without looking up, he'd catch the sticky mess in one hand. Crowds gathered to watch the Pizza Guy at Prisanti's. He grinned at their applause, always looking over their heads into the distance. She'd stood there, too, wrestling with the competing desires of wanting to be noticed and wanting to be obscured. The longer he went without seeing her, the longer she could look.

Andrea Cunningham still called out names. Ben placed a palm on the side of the bus for balance and adjusted his sneaker's crinkled tongue. He glanced at her mouth, licked his lips. "I bet your family's looking for you," he said.

The bus blocked the school, its fluorescent lights, her host family, the start of her exchange program. She would rather have stayed in the dark with Ben. But she had been dismissed.

"Right," she said.

He waggled his fingers at her, walking backwards. One of the Mexican teachers approached Mike with a stack of envelopes, and Mike drifted off without saying goodbye. He watched her from the corner of one eye, the way he would for the next seven months. Longer.

She took a deep breath, waiting a beat. When she followed Ben's path, he'd disappeared, swallowed by the crowd.

Andrea Cunningham consulted her roster, wiping her pink face with her polo sleeve. Her khaki pants looked permanently wrinkled.

"Halpern, Carey? There you are."

The whole Alarcón family waited inside to greet her. Tall, thin Lupe and her husband, the shorter, muscular Hector. Their teenage daughter, Alicia, with her skinny arms and legs, her puppy gaze. And Bartolo. Lupe's son from her first marriage, four years older than Carey, pockmarked and moody.

Carey's face felt dirty from traveling. Her mother told her constantly, "You could use some lipstick," but it had been hours since Carey had applied makeup. Her cheeks ached from smiling at the Alarcón family. But she continued to grin, nod, and shake her head. She tried to answer their questions, her stilted Spanish childlike.

Hector drove. Carey was wedged in back between Lupe on the right and Bartolo on the left. Fifteen-year-old Alicia sat up front and contorted her skinny body to better see Carey. She peppered her with questions. How many brothers and sisters did she have? What about a boyfriend? What's *Nueva York* like?

Carey answered her new teenage sister in Spanish, increasing in pitch and volume to convey meaning she couldn't find in words. She was an only child. No boyfriend. She'd never been to New York. Her life, to her own ears, sounded dull as cardboard. She wanted to tell them, 'I used to have a boyfriend—just not right now,' which was true. Or, 'I've been thinking about going to New York,' when in reality Chicago unmoored her. But her mind swam with the unanticipated difficulty of speaking Spanish, a language she'd studied throughout high school and college.

"Mija, calmate," Hector warned Alicia. He'd barely said hello back at the school; Lupe had hugged her. Spiky black hairs poked from the back of his neck, which was thick as a wrestler's. He was younger than his wife by a decade. His forearm muscles flexed when he gripped the steering wheel.

"Why not?" Alicia asked Carey.

"I don't know," Carey said. "New York's far from where I live."

"No," Alicia said, impatient. "Why don't you have a boyfriend?"

Hector cleared his throat. His eyes found Lupe's in the rearview mirror. He drove quickly and moved the little white sedan from lane to lane without looking, as if the cars would know to get out of the way, and they did. A rosary of black plastic beads dangled from the rearview mirror, constantly swaying.

Lupe brushed her daughter's shoulder with her long fingers. On her left hand she wore a thin gold band and diamond ring, and on her right, another diamond, pear-shaped.

"What?" Alicia protested. "It's a compliment. Es guapa."

Carey smiled at Lupe to assure her it was fine, then tried to catch Bartolo's eye. But his eyes were fixed on his lap, where his hands rested. Long, nimble fingers. He turned away. Yes, she was pretty, Alicia. No one challenged that point.

They passed through yellow-lit streets, a mix of brick and pavement, the park in the center of town with its Indian laurels and wrought-iron benches and cobblestone paths. Clustered groups wandered the plaza, ice cream in hand. The faces were brown, the clothes bright, the laughter loud. Someone strummed a guitar. Beyond the plaza were a few illuminated alleyways, wide-slab stone steps curving up a hill. Two blocks from a sixteenth-century church, an electronics store advertised a sale.

"Is this a good place to go running?" Carey asked Hector, and immediately his thick neck swiveled back and forth.

"Nunca por la noche." Never at night.

"Claro," she said, miffed. She knew to avoid certain potential physical threats—a dark alley or park, going home with a stranger after last call—the security system of being female. She had not yet discovered how closely Mexico guarded its women. And her host father could not provide the protection Carey really needed: a shield for her vulnerable heart and mind. At twenty-one, she wore little emotional armor.

The flashing neon of the bodegas and cafés dizzied her as they drove. In the car windows their faces reflected, half-lit and glowing: Bartolo's cola-colored skin pocked with acne scars made deeper by the dark, Carey's face white and pink with blank thoughts of tomorrow and the day after that. Possibility, the unknown, the wide expanse of who she might be in a place that did not know her. But she knew Ben, and he appeared in her versions of the coming year. She remembered seeing him once in the mall, wearing a Nirvana T-shirt. She'd gone to MusicTown and bought a CD, the one with the baby swimming underwater, even though she wasn't a fan and failed to become one. Looking for clues, filling in the blanks of Ben's life.

At the house, Lupe apologized again for keeping Carey up— You must be tired, but we're so excited you're here. Tall, elegant Lupe wore a yellow shift dress and flat sandals and a patterned scarf tied around her neck, like a timeless movie star. Her face was deeply creased around the eyes but still beautiful. Young Alicia carried a version of her mother inside her, velvety eyes and lush mouth waiting to upstage the baby-fat cheeks and large ears. Back home, a girl like Alicia would've drawn knowing glances from the women who lingered in her mother's gift shop. "Oh, she'll be trouble someday," they would say. "A real heartbreaker." Carey knew because they'd spoken the same words about her, loud enough for her to hear. A compliment that held you in place: Pretty someday. Not now.

Lupe led the tour. The kitchen smelled faintly of rotted fruit, though it was clean, with fresh mop tracks still drying on the tile floor. The open windows had no screens. Flies buzzed around the sink drain and the metal garbage can. Gross, Carey thought, trying hard not to wrinkle her nose. She immediately felt guilty when Lupe opened her arms wide and said, *Mi cocina es su cocina.* Her kitchen and food, offered up to a woman she'd met a half-hour before.

"Tienes hambre ahorita?" Lupe asked. Carey was hungry. On

the road Cesár had pulled over to a buffet restaurant where he had playfully sparred with the young male waiter who led the group to their tables. He knew someone at each stop; he likely had been paid to stop. But that was several hours before, and she'd only picked at the unidentifiable stews of thick red and green sauces, meats marbled with fat. What would Lupe offer? She didn't want to risk offending her host mother. Carey shook her head and stifled a yawn. "No, gracias."

"What do Americans think about Mexicans?" Hector wanted to know. It was the one thing he'd asked her all night.

"I don't know," she said in Spanish, which really meant she needed to think about it. She tilted her head, as if a script might be waiting on the ceiling. "That Mexicans are, what's the right word, more relaxed? Because of the siesta?"

Alicia giggled. Lupe busied herself with the tea tray, and Bartolo pursed his lips as if to keep from speaking. Hector grunted and headed to the stairs, muttering about a program on TV. Carey flushed, knowing she'd said the wrong thing, and called after his retreating form, "Buenos noches." The others ignored him.

Bartolo remained with the women in the living room, seated on the arm of a pink rosette chintz chair covered in plastic. Clearly their good furniture. But it was the kind of piece her mother laughed at when they drove by discount furniture storefronts. At Finer Things, Gwen Halpern sold a few end tables and lamps, not furniture; still, she'd point at the gaudy couches and particle-board kitchen tables and ask, Should I order that for next season?

Carey tried to smile at the expectant faces around her. She felt a pang for her father, who had checked her plane ticket three times and asked if she'd packed running shoes. Make this experience yours, he'd said. She even missed her mother's appraising eye, constantly evaluating Carey: You could use some lipstick. At least Carey knew how to talk to them.

"Give her the present," Lupe said to Bartolo. She and her son shared the same eyes, a deep brown, long fringe of lashes, symmetrically oval. They fit Lupe perfectly and had landed her modeling jobs when she was younger. On Bartolo, the eyes softened the rough appearance of his face. He presented her with an oblong white box, tied with a red ribbon like a valentine.

"Open it!" Alicia exclaimed, before Bartolo had even given her the gift.

"Un regalo para tí," Bartolo said.

She thanked him and carefully pulled at one end of the bow and removed the lid. Inside, on a bed of white cotton, was a dime-sized St. Christopher medallion, thin as a communion wafer, on a delicate silver chain.

"This is lovely," she said, and he smiled.

"It's from the store," Alicia said. "He works in his papa's jewelry store."

Bartolo's smile left his face, returning to its neutral mask. Lupe murmured indistinguishable words and crossed herself. Carey understood Bartolo's father was dead. She barely knew her host family and could feel their sorrow. Not quite as if the pain were her own.

How little she understood pain at that point. Bartolo and Lupe's sadness floated from them into the air, nested in the corners near the ceiling, blended into the gold-fleck pattern of the wallpaper.

"Would you put it on me?" she asked Bartolo, holding out the necklace's clasp and hook. She knew instinctively this was the right question, though she'd never received jewelry from anyone but her parents. The necklace was a gift from the whole family, even Hector, who watched TV upstairs, the sound filtering through the ceiling. But it was clear Bartolo picked, bought, and wrapped the medallion.

He silently took the ends of the necklace in each hand, and reached around her from the front. "Tu pelo," he said, and she lifted up her hair. He fastened the necklace. His aftershave smelled like spiced pears. He held his breath, his face flushing a purplish red, and Carey tried not to stare at his scars. He stepped back, making room between them.

"It is for luck," he said.

When she smiled and nodded, he said it once more: "For luck."

Carey touched the necklace at her throat when she reached the auditorium entrance on the first day of class. La Universidad Intercambio was once a private high school that now accommodated college exchange students. The program attracted more than 100 students from across the United States. In the auditorium, a brief flash of middle school who-will-I-sit-with anxiety entered her mind, and she willed it to disappear. So it did.

She surreptitiously searched for Ben. The seats were filling quickly, so she slid into a plush red aisle chair near the back. She looked up "relaxed" in her Spanish-English dictionary. Clearly, she'd said something wrong when Hector asked what Americans thought of Mexicans. She hadn't said relajado or tranquilo, two of the words listed, and her heart sank. She paged to the back for the Spanish word, *flojo*. Lazy, read the entry. Flojo also could mean weak, a poor worker. Hector had risen early to work at the bank, and Lupe left an hour later for her part-time job at a women's clothing shop. Carey wanted to cry; instead she distracted herself with pulling a spiral notebook and black pen from her shoulder bag. She placed them on her lap. She'd spent fifteen minutes that morning arranging her hair in a haphazard-looking twist. She touched it to make sure it was still intentionally out-of-place.

She'd slept lightly the night before, not only because of her uneasiness regarding Hector and vocabulary. Alicia kept her up for an extra hour in their shared bedroom. For all her teenage posturing, Alicia remained a young girl. Her bed held more than a dozen stuffed animals.

"I have always wanted a sister," Alicia had whispered across the darkened room to Carey.

"Me, too," Carey said, though she was just being polite. She loved being an only child: the attention and parental fussing, and also the way she was left alone. Her parents protected and cocooned Carey, unintentionally isolating her, teaching her how to isolate herself. Her bedroom and private bath were upstairs, the master bedroom downstairs. She loved her space, and they loved knowing where she was. Which made the Mexico trip something of a surprise.

As she had campaigned, the trip took on qualities of a dare:

perhaps she and her parents both wished to cancel the nonrefundable tickets. Even if the thought was fleeting, no one would admit to it. Instead, they over-planned. They fought over embassy advisories, concerns about drinking water, even the proper suitcase and clothing. But the arguments fizzled easily enough. The Halperns wanted to be open-minded, despite their many misgivings about sending their daughter to a third-world country. Carey was shoving herself out of the nest.

Growing up, she spent most of her time with her parents. The Halpern trio went to dinner and concerts, like peers. Once Carey reached college, they'd let her order wine at restaurants, even though she was not yet twenty-one. But sometimes she felt like a party-crasher. When they went out to dinner and she was too old for a babysitter, she made up games that only needed one player, or would fill the roles of both competitors in a game of checkers. Once, they had returned from a party to find twelve-year-old Carey playing a four-person Monopoly tournament by herself.

"I'll be the boot," Gwen had offered, slipping off her black kitten heels. Brian smiled, distracted, before going into his study. Even when he wasn't working, he was working. Billing hours.

"Mom, I'm already the boot," Carey had said. Her eyes were fixed on the board filled with game pieces, red and green plastic buildings. An empire.

"Well, what's left?" Gwen asked. "I'll be that."

"That's OK," Carey said. "There's not enough money in the bank."

If Gwen was hurt, she didn't show it. She got up, kissed Carey on top of the head, and went to pour a drink. She returned briefly, sipping her red wine and watching Carey's game, before going to bed.

Monopoly was a game Carey had mastered. She knew when to buy, when to sell. How to collect and accrue property, which she hoarded. She was less skilled at the real games of negotiation. All around her in the auditorium, students greeted each other and clustered around the most boisterous, those who bubbled continuously as fountains. Loners like Carey sat watching, waiting to make a move.

A man in a guyabera and khaki shorts walked to the lectern. The crowd quieted. Ben was seated in the third row, the unmistakable hair and white t-shirt; Mike was next to him. The day before, at a picnic for new students, she revealed she was from Indianapolis. "We'll have to compare notes," Ben said, disappointingly casual. He didn't ask about her high school, or if she hung out at Oakview Mall. He asked nothing. Andrea Cunningham approached Ben, and they huddled into a private conversation. She and Mike, cast off, discussed Guanajuato. "I'll show you around, if you want," he said. "We both can. Me and Ben."

Now she raised a hand and waved. Mike acknowledged her with a nod of the head and leaned in to speak to Ben. He was Ben's shadow, sidekick, sentry. Ben swiveled and scanned the crowd for a moment before turning back without seeing her. He appeared, briefly, to be picking his nose, which she decided was charming. Already, she'd blithely absolved him of mortal flaws.

"Bienvenidos," the man on stage was saying. "That means 'welcome.' Which hopefully you already know, if you're here."

A nervous collective laugh rose.

Don Hernando, the head of La Universidad Intercambio, was Mexican by birth, a rarity among the faculty. He loved his beautiful university. He loved his city, so tranquil, so filled with history.

"We're a friendly people in Mexico," he said. "Count on that. But if someone gets too friendly, come to me. If not me, talk to any teacher. Entienden?"

Did they understand? A collective nod: they understood. He added that Intercambio did not advocate dating, cross-culturally or within the program.

"It's more complicated here," Don Hernando said. "You are busy navigating the streets and the language. La cultura Mexicana. Focus on learning. You won't get lost."

He switched entirely to Spanish, about walking in pairs, avoiding the food and beverages sold on the street, taking studies seriously, the famous Mummy Museum. Her ears perked up when he mentioned the discoteca and cafés, and described which were acceptable and which were not.

After, Carey stood on the short stone steps, letting the sun toast her face and bare shoulders. Intercambio was in the mountains, less muggy than Mexico City. You could get away with a tank top until the undercut of cool breezes cancelled out the sun.

Eyes closed, she enjoyed the alternating warm and cool feeling on her skin, her face turned towards the sun like a flower. Most of the other students were leaving for lunch or heading to a class or milling around the building's entryway. Maybe if she spent lunch studying her dictionary, she'd avoid insulting her host family today. Maybe she could explore the park across the street for running trails.

Years of high school and college Spanish, a lengthy application process, and still she felt unprepared. Make this experience yours, her father had said. Study hard, learn something new.

"There she is." Mike's voice. He was often the one to pick her out, to find her, his blue eyes quick and roving, then still as a deer's when she looked back. She kept her eyes closed a beat longer, holding on to the sun and the feeling of waiting. She wanted to be found, just not by Mike. When she opened her eyes, Ben and Mike flanked her.

"Ready?" Ben asked, as if they'd planned a date. "Come on."

He and Mike grabbed her arms and led her down to the sidewalk in the direction of town. She laughed at first. American girls, for all their independence, learn a particular brand of giggling acquiescence. When Ben and Mike had marched her several yards without releasing their grip, Carey dragged her feet. Ben and Mike, each half a foot taller than her, stopped. They let go. Her arms still held the red imprints of their fingers. Carey asked where they were going, but she didn't get an answer.

"Indianapolites have to stick together," Ben said.

Mike laughed and his blond hair fell across his forehead. "Is that a word? Don't discriminate against a brother from Milwaukee."

"You're honorary," Ben said. "As long as you stop referring to yourself as 'a brother.' Uncool, white boy."

For the briefest flash, Mike's face betrayed his vulnerability. Carey saw it clearly. His availability. His frank, open gaze. His intelligence and aloneness. Mike was plain and obvious as a freckle. At Ben's words, hurt came across his face in a blink, disappearing just as quickly. Even in joking, Ben worked Mike's feelings and reactions.

Ben had that effect on people, Carey included. A small price to pay. His presence made them bigger, louder, street-smart, wise. Walking downtown became an event. People were drawn to him, as to a carnival barker or a celebrity in dark glasses. The possibility of being with him meant the possibility of being someone different. Why else do we seek the company of strangers, but for a foothold, a boost up to the window of our own lives? We search for advantages, a balcony view. We climb all over people to learn what they can tell us about ourselves.

They resumed walking, this time without touching her. "I'm not going anywhere," she said, believing it less and less. "I have class in twenty minutes."

Ben and Mike shared a look that contained a whole conversation in a glance. She knew only that it was about her. Ben smiled an in-charge smile, wolfish and dreamy.

"No you don't," he said.

"Yes I do." She reached into her shoulder bag for her schedule.

Mike waved a hand dismissively, and Ben encircled Carey's wrist with his thumb and middle finger, lifting her hand from the bag. His callused palms grazed her skin.

"You don't," Ben said. "We're teaching class today."

CHAPTER 3

LIBERATED FROM HER PATTERN of work, home, sleep, repeat, Carey now understood how limited her looping path of the Circle City had been. She'd missed major changes. Indianapolis, solid predictable Midwest mid-sized burgers and fries, morphed daily into a different city. More alien than Mexico had been when she'd first arrived.

Free mornings sans time clock, she lingered over the newspaper, examining numbers on immigration figures and photos illustrating the "new diversity": at the bus stop, uniformed Hispanic women in either the tight black pants associated with food service or looser, gray custodian's jumpsuits. Dark-skinned men in tri-colored jerseys kicked soccer balls in the park. Legs short and quick, black cleats still clumped with Mexican soil.

Hispanic executives who'd been at their companies for years were now featured in profiles. Caucasian female news anchors carefully enunciated Sink-Oh Day My-Oh, wrapping their lipsticked mouths around names like Gutierrez and Almogordo. In broadcast school, they had painstakingly mastered the Midwestern non-accent, only to land squarely in the Midwest, where they now learned to pronounce Spanish. Everyone loved Maria Cortez on Channel Two—bilingual, lovely Maria, quick to translate rapid-fire Spanish.

But TV was one thing. In Walmart, you could sense the wariness over the unfamiliar Spanish chatter. Cagey Americans, unaware that they were just as loose-mouthed in English. Just as quick to a bargain, fingering a cheap sweater on a rack, convincing a daughter that it didn't really look like it came from Walmart. English, Spanish—they were saying the same thing: Honey, cariña, nobody can tell.

Spanish, the language Carey loved, filled her ears. In the candy aisle at the Village Pantry, two boys fought in Spanish over how to spend their shared dollar. Alone in her car, she whispered phrases. "Dímelo. Quiero un Kit-Kat." The language brought Ben back to her, and she felt bruised by the need to conjure him and the need to forget. Small moments—his green eyes grazing her body in a way no one had before or since, his calloused hand resting on her bare shoulder—made more delicious and painful because they would never happen again.

In a matter of days, the spacious Halpern house began to shrink by inches. Carey grew tired of pretending she had a job, of the pointless dressing up in clothes that chafed her soul. Again she claimed to call in sick, though no one had noticed or asked.

Nicole had agreed to meet her for lunch at Edna's Diner on West 38th Street, a fixture in the African-American community. Back in high school, Nicole had a catchphrase: Wanna slum? And Carey would push aside her conscience to laugh. Slumming: two white teenage girls leaving their mostly-white subdivisions near 71st Street, driving four miles south to where gangs allegedly proliferated, unless the talk was high school bravado. 38th Street was lined with many of the same retail stores and restaurants as high-end 86th Street, north of their turf, but grittier. More litter, more bars. They were never asked to show identification at Ralph's Spirits & Tobacco. Neon billboards advertised strip clubs and adult video stores, which neighbored doughnut shops and fabric stores. A gentlemen's club sat isolated in a small field, with the back loading docks of Meijer on one side and Best Buy on the other. Wanna slum? Nicole would ask, and Carey always went. They'd occupy tables adjacent to blacks and Hispanics, but never mingled. This had been years ago, and they'd changed. But their shared history remained.

Nicole, in a cardigan and jeans over her black leotard, was

scanning the menu when Carey slid into the booth across from her. She'd pulled her dark blond hair into a loose braid, and the line between her eyebrows deepened.

"I've only got an hour," Nicole said.

"Hello to you, too. I'm fine, thanks. How's your day?"

Nicole's blue eyes softened. "Sorry. I'm so used to planning life around these classes. It's a grind." A grind, clearly, that she loved. Nicole, radiant and glowing, a supple-limbed dance teacher, a contributor. In high school, Carey had teased Nicole about her flamboyant arm gestures, or the health hazards of too much time spent in tights and leotards. Carey had run distance, endurance. Her arms pumped like thin pistons, biceps, trapezius, and triceps like hard fruit beneath her skin. In Mexico, Ben once had traced his finger down her arm, outlining the muscle, and whistled. On a good day, running had felt like flying.

Today she was conscious of the little fold of skin pouching over her jeans. And after showering, the wiggle of her upper arms as she applied lotion to a rash that had sprouted overnight.

Derek, the owner, stood tall behind the long lunch counter. He had taken over after his mother died. A decade later, some customers still complained Derek's pies and pancakes weren't as good. But business hadn't slowed.

"Be with you in mere minutes," he said.

Everyone knew Derek. He sponsored breakfasts for the Boys and Girls Clubs. He donated to charity auctions, and the year before hosted a well-publicized benefit for the family of a sixteen-year-old murder victim. He knew faces and orders but not names. "There's the man," he'd say by way of a greeting, pointing a long finger at a patron.

"Ladies," he said. "Ms. Jenks, you know you want a slice of my boysenberry pie."

Nicole blushed hotly. "Please, it's Nicole," she said. "And you remember Carey."

"Who could forget Strawberry Pancakes?" Derek grinned. He was maybe five years older than them, solidly built.

"I'll get your coffee," he said, winking. Nicole's eyes trailed after him.

Carey offered Nicole her napkin. "You've got a little drool going on," she said.

"Shut up."

"He knows your name."

Nicole wouldn't look at Carey. "His daughter takes beginning tap."

"So he's married."

Now she glanced up quickly. "He doesn't wear a ring."

High school was years before, but Carey could still hear adolescent Nicole in her head: "Wanna slum?" Nicole often had declared, "So many black girls at Township get pregnant by junior year, you'd think it was a course requirement." Gutlessly, Carey had said nothing.

"I heard he's single," Nicole said.

"What about Bob?" Carey asked, meaning Bob Kemper, who bartended at McAlestar's.

"That movie was OK." Nicole stared at the traffic out the plate glass window. At the next booth an older man in suspenders read the newspaper: Ben's passport photo was printed on the front page. Carey was relieved when the man folded the paper and laid it down, out of sight.

Derek returned with his notepad. "So, Ni-cole," Derek said. "Will it be waffles? Will it be pancakes? Don't keep me in suspense." He placed a palm over his heart and leaned down towards her.

"Chocolate-chip pancakes, please." She smiled at him.

"Sweets for the sweet," he said. "And for you, Strawberry?"

He did not call Carey by name. He did not lean down, swoonily awaiting a response.

"Chicken salad," Carey said. "On wheat."

"Huh," he said, frowning as he wrote it down. He retreated behind the counter, and Nicole held up her palm to preempt Carey's questions. They'd known each other long enough to converse wordlessly, but now the silence settled thickly around them. Carey couldn't read it.

They were out of synch, a poorly dubbed movie. After Carey had been sent home from Mexico, mired in a swamp of grief, Nicole coaxed her back into the world. Or at least out drinking at McAlestar's. In Chicago, they had spent days in requisite disappointing jobs, and nights in smoke-filled lounges. Bars with leather couches. Groping men they clutched, let inside. Brandon, who'd admired her eyes, slept with her, and never called again. A symbolically anonymous phase of Bills, three of them blending in her mind into one person, forgettable. But she remembered herself and Nicole, mascara-smeared, out for coffee on Sunday mornings, something to cut the gin breath, lighting cigarette after cigarette.

They kept it up for months, years, until one night Carey was sitting alone on the living room futon, between two men Nicole hadn't wanted to invite over. Nicole had to work in the morning, a new job selling classified ads for the *Tribune*, and she went to her room. Carey did not sleep that night. She began going for coffee alone. In the mornings Nicole would watch her from their kitchen breakfast bar, until Carey would finally ask, "What?" Nicole would shrug her shoulders and busy herself with a magazine, which she now stacked neatly on their secondhand coffee table. "It's just, when was the last time you had a second date?" she asked rhetorically. "Ben was your last boyfriend. Even if you won't talk, Carey, he's still gone."

She'd edged up to that uncomfortable truth, and for three days, Carey could barely speak—to Nicole, or anyone. She stayed out of the apartment. She spent a lonesome evening at Navy Pier amid the garish lights and tourists and rides, wandering aimlessly or sitting alone on a bench. Recalling other benches where she'd waited, when the wrong man appeared.

Carey and Nicole would turn twenty-nine this year. They'd hung on to each other. Nicole either hadn't heard the news about Ben's passport, or didn't care, and Carey said nothing. They made small-talk. Carey zoned out during Nicole's convoluted explanation of the dance studio's budget. When Carey mentioned the sickos she'd encountered in chat rooms, Nicole grimaced, implying that she, Carey, was a sicko by association. Derek saluted them when they left. "Until Tuesday, Nicole," he said.

Outside the restaurant, Carey lit a cigarette and held out her pack. Nicole shook her head. "I quit."

"Since when?"

She shrugged, wrapping her cardigan more tightly, arm muscles outlined against thin cotton. "The kids will smell it."

Carey paused briefly, looking up at the sky, which was largely blocked by a Hooters billboard. Carey dropped her barely-smoked cigarette on the ground, stamping her heel.

"You didn't have to do that," Nicole said, softening. "But thanks."

"I aim to please," Carey said.

"You do, don't you." Nicole studied her. "What's the deal with work?"

"What do you mean?"

"I mean, you're not there today, and you're wearing jeans." Nicole flipped her braid over one shoulder, waiting. She might've looked at her watch. She might've been scratching her wrist.

"I got let go," Carey said.

"Carey, no." Nicole sounded sympathetic but not surprised. "What'll you do now?"

"I don't know, get another job?"

"You don't have to be so sarcastic. Can you take me back to work? Bob dropped me here. My car's in the shop."

Carey unlocked the car and they got in. The interior smelled of smoke, less pungent than the inside of McAlestar's bar. Bob's bar.

"You quit smoking for Bob," Carey said. "And Derek. Your men don't smoke."

Nicole's blue eyes gleamed. "Can't I quit for me? Isn't that a good enough reason?"

Carey knew that the more she asked the less forthcoming Nicole would be. A characteristic they shared.

"Nope," Carey said, shifting into gear and driving north on High School Road. In her peripheral vision, Nicole smiled her Cheshire cat smile. They were back in synch. One of those rare instances when the action and the talk line up perfectly on a screen.

.

They passed the vacant strip mall where the chain grocery store used to be. Tenants had fled once the store relocated to the Northside. At one end of the plaza, a small white banner hung over the door of the old frozen yogurt shop. It read "Bienvenido a Nuestra Tienda." Colorful canned goods were stacked in the windows.

Years earlier, Carey's mother had complained about the influx of Hispanic immigrants on the West side. "They can keep their restaurants," she'd say, "as long as I've got the toehold in potpourri. Ladies who lunch pay out the nose for that stuff." Some months before Carey's study-abroad program in Mexico, she overheard her mother on the phone: "Maybe I should compete with them. Expand into a drive-thru. You want beans with that?" Her laughter pealed throughout the kitchen. Carey was certain that whichever friend was on the other end of the line was agreeing with her mother.

Carey tried to explain that the comments were inappropriate, but her mother claimed she was joking. Carey, a sociology major and Spanish minor, politely refrained from mentioning that Gwen Halpern was also a lady who lunched.

Now Carey pointed to the small Mexican grocery. "Looks new. Have you been?"

"Can't you get that stuff at Kroger?" Nicole asked. "And cheaper?"

A mile later, the new strip mall appeared from nowhere. The flat buildings sprouted and sprawled, prolific as mushrooms.

Casa Colmo had gotten a new sign since her lunch days before. Now red-and-green chile peppers flanked the letters. Last time, she hadn't noticed the cardboard sign in the window: Se Emplea. Now Hiring.

The shifting, weak sunlight highlighted the glass door's floor-to-ceiling etching.

"You could work there."

Carey had already turned on her blinker. Not because of Nicole's suggestion. The etched glass drew her as if her car's alignment had gone bad.

"I was kidding," Nicole said.

"No, it's a good idea."

"I have to get back to work."

"I'll just be a minute. In and out. I promise."

Nicole muttered an indecipherable complaint and pulled out her cell phone. Carey still didn't have—or need—a cell phone.

The restaurant door's wooden handle was smooth beneath her palm; she lingered over it. She could say the door was locked. She could appease Nicole and say she'd come back later. Somehow her hand moved of its own volition, the door opened, and she walked inside to a wave of fried tortillas, the upbeat trill of Tejano music. At a long table in the center of the room, ten or so Latinos folded new, laminated menus. They were laughing, speaking loudly. Only one woman sat at the table: the same woman from Carey's last visit, holding court. Her long, blue-black hair fell across the shoulders of her tight red T-shirt. The men were teasing her, and she shook her head. "Tell them to stop, Juan," she said in Spanish, turning to the waiter who had to be her brother. The almond-shaped eyes gave them away.

The mood was far cheerier than the other day, when Ben's passport was featured on the noon news. Now, the musical words, the scent of tortillas emanating from the kitchen—Carey inhaled it all. This place four miles from her house was not just a Mexican restaurant. Somehow she continued to enter new versions of a city she thought she knew.

Strangely, she felt homesick.

The man with the dark hair falling in his eyes noticed Carey standing at the door. He nudged the man next to him, signaling a chain reaction of quiet around the table.

"Buenos tardes," the floppy-haired man said in Spanish. He averted his eyes. The others just stared.

Carey said, "You're hiring? Quiero trabajar."

Spanglish. A few of the men snickered. The woman, perhaps a few years older than Carey, assessed her, and Carey became conscious of her jeans—stained on one thigh from a dollop of chicken salad at lunch—and her pilled black sweater. Her brown hair, shoulder-length and quickly blown dry, probably needed brushing. These things always occurred to her too late.

"Ha trabajado en un restaurante?" the woman asked.

"No, but you need someone who speaks English," she said in slow Spanish. "Hardly anyone in this city speaks Spanish."

Immediately she blushed. Of course, Mexicans in Indianapolis spoke Spanish. The city had a consulate, Maria Cortez at six and eleven. This table full of gaping men in front of her.

The woman crossed the room. She was a few inches shorter than Carey. She held out her hand. "Elena Morales," she said, without any accent. "I speak English."

Carey introduced herself, unsure of which language to choose.

"The church on the door—is it in Guanajuato?" Carey asked.

Elena appraised her. "Yes, the town of Dolores Hidalgo. Our home."

"I love that place," Carey said. "One of the most beautiful spots in Mexico."

A flexible truth. She'd visited Dolores Hidalgo, a small town about an hour away from the city of Guanajuato, on a day trip with other students. At its center, Dolores Hidalgo had a lovely, colonial square, the magnificent church, and streets of shops selling pottery, clothing and trinkets. Tourism was its main industry. But the outlying lanes showed disrepair, the vegetable stands measly and swarmed with flies. The outskirts were rough farming areas, covered with nopales and rocky hillsides. She'd been examining the tables of ceramics and skeleton puppets when a man had called from across the street: *Guera, I follow you*. Guera meant blond but also meant white. He mirrored her for a full block, never crossing over. But he could've.

Now she used Dolores Hidalgo like a bargaining chip. So she'd been there a day, when she was twenty-one. So she hadn't loved it. These were small matters.

Elena's mouth softened into something like a smile. "Maybe, we could use you," she conceded. "This is my parents' restaurant. I can't say yes or no until I talk to them."

"Que dice, hermana?" the man she'd called Juan asked.

"Momento," she told him, then turned to Carey. "My brother."

"You look alike," Carey said. Elena made a face.

Carey had never waited tables or worked in a restaurant, not even fast food. But she needed work. She needed to know what the whispers meant, even though she could translate: Yo lo conozco. I know him.

"Can I fill out an application?" Carey asked.

"Claro que si," Elena said, retreating behind the cash register. Juan smiled, waved. The one with the dark hair in his eyes examined Carey's plain black boots.

"Here you are." Elena pushed a piece of white paper across the counter and handed Carey a pen. The woman had written:

Name/Nombre: _____

Phone/Teléfono: _____

Carey completed the makeshift application, thinking they'd never call. Or worse, that they would.

When she arrived home, her mother was hovering over the answering machine, looking puzzled. She glanced up at Carey, taking in her jeans and black sweater.

"It's the temping service. They said your final pay sheet still needs to be signed. And that they're mailing a severance of contract form."

"I was going to tell you."

"So, tell." She pursed her lips, half concerned, half suspicious.

"The woman I replaced, Felicia? Who had cancer? She's better!"

"So now you're out of work. The agreement was you'd pay us back for helping with the credit cards."

"I will."

"Without a job?"

"I'm looking. I've got leads, maybe an interview."

Now her mother smiled, surprised. "Well, then. You're being proactive."

Carey stood up straighter.

"Hey, what do you think about my hair?" Gwen brushed a few strands off her forehead. It looked the same as always. "What if I changed it? What if I went super short?"

"That might work," Carey hedged. She imagined diet guru Susan Powter's close-cropped hairdo. Gwen sniffed—Carey should have been more enthusiastic—and headed to the living room. When Carey heard the sound of the television, she pressed play on the answering machine, listening to the nasal voice. She deleted the message. They had her address; they'd send the forms.

She grabbed the cordless handset and slinked upstairs to her bedroom, positioning herself on the floor of her bedroom closet. Growing up, she'd had the whole second floor to herself; still, she often retreated to the closet for phone calls. Wrapped in two sets of walls, two kinds of dark.

Dialing Mike's number felt like programming a time machine. He answered on the second ring. She pushed away the hem of her midnight blue prom dress, as if Mike could see her.

"Hey," she said. "It's Carey."

He inhaled quickly. "Hi," he said, a single syllable loaded with anxiety and excitement. Did she hear all that, or want to hear it?

"How are you?" he asked, just as she was saying, "It's been a long time." They finished tripping over each other, laughed, then fell silent.

"I'm glad you called," he said finally. "I'll be down in Indy, day after tomorrow. You free this weekend?"

"I could do Friday," she said.

"I'm having dinner with the Williamsons. Ben's parents."

She resented his explication, and the possessiveness she felt. She knew who the Williamsons were. They had never invited her to dinner. All she said was, "I have to work Saturday." A lie, albeit an optimistic one.

They agreed on meeting Sunday evening, and she suggested a bar in Broad Ripple. Her nails made tiny half moons in the flesh of her palms. She paused only a fraction of a second when he requested her email address. After Mexico, she'd cut him off, told him to stop writing, a decision she'd regretted yet could not undo.

"Hey, Carey?"

"Yes?" She stood and knocked her head against a tangle of wire hangers, the tinny clatter like wind chimes.

"What was that?" Mike asked.

"Nothing." Just hiding in the closet. As you do in your late twenties.

"I've wanted to get in touch before, plenty of times," he said. "I can't believe I'm going to see you again."

She could not let herself respond in kind. "So, see you Sunday."

"Right," he said. "Sure."

They were both quiet for a moment. "You still there?" he asked. "Where'd you go?"

There were so many ways to answer that question. She merely apologized. "Gotta run," she said. "My mom needs the phone."

She hung up the phone and smacked her forehead with it. My *mom* needs the phone, she thought to herself. Because I live with my parents. And don't have my own phone. Which is fantastic at age twenty-eight.

The answer to his question of her whereabouts was simple: she'd returned to that familiar retreat, the folds of her memory, to Mexico and the last time they'd laid eyes on one another.

Mike had come by the Alarcón house three times. She refused to see him. Ben had been shot and killed in an alleyway. Random violence, horrible, the Intercambio teachers said, skepticism tingeing their voices. Probably a robbery, said the old cop with the sad eyes, though Ben had little to steal. He worked as many shifts as he could get, and Carey assumed his money went toward bills. Besides pesos, he kept a superstitious nineteen dollars American in his wallet. He had a single credit card she'd never seen him use.

When the phone rang, she expected her host mother to summon her. Lupe, who pressed a wet washcloth to Carey's forehead, who rocked her when she woke up screaming, who couldn't watch when Bartolo had to restrain Carey's flailing limbs with his soft jeweler's hands.

She says nothing, Lupe had told other callers. She stares at the wall or the ceiling. No sleep. Yes, she eats a little toast or tortilla. But it comes back up, always. Her color is poor. Her eyes do not focus. Her body is sick, not just her heart.

The maid, Maria, had begun crossing herself in Carey's presence. As if La Americana was possessed. Lupe admonished Maria in the hallway outside the bedroom: *No. Está rota.* She is broken.

Sometimes Carey rocked on the bed, but mostly she was still. She imagined a computer screen swept blank by the delete key. The Alarcóns might've felt punished, though they were not to blame. She would speak to them if they asked the right questions. But no one asked who she was before she came to Mexico, or who she was before Ben. An unrecognizable woman, now. Nobody asked why she'd stopped showering and picked her scalp until it bled. She let a scab form, then scraped the hard shell away. Unconsciously marking the place Ben had touched her, hidden beneath her long brown hair, a place no one could see.

When the phone rang that day, Carey silently lifted the receiver on the upstairs extension. It was Andrea Cunningham, who told Lupe about the weekend memorial service. Lupe spoke on the phone in a hushed voice, the small *click click click* of her polished nails tapping the plastic receiver. A nervous habit.

The Williamsons were flying in from Indianapolis. Ben's parents had chosen Carey to give a reading. They were bringing a copy of scripture they thought Ben had liked, Andrea said.

Who did they think their son was? The Williamsons were Catholic, but Ben had never mentioned the Bible. Not once.

Carey managed to get dressed. She slipped out of the house and walked to the dorm, not seeing the vegetable merchants with their chiles and oblong green peppers spread on blankets along the sidewalk, not noticing the manic traffic. She climbed the steps to the fourth floor. Mike wasn't there. At the front desk she asked the clerk for a key to Mike Gibley's room. She explained vaguely, He asked me to get something for him. The clerk slid the key across the counter. A book, Carey added, but the man gazed beyond her to the street. The campus had been inhabited by zombies. The city, with so little crime, paused in shock over the American's death. *Es muy tranquilo,* every Mexican resident and tourist had said of Guanajuato. *Es tan hermoso.*

Then there was a blank period of time, like erased tape. She remembered when Mike entered the room, where she waded through piles of ruined jeans and t-shirts. Her hands were stained with black from the fountain pen she'd cracked, spilling everywhere. His boxer shorts were snipped into pieces, and she'd plunged the scissors into the mattress. Only the blue handle was visible. It looked like a neatly tied bow. Five iron bars covered the screenless, open window. She held Mike's laptop, still plugged into the wall socket, and she gave a violent tug to release it. The freed wires lay a few feet from where Mike stood at the door, his eyes widened.

"Please," he said.

She raised the computer to the window's vertical bars, perfectly spaced. Three days earlier, she'd stood in the same doorframe with him. For a split second, Mike's eyes reached her. The pain of what they had shared. Mike suffered, too.

The brief damp rot of sadness passed, replaced by anger. Maybe Mike called her name, issuing a warning to calm down. She couldn't remember. He lunged quickly across the room, stepping on the power cord. Carey released the machine. The laptop dangled for a moment before unplugging. The computer was only seven pounds of plastic and parts, and the crash was anticlimactic. Below, a handful of keyboard letters popped off and clattered into the gutter. Had she not been running out the door, down the stairs, and across the street, she might have paused over the cubes lying on the uneven stone. All consonants, no vowels. A word that made no sense.

They didn't send her home for that, though they could have. Andrea Cunningham and Don Hernando spelled out her situation. There was the memorial service to attend. There were marvelous grief counselors working with the students. Maravilloso, they said, reminding her of an elementary Spanish textbook, of boy and girl characters in everyday situations.

She did not go to the counselors or the service. Perhaps the Williamsons were disappointed, perhaps not. They were Northsiders; her family lived on the West side. She and Ben had grown up in the same city yet never knew each other. Or rather, he had not known her. How maravilloso, she had first thought, to become involved with a man from her hometown. To become involved with *this* man, in Mexico of all places, in a city wedged between mountains. Her mind fast-forwarding: brunch at Edna's, marriage a few years after graduation, a good story to tell their tall, green-eyed children. Now, thinking of home made her already-edgy stomach churn.

She did not want to return to Indianapolis and spot Ben's mother in the cereal aisle at Kroger. She did not want his family looking her up. When Lupe and Andrea explained that the Williamsons not only wanted to meet but had asked her to read scripture at Ben's memorial service, the movie projector in her mind sputtered to a stop. She knew she would regret her behavior. She knew skipping the service was like cutting a cord, even if she didn't know what the cord connected to. She knew all this and still stayed away, eyes trained on her digital travel clock, ticking off the minutes until the end of the memorial mass at the Basilica.

It was not just about Ben's parents. She did not want to see the body. She did not want to see Mike. If she could avoid seeing, if she could live with her eyes screwed tight, then it might be as if that night had never happened.

CHAPTER 4

THIS IS HOW IT WAS. Labyrinthine Guanajuato's steep cobblestone streets wended and branched, split into new avenues, reunited under different names. The blacktop roads, soft in the sun, circled around cool, leaf-canopied parks, around old buildings of earthen stucco and new ones of chromium steel. Between the buildings, alongside back-door taverns and apartment fire escapes, were narrow, dank passages—shortcuts through the maze.

At Banco Federal, two uniformed guards flanked the door to the columned building, machine guns cradled in their arms like babies they wanted to toughen up. Hat brims shaded their dark, inscrutable eyes. The sun cut a swath through the cool mountain air and burned Carey's white skin pink. Hot and cold at once. Ben instructed Carey and Mike to wait for him.

"Gotta forge a path," Ben said, and slipped into the alley. Carey felt relief in her chest, a loosening. She hadn't noticed that she felt constricted until Ben was gone and she and Mike were alone. She glanced at the guards and leaned against the newspaper box. Mike claimed ignorance of the plan.

"We'll just have to be pleasantly surprised," he said, and smiled grimly.

Mike was easy to be with, even if he barely looked her in the eye. When Carey spoke, he watched closely as if translating, even when she used English. His shifting gaze: to her mouth, the ground, then away. She knew and dismissed these facts. It was Ben she wanted to impress, Ben she monitored for signs of interest. On their fast walk downtown that morning, Ben had remained a stride ahead of them, loose-limbed, swaggering. They couldn't all fit across the stone sidewalk. She'd asked twice: where are we going? And they said she wasn't allowed to ask.

"Deep into the forest," Ben shouted, as they walked along city streets clanging with cars and the Spanish chatter of the business class, men in dark suits and women in pantyhose and knee-length skirts, shoes clacking on cobblestone. "Nature hike," Mike added.

She played along. Mike assured her the first day didn't matter. Carey, a solid though unexceptional student, tried not to think about whether the teachers would call roll, to forget about the fresh notebook and package of ballpoint pens in her bag, to ignore thoughts of her host family and what she might tell them about school at the oak dinner table. Not that she was beholden to them. They were being compensated for her lodging.

Before long, her full attention was on the back of Ben's head. Bulky-shouldered Mike walked beside her like a bodyguard. They'd singled her out. She lacked the assurance to turn them down, and hadn't wanted to, besides.

Occasionally, Ben glanced back, tossing random comments into the conversation: "She's a good professor. I've known her a long time." Define "know," Carey thought. "Don't eat at this place unless you want to want to be sick for a month." And he pointed to the dingy-looking window of a restaurant she would never set foot in. She wouldn't admit it, but sometimes she recognized her mother in her own thoughts and actions. A strange comfort.

Now she stared at the newspaper in the green metal coin box, translating the front page: "Faulty Smoke Alarm; Fire Kills Four." Mike squinted at the mirrored windows of the building across the street. He lost his sunglasses, he'd complained earlier, and the glare was killing him. When he turned to Carey, the hard lines at his eyes softened.

"I'm surprised you came," he said. He picked at the cuticle of his thumb with his index fingernail. His fingers were rough and red.

Carey's father's hands, nails bitten to the quick, looked the same way.

"I had a choice?" Carey said. "That changes everything. If I'd known that, I would have gone to classes and lunch and maybe gotten a manicure, too."

Mike hid his hands behind his back, feigning a stretch, pushing his chest out. The worn gray T-shirt said Property of Madison Athletic Dept. XXL.

"It's a great honor, actually, to be invited on the guided tour," Mike said. Smiled to himself, secretive. He knew where they were headed.

"A tour of what?" she asked. Mike only shrugged.

This attention was a welcome change from last year, when her boyfriend, Damien, had dumped her. Ceremoniously. She had tried and failed to keep up with the clever and challenging Damien, the underground magazine editor. He had humiliated her in return. Everyone knew he was sleeping with the graphic designer. Everyone but Carey. She wasn't sure which had hurt worse: Damien's betrayal, or that nobody had told her.

People in Mexico would learn only what she chose to reveal. Mike knew nothing of her past. And down the alley was Ben, a guy she'd cobbled together into an almost-whole person. The celebrity at the mall pizza shop. The University of Wisconsin decal on his car's back window. His hobbies revealed by the scuffed, brown leather hiking boots, caked in dried mud. He didn't know her, either: it felt like some kind of power.

"Didn't have to come," Mike continued. "I could un-invite you right now. Not too late for you to run back to school. It's what, ten o'clock? You could still slip into art history." The bank clock above their heads showed five past ten. Carey didn't want to leave. Mike joked, but issued a challenge, too: Run back to school, little girl. She could easily run the mile-and-a-half to the university from downtown, and fast, too. Losing herself, sprinting up and down the hilly streets, around unfamiliar landmarks.

"I'm sorry, would you like me to leave you alone with Ben?" she asked sweetly.

Mike's left shoulder twitched beneath his T-shirt. The sudden movement startled her, almost made her flinch, until Mike broke into loud, forced laughter. The guard nearest them, the young one with the baby-fat cheeks, followed Mike with his eyes. After a few seconds, the guard stared straight ahead. The other, also young but with a rough, scarred face, held his weapon in one hand to slip on a pair of mirrored sunglasses. Out of style, Carey thought, something her mother might have said aloud.

"You might be OK after all, Carey," Mike said. "I don't care what Ben says."

Behind them, a theatrical throat clearing. Ben. If he'd heard the conversation, he didn't acknowledge it. "Let's go," he said, a silhouette in the alleyway.

"I thought this was a nature hike." She raised her eyebrows.

They stepped into the cool dark of the alley, where wind rushed through. The baby-fat guard noticed their movement; Carey saw a barely perceptible lift of his small chin, almost an acknowledgement. Ben held one finger to his lips.

"Open your eyes," he whispered. "It's all around us."

He pointed to an oily puddle on the ground. "Water."

They walked a short distance before Ben stopped them, holding up both hands. He motioned to the stone wall, where fuzzy green moss clung. "Green. Part Earth."

Gusts of air echoed between the buildings and pushed the city's detritus down the alley. A rolling plastic pop bottle, a pink ponytail holder. "Wind."

"Now," Ben asked, steepling his hands to his chin. "What's left?"

Mike rolled his eyes. As if addressing a child, he asked, "Fire?"

"Bingo." Ben's mouth turned up in a half grin, only one dimple.

They stood in front of a gray door, like primer, the color of cars abandoned in Indianapolis lots. Halfway down the alley, connecting fire escapes nearly blocked out the sky. When the wind stilled, if you closed your eyes, you could imagine you were somewhere remote, natural. Ben lifted a hand to knock on the door, then stopped.

"I almost forgot." Ben reached into his pocket and handed Mike a pair of mirrored sunglasses, just like the ones the rough-looking bank guard wore. The younger guard, Carey remembered, had none.

Mike smirked and put them on, even though he didn't need them in the dark alley. "I won't even ask where these came from." Ben acknowledged Mike with a quick lift of the chin, just as the guard had done. Or had not done. A coincidence.

Ben raised his hand like a boy in school, his fist closed as if in salute. When he opened his hand, a silk scarf, the same green of Carey's tank top, fluttered to her shoulders. He shook it out of the folded triangles and let go, and she reached to keep it from the wet pavement.

"Pretty," Carey cooed. "Where did you get it?"

Ben ignored the question. His hand moved through his hair as if searching for a lost item. "It's practical. Tie it around your hair before we go in."

Ben knocked on the door in a quick succession, a practiced, specific rhythm, and Carey hurried to tie her hair back with the green scarf. When no one answered, Ben opened the door.

Inside was the outside: the sun beat down on a square courtyard, with cement paths and landscaped flower beds. Stone benches flanked a small reflecting pond. Bordering the pristine garden on all sides were run-down apartment buildings: layers of balconies climbed five or six stories, with clotheslines strung between them. Relief and disappointment ebbed and flowed in her, just like her alternating desires for adventure and predictability. She had thought they were taking her to a bar, or to the seedy side of town. The beautifully tended garden grew sprays of orange and red lobelia, low-growing hyacinth and green shrubs. The flowers emitted a fragrance more potent than a department store perfume counter. Some of the blooms still shaded by the buildings displayed buds waiting to open. Carey began to relax, and when a man stepped silently from behind a door with three folding metal chairs, she almost shrieked. He had a sharp face and hollow cheeks. Maybe a little older than Ben and Mike. He kept his head down and gaze averted.

"Octavio, my good man," Ben said, nodding approvingly. Octavio had slunk over to the wall, where he leaned his thin frame against the cement. He waved, but Ben had already turned away. He was a carnival barker now. "Take your seats, take your seats. Show's about to start."

"Is he going to tell us why we need the scarf and sunglasses?" Carey asked Mike in a stage whisper. Or, Carey thought, where he got them? Mike had chosen the center chair; Carey and Ben were forced to flank him.

Ben leaned forward and smiled genuinely at Carey, she could tell by the two dimples, his eyes locked on hers. "It's part of the show," he said. "Just in case we need them."

She smiled back. Inside her, a loosening again, a feeling of release and flight. As if her ribs could not contain her heart and lungs, and they would just sail, pumped with helium, full enough to burst. She remembered having this feeling with Damien, but it always came with warnings. The erratic behavior she tolerated, the tiny inner voice of her mother that she'd ignored too long.

This was different. She was different. She was in the mountains of Central Mexico, thousands of miles from home. Practically in the clouds, depending on the weather. She knew Ben. Or felt like she did. An important distinction.

She heard a distant screech and looked up. The balcony door to a second-floor apartment slid open. Out stepped a man in his forties or fifties, with a greasy gray lion's mane of hair puffed around his weathered face.

"Old Alejandro," Mike said with a quiet fondness, a shade away from mocking. "El Viejo." Mike had known. Everything planned, staged, presumably for her benefit. And if she'd gone to class? The show would've gone on, with another girl in her seat.

Alejandro placed two hands on the balcony railing. A small flask stuck out from the hip pocket of his tattered blue pants. He took a slow swig from the flask, his eyes on them the whole time. Carey felt—even welcomed—the odd flutter of nervousness, apprehension. They must have looked comical, like theater-goers, sitting in folding chairs before this man's apartment. If Alejandro thought so, he didn't let on. His face became utterly serious as he screwed the top back on the flask, tucking it into his pocket. In one corner of the balcony leaned half a black broom handle with a small piece of cloth wrapped tightly around the top, baseball-sized. Alejandro picked it up and extended the broom toward his audience.

Earlier Carey had wished Nicole were with her, helping her navigate, but now she was glad for distance. Not only to have the experience to herself, but to have someone to tell. The email wrote itself: Alejandro and the city making up the background of a story where Ben and Mike were the principal players. Ever since Carey could remember, Nicole had managed her love life like a juggler, keeping several romantic interests in the air at once. Or she was a stone-skipper, lightly skimming the surface, even as the rocks she threw sank deep. She kept it casual. Carey had been the opposite: falling into a bottomless crush, one boy at a time. Nicole had been excited and envious about Carey's year abroad. Already it was changing her, the proof here in the garden.

Now Alejandro smiled. He lifted a silver lighter to his lips and blew, like a man blowing out cake candles on an unwanted birthday: grim, sad, purposeful, perhaps a little angry. A fireball erupted from his mouth, for as long as his lungs would go, spewing out air and fire, shooting almost over their heads, and Carey gasped and scooted her chair backwards. The flame caught the cloth on his makeshift torch. The orange-and-blue fire continued to spew from his mouth, a direct extension of his body. Finally he closed his mouth and held up the flaming torch.

Alejandro took a short bow, and Mike and Ben clapped and cheered. After a beat, Carey clapped, too. Alejandro's eyes bored into her; he motioned with his free hand.

"Grrr-race Kay-ley," he said. "Vete aquí."

"What?" Carey said, looking at Ben and Mike. She understood "Come here" but wanted to buy time.

"Your little token 'do rag reminds El Viejo of someone," Mike said. "Seems he would like an audience with you."

Carey reached up to touch the scarf. In Mike's mirrored sunglasses Carey saw herself: brown hair swept back by green silk, a face already tanned, brown eyes alive and examining, trying in vain to see behind the reflection.

"You know. Grace Kelly?" Mike said. "Fifties icon? Married into Monaco royalty?"

They waved her forward, invested but unconcerned, like parents urging a reluctant child to sit on Santa's lap at the mall.

"Aquí, aquí," Alejandro said.

Carey stood slowly, unnerved by what he might want and knowing that Mike and Ben would be looking at her, both of them, the way men examine women when their backs are turned. A split-second judgment, followed by approval or dismissal. She didn't want to see their faces. The balcony was maybe fifteen or twenty feet high, and now she was directly below.

Above, Alejandro looked like a deposed dictator. Or a royal who'd seen better days: he needed a shower and a shave and a change of clothes, yet he tossed his shoulders back as if worldly things didn't matter. He shook out his shoulder-length hair, but it barely moved. "These boys," he addressed her in Spanish. "Americans I've known a long time. Good boys, maybe. I think." He squinted at the good American boys then returned his attention to the subject beneath him. "We'll see about you, huh," he said. Her brain worked fast to translate.

Alejandro winked at her and said one more word: "Catch."

He dropped the torch off the balcony. Crossing the short distance through the air, the flames diminished slightly, receding. She stretched her hands out and wanted to yank them back in. As the torch got closer, the fire gained momentum. The flames grew. The black handle bobbled in her hands, and she thought for a moment of the scarf, and how glad she was that her hair wasn't in her eyes or near the flames. Ben's token, as Mike had called it, protected her. Her fingers clasped the wooden rod.

She hollered and raised the torch like an Olympian, trembling, and Ben and Mike laughed and whistled. She turned and grinned. They stayed in their seats. Octavio moved forward, clapping. A second later Alejandro was next to her, the rusty hinge of the courtyard gate announcing his arrival, and he took the broom handle. She smelled gasoline, maybe lighter fluid, and wondered what he'd drunk from the flask. He motioned for her to return to the chairs, to become part of the audience again. Alejandro raised the torch, his spindly legs and protruding belly splayed sideways to give a better view, and stuck the flaming end into his mouth in a slow flourish and sizzle.

Smoke rose from his mouth and gathered above his head, and all three of them applauded. Alejandro tossed the dead torch to Ben. He mimed holding a camera, his index finger clicking an imaginary shutter.

"You were going to take my picture today," Alejandro said. "Where's your camera?"

"Loaned it," Ben muttered.

Alejandro sucked on his teeth. "You know better, hijo."

Ben nodded, eyes angry.

Mike patted Carey on the shoulder. "Muy bien," he said with genuine pride. "You barely flinched." She was still shaking. Rubber arms, pounding heart.

Ben and Alejandro were chatting a few feet away. The two shook hands. One hand white with a few calluses, the other brown, leather-tough. For a brief moment a flash of color was visible between their palms. Carey saw the flash and then wasn't sure whether she had seen anything. Maybe it was money. Or a small packet containing a small substance. Reflected light, an illusion.

The handshake happened quickly. She was distracted by Mike's conversation, by Octavio hovering in the background, and by her body's adrenaline. A light, cold sweat filmed her forehead. Dark spots two-stepped across her vision. Had anything been pressed between those two palms? What had been exchanged?

She didn't ask. She should have asked.

CHAPTER 5

AFTER GETTING THE CALL from Elena at Casa Colmo, Carey drove to her mother's gift shop on 86th Street. Her father had left an envelope on the kitchen island with a note asking Carey to deliver it to Gwen, and Carey's first shift wasn't until evening. Elena's job offer was more like a command: Come at 6:45. We give you the uniform and instructions. Carey had said she'd be there. A small well of dread gurgled in her throat.

Like ninety-five point seven percent of all stores in Carey's unofficial survey of Indianapolis-area retail shopping, Finer Things existed in a strip mall beside a larger mall. Her mother would grouse about patchouli wafting from the nutritionist next door. The walls were thin despite high rents.

A sign on Finer Things' door announced: "Back in 15 minutes! I'm down the strip."

Carey peered in the window. Her mother's store, with its heavy urns, thick rugs, and restored antiques, held little interest. There was only one item she loved: a heavy silver ball large enough to bowl with, which rested in a hollowed cherry tray. The decorative art came with an outrageous price tag of $1,999. Yet something drew her. The piece had remained in the store, unsold, for ten years. She ran her palm over it nearly every visit.

"Down the strip" was the sporting goods store anchoring the

plaza. Its new rock wall had attracted media attention, Gwen had mentioned repeatedly. Carey waded through racks of shiny running shorts and T-shirts to reach the tall, fake cliff face.

There she was: dangling from a harness twenty feet off the ground, wearing tight gray trousers and a hot pink cashmere sweater and new climbing sneakers, her face determined as she reached for handholds. Next to her, a twenty-something female climbing coach offered encouragement. There was something comically shaming about seeing her mother dangling from a rope in a hot pink cashmere sweater. Carey tried to think of something funny to say when a man broke the silence, cupping his hands to his mouth.

"You own this wall!" he proclaimed upwards. His tanned, leathery skin turned craggier with the smile beneath his beard. Gwen looked down. Her face had a sheen to it. A bloom. She started to respond, but caught herself. Her forehead wrinkled.

"Hello, *Carey*," she said, loudly. The man glanced briefly at Carey and then away.

He motioned to the climbing wall, where Gwen and her instructor still dangled. "They're doing great," he said to nobody, and faded into the maze of racks. Her mother fluttered to the ground like Tinkerbell.

"Exhilarating!" she said. "There's nothing like it. You go next."

Carey craned her neck, examining the wall. She used to run upwards of thirty miles a week. Now, her muscles quivered after a few flights of stairs.

"I'll pass," Carey said. "Dad wanted me to give you this." She handed her mother the white envelope, which she opened.

"Your father sent this? And you?" Inside was a gift certificate for Ross Jewelers. Gwen stuffed it back inside the envelope, but not before Carey saw the three zeroes.

"What's wrong?" Carey asked. "It's a nice gift. Maybe for your anniversary?"

"Right. And not because he feels guilty." Her mother faced the climbing wall. "I just wonder why he didn't come himself. Though you don't have too much on your plate, do you."

Carey was in good enough spirits to let the jab slide. "Actually, I found a job."

Her mother exhaled loudly. "Why didn't you say so?" She hugged Carey with thin arms. "Let's celebrate. We haven't been to the Tea Cozy in ages. What's the job?"

"At the Mexican restaurant on High School Road."

Her mother took a half step back, as if feeling for balance. "I don't understand."

"That's about as clearly as I can say it," Carey said.

"Watch your tone."

Carey half-smiled, an insincere apology. "I start tonight."

"But you've no experience. What on earth will you do?"

Carey shrugged, picking imaginary lint off her sleeve. "I'll learn."

Her mother was scanning the store.

"Who was that guy?" Carey asked.

"What? Who?" She shook her head as if to clear it. "Is this restaurant one of those health code nightmares? Is it reputable? You know, Beverly Anderson's daughter worked at Don Pablo's to put herself through graduate school. Did I tell you she owns a house in Fishers? Not married, just up and bought a three-bedroom. Kind of curious. Anyway, I could ask Bev to ask her daughter to put in a word for you."

"No," Carey said, louder than she intended. "I'm going to give this a shot."

"You don't sound terribly enthusiastic about it."

Carey hated when her mother was right, or when her mother read her so easily. To be known by another person: a comfort and a curse. She tried to arrange her face into pleasantness, to fall behind the veil that would block her mind's scrolling thoughts. That people, say, Bev Anderson's daughter, only worked in restaurants while pursuing graduate degrees. That Carey lived at home, age twenty-eight, once again financially beholden to her well-off-yet-stingy parents. That she had been released by a temp agency. That if she invited a lover over, it would take serious logistical maneuvering to get him inside the house, and then an act of willpower to be silent while intimate. That she had no lover. How greatly she wanted to live behind that veil, hiding what was real. How often she failed.

"It's a job," she said. "It's a step toward paying you off."

"*Back.* You mean paying us back." Her mother's lips twisted like a licorice vine.

"Semantics," Carey said. When she smiled, this time it felt genuine.

Seat them, but do not forget the menus. Take the drink orders after two minutes. Maybe even one-and-a-half minutes. Chips and salsa, but do not fill too full. They are free, so they always want more. Wipe down the tables with this rag. Not while they are sitting there! You do it before or after. Write the orders on this pad, and give the sheet to Roberto. My cousin, Roberto? *El guapo* with the hair in his eyes? Yes. He will nod when the order is ready. You know because you have to look at him. Watch for the nod. No, a bell is too loud. Customers do not like a bell. Hold the tray this way. You are crooked. Try now. Maybe your other arm is stronger? Use your legs, not your back. There. That might work—not too bad. Ay de mi. Just water. It dries. Well, I suppose you could be the hostess, but *I* am the hostess. What we need are waiters and waitresses. That is why we called you, Kah-ree. Mis padres dicen, Porque no? You understand, right? They said, Why not? Yes, you know Spanish. But you so often speak English, no? Are you feeling lack of comfort? You have in your eyes a look. That is how I know. And you are quiet. This is not to say something bad, but most Americans are loud, no? And so thirsty. Remember the refills. The bathrooms need to be checked once an hour. For extra paper, cleanliness, these such things. Go to the window for the food, once you see Roberto nod. Stay out of the kitchen because you do not wear the hairnet. The cook makes dinner after the shift; eat with us. This is our way. You get used to it in no time. Welcome. Bienvenido. No, hold the tray a little to the left. Bueno. Good enough.

•

She kept missing the nod. Roberto's all-important nod. She forgot each time, and he would appear from nowhere, his hand gentle at the small of her back, with a quiet, Esta lista. It's ready. A sparse selection of customers inhabited the restaurant, half of them seated in her section. She and Juan, Elena's brother, bustled about while two other waiters sat at the bar watching the news. "It is not their shift," Elena said, following Carey's eyes to the bar. Juan, a few years younger, winked at Carey each time she passed, nodding his encouragement.

By seven-thirty she'd swung her ponytail through Table Six's sour cream ramekin. Her arms shook beneath the serving tray. One table tipped her with a fifty-cent piece, and the waiters, men she'd met two hours ago whose names she'd already forgotten, told her to bite the coin to make sure it was real. "You bite it," she muttered, and they roared with beer-infused laughter after Juan translated. Around eight-thirty, she realized she'd been grinding her teeth to the rhythm of the words "What am I doing? What am I doing?" At nine she told Juan she needed a break and stalked off to the bathroom to weep.

You can always quit, she told herself, face in her hands. Her too-tight black pants were bunched around her ankles as she peed and cried. What's more pathetic than a breakdown in a public toilet? The Casa Colmo ladies' room was clean, painted in warm shades of brown, with pictures on the wall and a potted cactus on a shelf above the mirror. Of all the places to feel sorry for oneself, this bathroom wasn't bad.

You can always quit—that was her real mantra.

To quit or not? The biggest disappointment to her parents, her mother especially, was Carey's incomplete education. Gwen was a first-generation college graduate. Carey, who'd never gone back to school after she was sent home from the exchange program, had been expected to carry on the tradition. Intercambio had given her credit for her junior year though she hadn't completed the coursework. She might've finished the Guanajuato program, she sometimes rationalized, had they not been so quick to pack her off to Indiana. The reality she tended to forget: she could not get out of bed to brush her teeth until Lupe intervened. She was nearly failing out for nonattendance before

Ben died. She never would have passed. Charitable Intercambio kept giving.

If she accepted the credits, she would benefit directly from her boyfriend's murder. Life would return to normal, to pleasing her parents and getting a better job with better pay and driving a Saab and getting married to not-Ben and having two-point-seven children and a fieldstone house in Fishers and maybe a golden retriever. She would move on. Ben would continue to be dead.

Quitting had worked in the past. She'd pull up her pants, wash her hands, fix her ruined makeup, walk out of this bathroom and quit.

She picked dried sour cream from her hair. In the mirror's reflection was a framed photograph: the picture had been taken in daylight against a bright blue sky, but it was unmistakable, even in its reverse mirror image. Ixtaccihuatl. The Sleeping Woman. Not as mysterious as the version Carey had seen at dusk almost eight years ago. In this picture, the sun lit up the entire mountain, making the curves of the sleeping princess less distinct. Carey might not have recognized the shape had she not known what to look for. Up close, she saw that it wasn't an actual photograph but a page torn from a magazine.

Signs appear to those who want to see them. Did the picture somehow speak to her, via divine intervention from Our Lady of the Backwards-Looking? Maybe. Or possibly Carey, with no other prospects, had been searching for reasons to stay. She'd entered through the glass door depicting a church from another life. Her bosses were a kind family she barely knew and strangely did not want to disappoint. Now this sign: an image torn both from a magazine and her memory. She'd even chosen the volcano for a screen name: La mujer.

She salvaged her eye makeup and emerged. Juan watched her clear glasses of melting ice. "Long break," he said. "We take that out of your pay."

He wore a mock-serious expression, then winked twice for effect. The waiters at the bar laughed and laughed. She smiled and carried the fingerprinted glasses to the counter, her newly-aching back creating a foreign, pleasant sensation all the way to her heels. This was work. Work mattered. She would break her back if she had to, anything to make up for her failures. She would compensate for becoming spoiled and soft, the kind who quits everything easily and without conscience. She sipped Coke from a straw at the bar, guzzling refills before heading back out on the floor. This time, she decided, quitting would be the difficult choice.

The caffeine kept her up that night. She prowled the dark house. In her father's empty study, the computer lit up the room with its geometric-pattern screen saver. She eventually found him on the back deck, smoking one of her cigarettes.

At the sound of the sliding glass door, he appeared neither surprised nor ashamed. He took a long drag, exhaling a thin line of smoke.

"These are *good*," he said. "I haven't smoked since college."

"Dad?"

"Takes the edge off, you know?"

"I would've given you one if you asked."

"Would've been awkward."

"Unlike digging through my purse."

She'd always wished her parents acted more like parents. Most teenagers naturally want to separate, not drink wine with them at dinner. Gwen and Brian had anointed her with a maturity she did not possess. Because they were open about things other parents considered taboo—drinking, smoking, even her mother's frank talks about sex—she found herself hiding more innocuous things from them. Details about trig class. The name of the guy in the old station wagon who dropped her off once. ("Was that a date? Honestly, Carey, does that car even have a muffler?") Withdrawing gave her more room. She made her parents into authorities.

She appreciated the irony of her father sneaking one of her cigarettes. Had her mother gone through Carey's purse, that would have been another story. Her father, who lately bumbled through the house like a clumsy afterthought, made the action pardonable, even funny. She took a cigarette from the pack and clicked her lighter, which he had also borrowed. An empty tumbler with a lone ice cube rested on the wrought-iron patio table.

"That can't be good for your running," she said, gesturing with her own lit cigarette.

"Nor yours," he said.

"I stopped running," she reminded him. "That's your thing now." It had always been his thing. He'd introduced her to running, and they'd competed together in 5Ks and half-marathons when she was in high school and college. He'd stopped asking her to join his regular jogs in the nearby woods of Eagle Creek Park.

"Chicken or egg?" he asked cryptically. "You can't run because you smoke, or you smoke so you can't run."

"That doesn't make any sense."

"Exactly."

She fumed inwardly. "It's bad etiquette to bum a smoke and criticize the smoker."

"Point taken," he said. He crushed out the cigarette on the table, and ashes fell from the ironwork slats onto his jeans. Like her, he changed from work clothes immediately upon arriving home. Carey knew that the desk chair in her parents' bedroom would be wearing her father's rumpled shirt and jacket and tie. And her mother would be asleep, ignoring the clothes until they found the closet.

"That was some gift you had me give mom," Carey said, trying to change the subject.

He brightened. "Did she like it?"

So her parents had not spoken yet about the exorbitant jewelry shop gift certificate. It had been a mistake for Carey to bring it up. She shrugged, trying to back out. "I'm sure she did. She just seemed kind of confused."

He nodded quickly, grinding the cigarette on the table until it was flattened.

"Gwen's not going to like ashes on the deck," Carey said, trying to lighten the mood. They had always bonded over mutual defiance of Gwen Halpern's attention to household minutia. There was a time, long since passed, when Gwen took the teasing in stride and laughed at herself.

"I doubt she gives a shit, one way or the other," he said, pushing back his chair.

"Dad," Carey started, but he was finished. He ruffled her hair like he did when she was a child, leaving her alone with his empty glass and ashes.

No new email messages, from Mike or anyone else. Two chat room members were engaged in verbal foreplay. The scene left her cold. She rewound the day. Her first shift had ended with delicious quesadillas, almost as good as Lupe's had been. She could still remember, all these years later, the taste of Lupe's quesadillas.

She had anticipated with dread the focused attention her parents would provide when she moved back. Now she was miffed by their self-absorption. She was their buffer, pawn, bargaining chip. The deliverer of dated anniversary gifts, the messenger about to be shot.

She shut down the computer in the dark, letting the fading screen slowly darken the room. Out the window, tree branches outlined by moonlight disappeared and reemerged with the cloud cover. She grew sleepy in the light's tidal rhythm.

Her dark room lit briefly with light from outside, as headlights turned down their cul-de-sac. The car pulled into the Halpern's driveway. Slowly, quietly, practically idling, her mother rolled her black Jetta into the open garage at 3:23 a.m.

CHAPTER 6

BARTOLO ENTERED THE CAFÉ with his friends, unaware of Carey sitting alone at a table across the room. When he saw her, his face stiffened. He strode to her table.

"What are you doing?" he said. "You shouldn't be here alone."

"Why?" she challenged. "I'm waiting for a friend." The "o" in amigo gave her away. Gendered language offered less room for vagaries, for games.

Bartolo surveyed the three empty seats around Carey's square wooden table. His three friends were settling into another table across the room. One too many. The old man behind the long wooden bar dried glasses with the concentration of a meditating monk.

"I'm fine," Carey said. "Go sit with your friends."

"You are welcome to join us," he said, sweeping his hand formally to his party. "We will add a chair."

She said, No, no, I couldn't intrude. He said, But it is our pleasure. They batted the invitation back and forth. She remained firmly planted. The men in her host family, Bartolo and Hector, hemmed her in with their curfews and questions. They were unused to American women who said and did what they pleased. Carey merely wanted to go running alone, or opt to sit by herself at a café table.

"Insisto, insisto," Bartolo said, now doubtful.

"He'll be here any second," Carey said.

Bartolo shrugged, nodded, and crossed the room. He sat with his back to Carey, occasionally looking over his shoulder. Serious, even grave, as if she were not smiling at him but sticking out her tongue.

Ben had emailed her late the night before, to invite her to the café for a drink after classes. They'd been in Mexico a little over a month, going out in packs, or it was the three of them: Carey, Mike, and Ben. Never two.

What made Ben's no-show worse was that she'd emailed Nicole to brag. Nicole responded promptly, full of unsolicited advice: "It's up to YOU to do something! DON'T wimp out! He's waiting for a sign."

Carey had been sitting alone for forty minutes, according to her silver wristwatch. Her pint of Dos Equis perspired onto the ringed table. Her fingers unconsciously picked at the sleeve of her white peasant blouse. Sweat adhered the backs of her thighs to her jeans skirt.

After half a beer, she stood to leave. Bartolo hurried to her table as if summoned. He smiled, less shy after a couple drinks.

"I'm sorry, I think your friend is not coming," he said. "Perhaps something came up?" His words translated as "something got in the way." She unconsciously altered the meaning, as she was taught to do with idiomatic expressions.

"Está bien," Carey said brightly. "No problemo."

"Please, join us." His words slurred slightly. "Truly, we would be honored."

Carey wanted to. But she felt foolish for snubbing the group. One of Bartolo's friends, a shade more attractive than the others, turned his head. He was confident verging on arrogant, evident in his swagger up to the long oak bar, or how he'd stare, then look away before she did. Letting her know she'd been caught watching.

"I think I'll go back to the house," Carey said, walking out. Bartolo was still as a statue. His table of friends howled, and Carey burned with their drunken teasing. Ay, Bartolo, you drove her away! What did you say to her, guey, when will you learn how to talk to a girl!

He waved them off and followed her outside, two steps behind her.

"It's dark. You shouldn't walk alone."

She said nothing.

"I'm ready to go home anyway. I'll walk you."

Again, silence. Carey ran a hand through her hair, expending all energy on indifference.

He stopped. "You're going the wrong way."

"Fine," she finally sighed, turning to follow him. She would have figured out which way to go. Or she would've wandered for hours, days, weeks, lost as an amnesiac. There seemed to be countless ways to get from one place to another, though the parks and buildings allegedly never moved. Maps helped little—many of the streets and callejones dead-ended once you'd climbed to the top of their winding paths. Or they were renamed.

They walked quietly for awhile, strides falling into rhythm. She tempered her irritation toward Bartolo—she was angry with Ben. Hurt by Ben.

"Thank you again for my necklace," she said, making amends, touching the hollow of her throat where the St. Christopher medallion hung. "Alicia said it's from your jewelry shop?"

"Yes. But it was on a different chain before. I liked this one better."

In the dark, walking side by side, she could almost feel him blush. They passed the darkened bakery window, their reflections illuminated under the yellow street lamp. He was slightly taller, a bigger, older brother. Hermana y hermano.

"It was a simple adjustment," he said. "I do it every day."

"But you hadn't met me. How did you know what I'd like?"

"In the picture you sent, you wore little jewelry. You prefer simplicity, I think."

In Carey's high school senior photo, her last formal portrait, her mother insisted on the salon for a professional hairdo. But Carey had drawn the line at the strand of pearls her mother offered to loan. Her neck, bare and unadorned, had been what she liked most about the picture, and the first thing Gwen Halpern critiqued.

"You're right," Carey told Bartolo.

They continued along the sidewalk bordering a small park, a square block of green space. City grit lodged between Carey's sandaled toes, but she felt at ease, if resigned. Cars passed, going out or going home. A few lamps cast light: couples on park benches, teenage boys skateboarding up and down narrow park paths, and cats, nimble and sly, pets or strays, slinking in and out of the darkness. Shadows played among the trees and bushes, and a rustling that could have been— what? wind, animal, human, newspaper—unsettled the stale, warm air of the day. She was glad not to be alone.

"Cuidate," he said, gently reining her in by the shoulder, switching places so he would be nearest the traffic. His friends, honking and shouting from a passing Toyota, stopped at the curb.

"Perdoneme un momentito," he said, walking to the car. He put his hands on the window frame and leaned inside, talking quietly. She bent to fiddle with her black sandal strap. The one with slicked hair spoke in a teasing voice, but not loud enough for her to hear. Bartolo laughed and slapped the roof of the car, said Goodbye, I'll see you.

"What did they say?" she asked.

"Ay," Bartolo said. "They think I am, how to say, having bad intentions."

She laughed out of embarrassment. "Just tell them I am your sister," she said.

"I would if you were." He focused straight ahead, and they were halfway down the block before she translated the verb tense. Past perfect, subjunctive, she couldn't remember. She had little time to dwell on her sub-par Spanish grammar.

"Who were you waiting for?" he asked.

"A friend from the school," she said.

"Americano o Méxicano?"

"Americano," she said. "Por qué?"

"Por nada," he said. For nothing.

When they entered the foyer, Hector was hunched on the small upholstered bench, tying his shoes. A flashlight peeked from the pocket of his light jacket. He straightened and stared incredulously.

"Do you know what time it is?" he asked in Spanish, his voice low and level.

Carey began inventing apologies, excuses. Hector intimidated her. Even though she could see his scalp through his thinning hair, pinkish, vulnerable as a baby's.

Bartolo spoke breezily for them both. "No hay problema."

Hector grunted and began untying his shoes without a word.

In the kitchen, Lupe filled the copper kettle with water. When she saw Carey and Bartolo walk in together, she smiled. A trace of worry remained in her eyes.

"Buenos noches, niños. Están muy tardes," she said.

"Está bien, está bien," Bartolo said, placating her. "Estábamos juntos." We were together.

"De dónde?" Lupe asked.

"En el café cerca del parque," Carey said, proud of her Spanish reply.

Lupe asked if they'd had supper. It was nearly eleven, and the family normally ate at nine. She heated the cast-iron pan that lived on the stove's back burner. She lit the pilot light, drizzled a little oil in the pan. When the oil hissed, she dropped in perfectly round and flat tortillas. Flipping them once, she added fresh white cheese to each circle, folding them in half.

Lupe moved confidently in the kitchen, a surprise. Maria had cooked all the other meals and cleaned up afterwards. Carey had assumed that Lupe, with her impeccably manicured hands, would fumble cautiously with the oil, hunt for a pan, burn the tortillas. Instead she practically commanded the spatula to her hand, her long, thin arms stretching from her station in front of the stove, graceful and easy. The simple quesadillas browned lightly and perfectly.

"Mama was a model," Bartolo said, noticing Carey watching.

Lupe smiled, modest, and pinched a bit of extra flesh at her waist. "Not anymore. Not like your Julia Roberts, from *The Pretty Woman*."

"Bartolo has your eyes," Carey said. Bartolo reddened with the effort of suppressing a smile.

Lupe studied her son, as if this were new information to her. "Hmm," she said, not agreeing or disagreeing. "He takes after his father, bless his soul."

Bartolo's face drained of all expression, reforming into a stony mask. He attacked his quesadillas, pausing only to drink the chocolate from the matching stoneware mug his mother placed by his plate. Lupe watched her son as if he were a suspenseful movie.

Bartolo's father was Lupe's first husband, her first love, and they talked about him obliquely, as if he were in the other room and might hear. Carey had gathered that the man was dead; no one told her. She didn't know them well enough to ask, nor did she know how to ask. She'd barely known her own grandparents, who died when she was still a child. Her parents kept no photos of them around the house. In her family, the dead stayed dead through silence.

A few pictures of Juan remained on the walls: a young, pregnant Lupe in a colorful shift dress, holding Juan's hand. Walking on a beach with a toddler-sized Bartolo atop his shoulders. He was tall, taller than Lupe, clean-shaven, and combed his black hair back with pomade. In the pictures, Juan and Lupe looked like a famous couple, grinning in sunglasses and fashionable clothing. Hector was shorter, balding, and serious, and turned Lupe into who she was: a fifty-something woman on her second husband. Juan had to be dead. Why else would Hector allow photos of his wife's first husband to remain on hallway walls and in frames on the parlor bookshelves?

Lupe placed the pan and spatula in the sink. She'd cook, but Maria cleaned up.

"Lupe," Hector summoned from upstairs, his warning voice. She wiped her hands on a dishtowel and sighed.

"Just remember, niño," she said to Bartolo. "You have the world in front of you." She leaned down to kiss the top of his head. He accepted with a grunt.

She walked to the doorway and Carey could see the model's stride, shoulders set. Barely turning her head, she addressed Carey. Slowly, lazily.

"You too, niña. The both of you, no?"

From above, Hector cleared his throat. He must've been listening through the heating vent. "Basta, Lupe," he said. Enough.

None of it sunk in—Lupe's pushing, Hector's reluctance to

embrace an outsider. Carey, eager to check email, used Lupe's exit as her cue. She offered to take Bartolo's empty plate to the sink with her own. He shook his head.

"I'm going to stay here awhile longer." He watched her carefully.

"Well. Goodnight, then. I have some things to do for school."

He poured more chocolate, concentrating on each drop. She sensed, just as at the café, that she'd said the wrong thing, made the wrong choice. Yet she didn't care enough to fix it.

In the parlor she plugged the phone jack into her laptop. She'd learned from classmates that the Alarcóns were unusual, one of the only host families with dial-up Internet access. On rare occasions, Hector brought home a computer from the bank and logged on; his line was the designated backup when the bank's system failed. It was late enough that he wouldn't mind if she tied up the phone.

Her inbox held nothing new, save for a message from Nicole that she briefly scanned and decided to answer later. She went back to Ben's emailed invitation, a flirtatious note, asking if he could "corrupt" her, pull her away from her studies, and she should say Yes. She'd done as he asked. He did not arrive.

Date: Tuesday, August 22, 1995, 11:47 p.m.
To: Ben Williamson <bensays@freenet.com>
From: Carey Halpern <chalpern@intercambio.edu>
Subject: missing in action

If I didn't have your e-mail in front of me as proof, I'd swear I'd gotten the time or place wrong. Nope. I was there. Where were you?

My host brother walked me home. A gentleman and a scholar. Hasta mañana. Unless you skip class, too.

C

As soon as she hit "send," regret washed over her. What if something had happened, what if he was sick, or in some kind of trouble? She tried to sedate that voice in her brain. She'd been stood up, after all.

She crept barefoot down the hallway, sandals in one hand. Lupe and Hector were speaking rapidly behind their closed bedroom door. Hector's gruff, repeated words: "A bad idea, Lupita." Mala idea. That she'd been out at night. That they'd been together. Hector had been concerned enough to look for her. Why hadn't he been reassured she was with his stepson? Another thing she failed to understand in the moment: Hector was less interested in her protection than in Bartolo's.

Silently, she opened the door to the room she shared with Alicia, whose sleeping face, washed and slack, looked younger than fifteen. Carey tiptoed to bed, imagining what the night would be like if Ben had shown up. She invented their conversations, an ease that did not yet exist. She envisioned the painfully long, exquisite process that would lead them to bed. In some ways, the anticipation of seeing Ben was better than the fact of seeing him.

She was merely a host body, controlled by brain chemicals and pulsing blood. She wished to be logical. Reason and logic keep us, allegedly, a chromosome away from our animal ancestors. Yet she squandered her brain power in the most predictable of ways: plotting a love life, a social life, but mainly just plotting.

The other students in the exchange program were business majors with minors in international finance, future PR execs, one girl who wanted to be a Spanish literature translator. ("All the classic novels," Sylvie said with a perfect accent.) Carey still didn't know what she'd do with her sociology major and Spanish minor. They had seemed like worthwhile pursuits, interesting, fulfilling. That had seemed like enough.

Carey rolled onto her side and watched Alicia sleep. How easy fifteen seemed, with a summer break and an uncomplicated life still dictated by parents. Carey longed to be that age. Older was fine, too. She wanted to be whatever she was not.

The next morning, she went directly to the computer lab before class. There were two new emails from Ben.

Date: Wednesday, August 23, 1995 12:01 a.m.
To: Carey Halpern <chalpern@intercambio.edu>
From: Ben Williamson <bwilliamson@intercambio.edu>
Subject: homework reaps rewards

Ch. 3 for culture class: pay close attention to the Rivera reference. A giant, flawed man, but he did all right with las mujeres. Women posed for him. Nekkid, as my Uncle Vern would say. I ain't got a paintbrush. But I do have a camera.

—B

Date: Wednesday, August 23, 1995 3:37 a.m.
To: Carey Halpern <chalpern@intercambio.edu>
From: Ben Williamson <bensays@freenet.com>
Subject: re: tonight

Ooops. I forgot about the café. I was hanging around the dorm and got to talking with people on the floor. I'm not usually such an airhead. Must be the altitude…

Ben

They'd talked about touring the Rivera house and the murals downtown. They could have gone yesterday. She'd feel a mad rhythm in her chest when she walked into Profesora Schwartz's history class. She couldn't stay angry, not once she saw Ben's hair, sticking out at odd angles like a cartoon mad scientist. He wore a wrinkled white t-shirt, baggy khaki shorts, the brown lace-up hiking boots. The same boots Carey had followed down the corridor of Oakview Mall back home, clumps of dried mud falling from the soles onto the tile. She'd been enough paces behind to stay invisible. She had thought, *So he hikes.*

History was held in the chemistry classroom. She sat next to Mike at a lab table. Across from them, Ben was talking to Jennifer, she of the canary-colored hair and loud, attention-getting voice. She announced she was going dancing on Friday. Probably the type of girl Ben normally went out with, like the ones from Trinity whose mug shots were in the paper the year before for hazing underclassmen. Tough and pretty, steel-eyed and fierce. When you looked at those pictures, you knew: Those girls feared no one.

Ben rifled through his green backpack, pulling out notebooks and papers. He set his camera on the table.

"Take your picture?" he asked Carey, grinning.

"No," she said flatly, even though her anger had dissipated. He raised his eyebrows, watching her. A few glossy photographs fell from the textbook in his hand. She tried in vain to see, but he scooped them back inside in a single deft motion.

"I've done some modeling," Jennifer supplied. "You can shoot me."

Carey said, "You *should* shoot her, Ben."

Mike concealed a smirk, but Carey's remark sailed past Jennifer. "Modeling was actually a pain," she said. "Standing around like a dressed-up doll, sucking in my cheeks." She imitated a pose, which would have been funny if it didn't enhance her beauty, bringing out her cheekbones and enormous blue eyes. Pretty people cannot be self-effacing, not about their symmetrical bodies and features.

Ben picked up his camera. "Come stand by the window," he told Jennifer. "For the light."

Carey turned away. Mike massaged his left shoulder through his red-and-white "Big Mike's Sub Shop" shirt. He looked at her mouth instead of her eyes.

"Didn't see you at the theater last night," he said. He pronounced it *thee*-a-tah, with a failing British accent. A series of short plays had been performed by Mexican university students in the plaza.

"I was busy," she said. "Well. I was supposed to be busy." She glanced at Ben, immediately wishing she hadn't. She saw his back, tensed with concentration. She saw Jennifer's face, lit up in its posed way.

"Aha," Mike said. "So, did you two…are you two…?" He gestured between Carey and Ben with a flip of his wrist.

He meant to be casual, she could tell, even as he finally looked in her eyes.

"No," she said. "We didn't. We're not."

Mike nodded quickly as if to say, Understood. But he concentrated on the table. He traced his finger along the carved graffiti, a knifed epithet: "Chupacabra '87!"

The shutter clicked again. Ben had taken a candid photo of her. Possibly Mike, too.

Ben grinned. "Everybody wants their picture taken," he said.

"You could've taken it last night," Carey said.

"True," Ben said. "I wish I'd had the chance. But there's always tonight. And noon tomorrow. And what are you doing at three, the day after that?"

She took this as his apology.

Later, rehashing the conversation, she assigned more importance to the exchange than it deserved. Memory: a sifting of glances, words, expressions. Discarding the ones that don't fit, assigning meaning to the ones that do. Getting it wrong, always, via an imperfect brain.

In a social psychology class, she had learned that eyewitness accounts of crimes and criminals were usually wrong. The criminal was a foot taller or a foot shorter than the witness recalled; the suspect had blond hair or red hair, not black. New information in the brain is touched by the millions of other pieces already stored inside. We didn't see what we thought we saw. To imagine her own brain misfired over someone she knew, someone she loved and had been intimate with. Someone she'd imagined she knew better than she actually had.

A small glowing forest of birthday candles lit up the iced chocolate cake the waiter had placed on the table, and the Americans cleared glasses and beer bottles and the ashtray to make room.

"We're eating pastel at Pastel!" yelled Jennifer, the birthday girl.

She was already tanked, her face red and puffy from drinking. She'd curled her blonde hair, framing her face and bare shoulders. Jennifer wore a beige satin spaghetti-strap tank top—practically pajamas—for her twenty-first birthday, which meant less here than it did in the States. Alicia probably could get into Pastel. No one had told Carey there would be a birthday party tonight; she'd arrived empty-handed.

Ben, Mike, and a few other students—Mimi from NYU, Alex from Ohio State, and Sharese from Alabama—crowded around the small circular table. Sharese and Mimi shared a cigarette. Mike argued with Ben over singing "Happy Birthday."

"We're in Mexico," Mike said. "We ought to sing 'Las Mañanitas.'"

"I heard you the first three times," Ben said. "Control yourself."

Mike glanced quickly at Carey and at the cake. He rolled his eyes and raised his beer bottle, toasting to nothing in particular, deflecting his embarrassment. She tried to smile at him. He wouldn't look.

Ben wore a gray button-down shirt Carey had never seen before. A change from his T-shirts and used polyester. Still, the cotton material was deeply wrinkled. Old or new, Ben's clothes bore creases. He didn't own an iron and couldn't be bothered to borrow one. Years later, Carey thought of his wrinkled shirts as one more sign she missed. Maybe he knew his time was short. He had better things to do than iron.

Pastel was made of cloying cologne and perfume and cigarette smoke and sweaty dancers. The club catered mostly to Mexican patrons, such as the man in his early twenties who shook Ben's hand at the door. "El fotógrafo!" he exclaimed drunkenly, and Ben patted the man's shoulder. The Americans mixed with the locals. The Intercambio students agreed that was the best part: Pastel was *authentic*. Never mind that the club (or el dees-co, as Bartolo called it), played dated American music—Bon Jovi, Madonna—or that the pursuits of dancing and drinking and flirting were the same as any club they'd been to on their respective college campuses. The white Americans played the unfamiliar role of minorities. They relished it because they knew it was temporary, part of *the experience*, part of *what you get out of it*. Small, new pieces inside themselves to take back home.

An older man strode to the table. Maybe sixty years old, in a stiff white suit with brocaded epaulets, brandishing a guitar. A sombrero hung from a cord around his neck and bounced on his back; he lifted it to his head. His thick, grayed eyebrows pushed together in concentration. After strumming a few chords, he serenaded Jennifer with the traditional birthday song. A throaty and sweet voice, eyes closed.

"The lyrics never actually say birthday," Carey remarked. Nobody responded. She silently accepted a third Corona from Mike and tilted it to her mouth.

"So sweet," Jennifer said, as the others fumbled for coins. "Did you guys do this?"

Modest Ben smiled his most humble smile.

The cantador accepted a twenty-peso note from Ben and bowed slightly. "Que bonita su novia," he told Ben. Carey's smile froze when she realized the singer meant Jennifer. Worse, Ben only shook his head, saying nothing.

Her possessiveness had been growing; now it blindsided her. The mood had been wrong all night. Carey first had tried to be witty, a crack about Jennifer having to watch out for wrinkles, and even she could hear her stilted, catty voice, too late to draw it back. The pause before Mimi laughed, politely, the same as stamping Carey's forehead in big red letters: SHUT UP. Which she couldn't see, but only felt, burning on her face. Eventually she lapsed into silence alongside moody, acidic Mike, until they were singing to Jennifer to tell her they were glad she'd been born, though truth be told Carey wasn't. Nicely, she allowed, Jennifer ought to have been born sooner, later, placing her in any junior year study abroad program but hers.

Still, she knew: There would always be Jennifers. There was an army of them, their mothers had all watched "Love Story" in the 1970s, admiring the long dark hair of Ali McGraw as Jenny. And some of the Jennifers had other names, different colored hair.

Her eyes burned from the dance floor smoke machine. She abruptly stood and wove around tables and through the crowd at the bar to get to the bathroom. A man Nicole would've described as hot smiled at Carey. Medium height, Mexican, and stocky in a dark tan suit with an open-necked shirt. He made Carey feel underdressed in her black pants and tight red sleeveless blouse. He brushed his arm against Carey's as she walked by, silky fabric against her bare skin.

"Perdoneme," he said, adding to his apology a hand on her upper arm. He wore a thick gold band on his pinkie. "Quiere bailar?"

"Sorry," Carey said, promising nothing, motioning vaguely to the other end of the club where the bathrooms were.

He nodded, looking her up and down. "I'll be right here." The Spanish words rolling off his tongue.

In the bathroom she washed her hands and checked her hair in the mirror. The same Carey who went running this morning, but showered and in a change of clothes. Hair loose, fairly shiny. But not blonde or curled, not hanging down around her shoulders. No skin-exposing tank top. She tried to imagine Jennifer's flaws: the aspiring broadcast journalist could not stifle the twang that revealed her rural Illinois roots. The hard vowels stretching "You guys" into five syllables instead of two. All those stories of growing up in Chicago, when really she'd lived in a dumpy little river town. She pronounced Chicago like the "a" might break her face.

Jennifer swung open the bathroom door as if summoned. Her eyes were red. A small flaw, Carey noted.

"You all right?" they asked simultaneously, a rare show of camaraderie. Then the image popped into Carey's head: Jennifer scooting her chair closer to Ben's at the table as she sliced her birthday cake. "Que rico," she'd said, licking her chocolate-covered fingers. She was not a friend. She was danger, a threat, a red flashing sign on a dark, curving road.

Jennifer spoke first, her nasally voice twanging and echoing in the small bathroom. "My contacts are bugging out. I wish to hell Mimi and Sharese would quit smoking."

She said "Sha-reesh" instead of "Sha-reese." She flipped her hair around, fluffing it out, losing her balance and falling off one heel. The sandals were beige rubber, cheap-looking.

"Other than that," Jennifer said, "I'm great. It's my birthday, goddamn it!"

She waited for Carey's response, which didn't come. "Anyway," Jennifer prompted, "Mike thought you were upset."

"No," Carey lied. "I just had to pee."

"God, me too. Wait for me?"

Carey leaned against the sink, her hands bracing the countertop's tiles.

"So, Carey," Jennifer said from the stall. "What's up with you and Ben?"

Carey's pause gave her away. "What do you mean?"

"What do you mean?" Jennifer mimicked. "Are you guys dating, or what? Inquiring minds want to know."

"*I* want to know," Carey said, imitating those National Enquirer commercials from back home. "We hang out."

"I know *that*." Jennifer sounded annoyed. "So are you together?"

There was no way to answer: Yes, but he doesn't seem to know it. No, he's all yours. Loud, pulsing music erupted outside the red bathroom door. Carey felt it in her heartbeat.

"Maybe," she said, realizing how silly she sounded.

"S'cool," Jennifer said. "Just asking." She emerged from the stall with toilet paper stuck to her beige high-heeled sandal. Carey followed her out of the bathroom. Anyone who wears beige rubber shoes, Carey thought, deserves toilet paper stuck to them. An arbitrary bias rooted in Gwen Halpern logic. Still. Carey stepped on the white tissue and freed Jennifer, who flounced away, oblivious.

At the bar, the man in the suit stood in the same place. He grinned so widely she could see the small silver filling of his upper molar. He asked again: Did she want a drink? Did she want to dance? He wasn't bad-looking.

"Both," she said.

He held tightly to the small of her back as they moved across the dance floor, increasing the pressure to turn and twirl her. His musky cologne filled her air. She didn't recognize him, but he knew her.

"I am a good friend of your brother." Luis spoke hotly in her ear. "Since we were young."

"Is he here?" She craned her neck. She would behave differently if

Bartolo were present.

Luis's silver filling glinted again. Bartolo only went to the disco when forced.

"Were you at the café a few weeks ago?" she asked. "The day I was there?"

"Yes," he said. "I thought you were very pretty."

Normally, she'd be put off by such unvarnished flattery. Tonight was different.

"Gracias," she said, attempting for the kind of inflection she'd heard Lupe use when responding to compliments: grateful but unsurprised. She even flipped her hair a little, scanning the crowd over Luis's shoulder. Jennifer, Mike, Sharese, and Alex in a discussion. Off to the side of the table was Ben, his back against the wall, watching her. Unsmiling.

She threw back her head and laughed, though Luis hadn't said anything. He pressed his cheek to her cheek, his body to her body, twirling her out by the arm. She ran into the couple on her left. "Lo siento," she said, though nobody heard or noticed, not in the flail of limbs and pulsing beat and strobe lights. The room sweated in unison.

Now she didn't need to look. Ben's eyes burned into her back, the side of her face as she spun, the narrow runner's hip that jutted with her momentum.

They danced to three songs. Back at the bar, a salt shaker and small dish of lime wedges flanked the two shot glasses of tequila. They were filled to spilling, meant to be sipped, taken with the salt and fruit. She wanted something that burned. There were rules being established tonight, ones she could not name. She would make her own.

Then Ben was there, at the bar, clapping one hand on her shoulder, one on Luis's.

"What're we drinking?" He spoke in English. It was clear Luis didn't understand, but he reached out his right hand to shake Ben's. Neither asked the other's name. Maybe they recognized each other. Ben slowly removed his right hand from Carey's shoulder, pausing briefly at the back of her neck.

"Es tequila," Carey said, picking up her shot. Irritated he was speaking English.

Luis, still confident, smiled his winning smile. He was a couple inches taller than Carey, which meant smaller than Ben. "Uno más." Luis signaled the bartender with an index finger.

As soon as Luis turned his back, Ben picked up the remaining shot, tilting it to his lips. Gone in one long gulp.

Luis turned to Carey and Ben, smiling tightly. "Son novios?" he asked. Everyone wanted to know their status. Luis reached for his glass and found it empty. He probably would've given the shot to Ben anyway, out of politeness. Ben grinned like a misbehaving boy who wasn't the least bit sorry. The heavyset bartender was occupied at the other end of the bar. Luis's smile disappeared. He held up both palms. "Que pasó?" he asked.

Nobody answered. "Let's go," Ben said, his arm snaking back around Carey's shoulder.

"No," she said.

"Carey. Come on."

"No entiendo ingles."

Luis gave her an odd look, his face flushed. She was with some cabrón who stole his tequila. She couldn't hear Luis's rapid Spanish above the music. But his face said all she needed to know.

Ben smiled at Carey with admiration. He leaned down to her ear, staring directly at Luis. "Vamonos," he said.

It wasn't as if she decided, or made anything like a conscious choice. It was her feet, she told herself, that just began walking. Then running. Always following.

Bartolo would hear about it, of course. Luis had been a gentleman. But she couldn't help what her feet decided without her consent.

On the sidewalk, she put up a good front. They'd gone far enough from Pastel that they couldn't hear the music. They walked uphill, beyond town, catching their breath.

"What were you thinking?" she asked, amazed and incensed. "I know him. Do you think you can just drag me away when I'm talking to someone?"

For a moment he didn't answer, then sighed a heavy, tequila-infused sigh. "You don't want to hang around that guy," he said.

"How do you know?"

"Because I'm better," he said simply.

She smiled to herself. The street seemed unfamiliar until she saw a house she recognized by its bright red-and-yellow-painted door. Soon they were turning down lanes with unrecognizable doors, then fewer homes, then stretches of weedy fields between buildings.

"Oh! Jennifer." Carey suddenly remembered. They'd never returned to the table.

"What about her?"

"Think she'll be upset we ditched her party?"

Ben shrugged. "Who cares?"

He bumped against her, sideways. Grabbed her hand with a damp palm. He said he knew a place with a good view, if she wanted to see.

"I've seen El Pípila," she said. Everyone had. The statue of the town's revolutionary hero raised a fist from atop a southern hill, looking down on the old river basin where the city clung like colorful moss. The overlook filled with camera-wielding tourists, vendors selling tamales and Chiclets, T-shirts and silver jewelry. Great floodlights illuminated the figure after sunset.

"That's on the other side of town."

"Fine," she said, an edge in her voice. She didn't want him to forget she'd been angry.

They hiked uphill for several more minutes, and Ben led her to an alley with winding stone steps. Weak yellow lights cast shadows. She took a step back and he squeezed her hand.

"I know who lives here," he said. "It's fine."

And her feet kept moving. They passed several clustered houses, much smaller than the homes in Lupe and Hector's neighborhood. A television set radiated canned laughter. A dog barked. Up another staircase, this one narrower. He insisted she go first. He put his hand on her hip, gentler than Luis's had been on the dance floor. Ben's hand rested there, not moving her in any particular direction.

The top of the staircase unfolded onto a flat roof. It was very dark. She climbed the remaining steps. Below, lining the valley, hanging on the hills, the city lit up in a muted yellow glow. As if the light came from within. She remembered patchy details from a recent lecture: a flood hundreds of years before, the teacher said, had buried parts of old Guanajuato. A city beneath the city. Nothing remained but ruins, yet she had the idea the underground city caused the soft light in the bowl of this old river valley. Lighter than phosphorescence, yellower, more beautiful.

"I've never seen it like this," she said.

Ben was a few steps below her. When she turned, his forehead pressed against her side. She couldn't see his face. His hair brushed her skin, where the red shirt had risen up half an inch. He put his lips to the exposed flesh. It was happening, she told herself. He nudged her forward, admiring the city briefly.

"Come here," he said. He stretched out on the pebbly rock surface; she joined him. The straw broom in the corner leaned against the wall near a rounded pile of debris. Her mind flashed: Is this going to be it? And, Is this all it's going to be? It was not her first time, that forgettable event had happened the summer after high school, but the idea of *this* first time made her drunk with excitement. Maybe she should tell. Back home, I knew you. You didn't know me.

"I promised you a view," he said, "and you're not even going to look?"

She turned her head, following his gaze up to the sky. Down in the city, the lights made it impossible to see what was overhead at night. Of course they were there. The stars. Brighter than she'd ever seen, suspended.

She stretched out beside him. Their arms touched, barely.

"This would be a good place to shoot," he said. "You'd have to pose. You're always moving, too quick for film. But I'll try." When she didn't answer, he added, "If you want."

She felt the same calm as when diving into a swimming pool: everything slowed down, heavy, bathed in blue-green light. "Of course."

He raised his finger, the pointer, and traced out shapes in the stars.

"Connect-the-dots," he said.

Not the Crab or the Hunter or the Dippers, but an ice cream cone. A VW Beetle. A beer bottle. With one finger he spelled their names, taking up half the sky.

She traced, Why haven't you kissed me?

"That didn't exactly connect the dots," he said.

"Shh." She was making rules. He laughed.

He traced, I did. Sexy hip.

She traced, Why not before?

He traced, Why haven't YOU kissed ME?

She adjusted her slipping bra strap, trying to be subtle. She rose on one elbow. Untucked his wrinkled button-down, exposing a half-inch of skin over his stomach and hip. His breathing changed. Her fingers brushed against the bare skin over his hip bone, boyish and jutting, and she placed her lips there, in the spot where it was hollow, a valley glowing with heat rather than light.

CHAPTER 7

SHE BACKED HER RED Mazda out of the garage's third bay. It was Saturday night, and she had forty minutes to kill before meeting Nicole, who'd invited her out on a whim. Sitting by herself in McAlestar's was not an option. She could tolerate the dive bar only in the company of Nicole. To sit alone would be sad. To sit alone in her childhood bedroom, with her parents below, restless as tigers, would be sadder.

The Mazda hacked and coughed, deep and tubercular in its engine. The car showed its age: rusted, braying doors, nubby cloth seats, seat belt worn soft as velvet. Her father had offered a loan, a down payment on a new car, but she wanted no new debts. The Mazda was her first, her freedom. She loved the thing senselessly, as a child loves a security blanket.

Carey got the new car in high school, when her small orbit only included school, cross country practice, and weekend nights out with friends. Indianapolis lapped outside the I-465 beltway, but she rode elliptical circles around her Westside turf.

One fall day, a few months into dutifully driving her little circuit, her coach ended cross country practice early—a rarity. Carey wasn't expected home for another hour-and-a-half. On a whim, she drove east, beyond city limits, where houses were interspersed with fields. Indian summer, windows down, WTTS blaring. Happiness. In the small town of Fortville, a giant pink plaster elephant guarded a flat-roofed liquor store, its trunk curled around a martini glass. Then she drove home, failing to mention to her parents that practice had ended early, that she'd been exploring.

She cruised more frequently, sighting landmarks her parents once had pointed out to her—the towering "Mr. Bendo" statue outside a body shop on the far Westside, and the dilapidated old baseball stadium where, at an Indians game, Gwen told Brian she was pregnant. Her own discoveries were the more important landmarks: that pink elephant, or the scraggly tree alone in a cornfield like the one on the cover of U2's *Joshua Tree* album. People and places became familiar, like the old black man who stood at the corner of 38th and College Avenue. Instead of begging for money, he danced to hip hop for donations, holding out a purple Crown Royal bag. The first time she drove by, she looked away from his gritty street corner. The second time, she slowed, wishing the light hadn't changed so quickly. He was good. Eventually, finally, she parked at Church's Chicken and dropped a dollar in his bag. "All *right*, baby doll," the man said, like a kindly uncle.

Soon after, her father was paying bills when he frowned over the rims of his reading glasses. "This isn't good," he said. He studied the Shell bill. "The new car isn't getting the gas mileage it should."

Her father attributed the spike in their gas card purchases to a mechanical problem. She knew her mother would be suspicious (probably already was, glancing sidelong at her daughter when she said, "The mechanic said it's fine.") Sometimes, it seemed her parents were blind to the things most people's parents disapproved of—occasionally drinking at high school parties, sneaking out with Nicole to meet Tommy Pritchett and Josh Siders in the park after curfew. But their radar would pick up the frequency of her innocent, aimless, maybe even spacey ambitions, and they would be worried. She drove less, explored less.

Her desire to drive, to be elsewhere, was inexplicable to her. How could she describe it? *I don't know if what I'm looking for exists, because I don't know what it is. I'm searching for the right shade of sky, for a signal from lightning bugs in a cornfield, for a boy-ghost who tosses pizzas. I'm teaching myself how to leave.*

She understood, seven years after Ben's murder, how you could become a constant tourist in another person's country. How you could live most of your life in one city, yet relinquish ownership and possession of it to a memory. Indianapolis, a place where Carey and Ben had both lived, where they had never spoken, never touched.

Here, she told herself, out driving, is where you saw him for the first time, practically a boy, tossing pizza dough at the mall. The one place you knew to find him. Every other sighting just chance, or chance plus engineering. Here is Trinity Catholic Academy. Ben is missing from the uniformed students milling around the brick building's sidewalk. Adjacent, the soccer fields where you never saw him play.

See it. Here is the house you've never been inside, the small two-story, painted white with gray shutters and a black shingled roof. Tending to the swaying daffodils in the immaculate garden are the parents you've never met. Upstairs, his sister Molly listens to CDs, ignorant of your existence. She is forever a teenager in your mind, unknown and unknowable.

Here are chain restaurants where he might have eaten. Sporting goods stores where he might have shopped. On a trail near Eagle Creek Park, the path you drive by instead of run, are people he might've known walking dogs he might've petted. You once saw him driving this road, or thought you did.

She told herself that she knew Ben. She knew his hands on her, his eyes on her. A feeling, a sensation, more vivid than sex. And nothing had been wrong with the sex. Sex with Ben was the standard by which she judged all others. But his hands, his eyes. Something about to happen. A precursor, a permission slip, a gauge. Anticipation flooded her system like a drug. All he had to do was look at her. All he had to do was touch her. The memories had not gone stale. She replayed the tape in her mind. Stop. Rewind. Pause. Keeping the experience alive. Keeping Ben alive.

Ben, whom she had betrayed. In moments when she was alone in the car, she found herself whispering, I'm sorry. I'm so sorry. Knowing and not knowing who she was talking to: Ben, or herself?

Sleeping with Mike had been a mistake, a terrible choice. But there were much worse decisions being made that night. Carey had never held a gun in her hand.

If this was a consolation, it was not enough.

In the year after the murder, she saw the Williamsons being interviewed on television. The subject was surviving the violent loss of a loved one. They were both pale and thin, and though Carey had never met them, she could tell that they'd lost weight. They needed and had not purchased smaller clothes. Andrew Williamson kept his eyes on his wife and didn't say a word. Lida Williamson spoke for them both. She smiled slowly, her eyes weary, and said, "We hurt every day. But we also forgive, even if we're forgiving a stranger. It's like opening a door. What choice do we have?"

You have many choices, Carey had thought reflexively. You can stiffen with hate. You can resolve never to let someone in again. You can slam shut any door you choose, real or imagined.

You can drive. You can go nowhere at varying speeds. Here is the cemetery you've never visited, the grave you've never seen, the body—the hands, the eyes—beneath the earth, somewhere.

Here. But where? Carey did not know.

She did not know where he was buried.

She did not know where he was

She did not know where he

She did not know where

She did not know

She did not

She did

She

She tried to stop thinking about cemeteries and grave plots, and the mental routes she knew by heart, where she was both the guide and the tourist. Inevitably, she returned. Back to the time when her largest concerns were when he would touch her again, when he would see her. As if by being seen, she became real.

•

At McAlestar's, Nicole stood at the bar in jeans and a fitted black T-shirt, her spine planked gracefully forward as she whispered something to Bob Kemper, the bartender she kept on a string.

Carey wove around the half-empty tables, blocked by a waitress delivering red plastic baskets of cheeseburgers and chips to two couples in a booth. The men wore jeans and fire department t-shirts, and their dates showcased off-season tans. On the big screen, an old IU basketball game featured hulking men in ridiculously short shorts.

"Now the '87 Hoosiers," the thick-necked firefighter declared. "That was a team."

"Should've kept Coach Knight," the other firefighter said.

Both nodded sagely, their dates contributing nothing. The waitress departed, moving her large server's tray in a deft motion Carey couldn't help but admire.

Bob lifted his chin in greeting, and Nicole turned. "There you are!" she grinned.

Carey supposed the extra enthusiasm was for Bob's benefit. The presence of a man can torque a woman's bearing, even if he isn't the right man.

Bob pulled the tap and sang along to the jukebox, his neck working to Elvis.

Every so often, he checked himself out in the mirror behind the rows of neatly lined liquor bottles, as if his head-bobbing might have dislodged his short blond hair. Three years ahead of them at Township, he'd been a friendly loudmouth, tall, bulky, hard to miss. He'd changed little.

Bob wiped down the already-clean laminate counter, sliding coasters in front of them. He delivered the beers with a flourish, the amber liquid sloshing but not spilling. A smoky haze perpetually lingered, despite the noisy ventilation system that clung to the ceiling and sucked up the pollution of cigarettes and deep fryers. The ceiling's once-white foam tiles were stained yellowish-brown. McAlestar's kept the lights low.

"Tell me about that restaurant," Nicole said.

"Not much to tell. Seems like an OK job." Carey had broken

four glasses at once, ramming her tray against the swinging door and covering herself in leftover margarita sludge. She had broken down twice in the bathroom. And she had not once raised the courage to ask her Mexican co-workers about Ben.

Nicole smiled sympathetically. "Well, you don't have to do it forever," she said.

"Right," Carey said. "But I'm not going to quit, either."

Nicole didn't respond. They drank their beers and two more automatically appeared. She glanced briefly at Bob. "Don't look, but those men won't stop staring," she said.

"Who?"

"Those Mexicans who just walked in."

A contingent from Casa Colmo stood in the doorway. Juan, Roberto, and three of the other cooks. They were out of uniform, in jeans and button-downs, hair combed just so. That restaurant, those Mexicans.

They headed straight to the bar, to Carey and Nicole. The firefighters were watching them, stone-faced.

"Here we go," Nicole groaned.

"No," Carey said, "I know them."

Juan led the way. His loping stride evoked energetic guilelessness. His too-large ears made him look innocent, boyish.

"Que tal, Kah-ree," Juan said. "You tell us to come, we come."

Carey made introductions. Bob took orders, cupping his hand around one ear and squinting at the thicker accents. Nicole stiffened in her seat, understanding only the few English words cut in among the Spanish.

"Would you like to have a table?" Roberto asked. Some of the men had already claimed seats at the center of the room.

Nicole's eyes said no.

"Maybe in a little while," Carey told him.

Once the men were out of earshot, Nicole asked, "You invited them?"

"Not specifically tonight. I just told them this might be a good place. To meet people."

Nicole turned toward the table, and one of the cooks, Rafael, gazed back intently. Rafael's wife and children were in Mexico. Nicole swiveled to face the mirror, herself.

"Who're they going to meet?" Nicole asked. "Maybe the one with the floppy hair's slightly cute."

The bitter beer slid down Carey's throat like the solution to an unnamed problem. Bob, quick with refills, helped her lose track. She was closing in on a decade of regular bar-going. Different bars in different cities and even different countries, and what you learned was that they were all the same. At some unrespectable hour there's your puffy face in a mirror, your flooded brain deciding either that you're beautiful and wronged, or ugly and righteous.

"I like your shirt," Bob told Carey solemnly, to ingratiate himself to her. Carey wore a pilled purple sweater. She'd bought it for the color, though its iris hue had faded several shades over the years. It was not, as Bob stated, a shirt, nor a sweater worth complimenting. She warmed to him regardless.

"Yours, too," Carey said. Bob wore a white short-sleeved polo with an embroidered leprechaun and the bar's name on the breast pocket.

Nicole giggled and shushed her. "Too loud," she said.

Carey leaned forward, confidential. "Bob. I need a round for my friends."

The jukebox played faintly beneath conversations. Alone, Carey edged to their table, her hands full of drinks. The men stood, accepting the pint glasses, offering her a chair, waiting for her to sit before taking their seats.

"Where's Elena?" Carey asked.

"This is no place for a…" Juan paused, "…for my sister."

"I see." Carey narrowed her eyes, and the men laughed. They drank. Nicole gave a coy wave over her shoulder, and Carey beckoned her over; she didn't come. The basketball highlight reel ended and the Pacers, playing on the West coast, took over. The streaming, constant timing of television, nothing like life. Yet we crave those punctual beginnings and endings.

Roberto fed money into the jukebox, disappointed when he

returned to the table and could not hear his songs over the growing din of the bar.

"Bob!" Carey shouted across the room. "Turn up the music!"

Bob obliged. "Hello, I Love You" by The Doors took over the room.

"You like this band," Roberto said, reading Carey's face.

Juan tapped her shoulder. "Your friend has a boyfriend?" he asked, and Roberto sighed, staring into space. One of the firefighters' dates, the one whose white shirt made her tanning-bed skin nearly glow, gave Roberto the once over on her way to the bathroom. His mouth turned up lazily and the lids of his dark eyes drooped, like a model in a cologne ad.

"Shh. Just a minute." Carey closed her eyes, waiting for the part about the woman whose arms were wicked and legs were long. Ben once had remarked, off-handedly, "That line is you all over."

Just before the lyric, somebody hollered, "Good song, Pancho," and her eyes snapped open. Juan and Roberto watched her for instruction. Pedro, Rafael, and Hugo paused in their pool game. None of them were named Pancho. The voice had come from a far booth along the wall.

"Ignore it," she advised. They settled back into their seats, and the song tapered away into another, the volume lowered. The beer made her drowsy. "Nicole's got a boyfriend. Boyfriends. And she's too old for you."

Juan laughed. He tipped back his glass and promptly dribbled beer on his chin. He wiped his mouth, darting a glance at Roberto, who paid no attention. "Pues, quien sabe?" Juan asked. Who knows?

Carey returned to the bar.

Nicole tossed her blonde hair over one shoulder and into Carey's pint glass. "Everything OK?" Nicole asked.

"Why wouldn't it be?"

Bob mixed whiskey and soda in a low tumbler. "She's only looking out for you, Carey."

At her co-workers' table, one of the firefighters had taken her seat. His thick neck nearly creaked as he turned his head slowly between Juan and Roberto. Without thought, her body glided to them, quick and forgettable movement, alcohol's eraser effect on travel.

The firefighter was speaking in low, confidential tones. "You all the ones been spray-painting gang bullshit on the municipal center? Listen. I'm just asking. A simple friendly inquiry." In-KWI-ree.

"I work with them," Carey announced. An assumption that she gave the men clout by association. That she had clout, by dint of whiteness, birthright.

The firefighter lifted his fleshy face to her. Pinned to his t-shirt was a small, metallic American flag, with the words *Never Forget* in ornate script. "Well, good for you," he said. "That's real good."

The man's date returned from the bathroom with a newly-painted mouth, hot pink and glossy. The woman searched out Roberto, who was examining his fingernails. Her face turned sour when she saw the firefighter.

"Denny. Leave these poor people alone."

Denny stood, but slowly. "Just chatting," he said. "Getting to know each other."

Soon, Carey's co-workers were yawning, gathering their light jackets, hanging up their pool cues. They told her to have a nice night, they'd see her at work. She did not try to convince them to stay. Not in a place where they stood out like cardinals in a leafless tree, yet were assumed common, even generic.

They had names. They were specific in ways she was still learning—Roberto with his unexpected commentary, Juan's impish grin and constant, awkward interest in girls. The echoes of other people's words rang in her ears as she watched them go. These people. Those people. These poor people.

CHAPTER 8

SHE DIDN'T LEAVE THE rooftop, didn't leave Ben, until the sky was turning new shades of purple in preparation for day. She slept maybe two hours in the twin bed across from Alicia's. No one in the house woke when Carey returned. Had it been a weekday, Maria would've emerged from her narrow room on the first floor to soak the wash, or to prepare coffee. It was early on Sunday when Carey crept back into the house, and Maria took the bus back to Dolores Hidalgo for the weekends. The Alarcón house was especially relaxed on the weekends, and it took Carey some time to realize it was because of Maria's absence.

Back home, the Halperns used a cleaning woman once a week. But the idea of live-in help baffled Carey. The first time Carey had taken her laundry to the walled-in backyard, Lupe admonished her: Let Maria do it. Carey tried to wait for weekends to do wash. She'd lie to Lupe: I forgot. Now I'm out of clean jeans. Shrugging helplessly, a ditz who couldn't be bothered to give her dirty clothes to the maid. Ben smirked when she had described her predicament. "Why not mop the floors for her, then?" he challenged. Intercambio had a laundry service, twenty dollars a month, but Ben washed his clothes by hand in the dorm basement's industrial sink. He used the same product he showered with: Dr. Bronner's peppermint soap.

When Carey snuck into the house that morning, she was wired, replaying the night before. Her throat was raw from talking, from not sleeping. Her lips tender. Her hip deliciously sore from lying on her side, on gravel, facing Ben.

Lupe's muted voice filtered through the bedroom floor vents. Carey recognized the tone: worry, frustration, upset. Over the missed curfew? Ben was worth it. Across the room, Alicia slept, occasionally sighing and burrowing into the pillow. Carey stretched her arms overhead, contented, feeling sorry for Alicia, who hadn't spent most of the night on a rooftop with a magnetic semi-stranger who wanted to know her. And Alicia wouldn't for years, if ever, because she was a young Mexican woman in her father's home.

Carey dressed quickly in jeans and a white long-sleeved running shirt, jamming her feet into slippers. Bare feet were not only unacceptable but rude. Carey loved being barefoot, even when the soles of her feet turned black with dirt in the summertime. Sometimes she forgot the slippers, especially for a quick trip to the bathroom late at night. Sometimes she forgot on purpose, if she thought she could get away with it.

At the kitchen table, Bartolo spooned cereal into his mouth while Lupe continued her tirade. Maria hadn't bought enough produce for the weekend. Carey hadn't been found out. In a way, she wished she had.

"Kah-ree," Lupe said, breathless. "Ay, bien. Puedes ayudarme ahorita?" She needed Carey to go to the market with Bartolo. Carey said sure. Seguro. As of late, she was the type of person who did spontaneous things before breakfast.

Bartolo crunched his cereal loudly, his jaw working deliberately. The cornflakes box on the table—"Hojuelas de Maiz"—had the same red, yellow, and green rooster. When Carey poured a bowl, Bartolo took one last spoonful and pushed back his chair, placing his dish in the sink. He didn't look at her. Lupe leaned against the counter with the phone pressed to her ear. She stood with one hand on her narrow waist, sharp fingernails splayed over one round hip. She wore all her jewelry, a diamond ring on each hand. Both looked like engagement rings. Her eyes tracked her son as he moved out of the room. Bartolo ignored his mother, too.

"Bueno," Lupe said, and proceeded to place an order for meat. Another errand. "Bartolo y su amiga vengan pronto. No. Solamente amigos."

Carey munched her cereal, studying the foreign/familiar box. In Mexico, the word "no" was drawn out to three syllables, alternating pitch. She listened to Lupe's extra-long no, as her host mother assured the butcher that Carey was just Bartolo's friend, nothing more. Why the butcher cared, she didn't know.

She chalked up the silence in the car to the early hour, though a part of her wondered if Luis had already spoken to Bartolo. Told him about last night at Pastel. What bad manners his visiting sister had, what obnoxious people she hung out with. Such an act Ben had put on. On the roof he'd been a different person. He brushed her hair off her face and told her he'd been waiting a long time to do that. She wanted to say she'd been waiting longer, since Indianapolis, which he still didn't know.

Bartolo probably had stayed home. Despite his growing comfort with her, he still could be shy. Sometimes they'd eat an entire meal without speaking, exchanging amused glances over Alicia's description of a pop song or a good-looking boy. On the sidewalk in front of the jewelry shop, he'd wave when she walked to school, one day asking about her classes, the next, giving a nod and a smile. He always saw her coming.

Carey's Spanish had improved dramatically in mere weeks, but some of her most enjoyable interactions were wordless conversations with Bartolo. Infinitely easier than talking to most people, in Mexico or back home. He felt like the brother she was supposed to have. She imagined all siblings shared such closeness, inside jokes and easily forgiven annoyances, discussions spoken in glances.

Bartolo ignored her now. He drove like his stepfather: a constant weaving and avoiding. The short trip to the market was filled with narrow misses. The breeze funneled through open windows of the little white Renault. Carey was relieved to get out at the giant Mercado Hidalgo. It reminded her of the fieldhouse where she went to her high school's basketball championships: an arched ceiling with lots of windows, and a second tier almost like bleachers. Even when it was packed with fans, you had breathing room in the fieldhouse, staggered seats, the open space of the court below. At Mercado Hidalgo, the main floor stalls sat stiflingly close: vegetables and fruit here, bootleg CDs and rough-hewn leather purses there. Whole plucked chickens, fish and mariscos uncovered atop beds of ice, surrounded by a cloying, rotten smell. Buzzing flies. On a long table were leather-bound journals. Just Ben's style, especially the brown with the dark-burnt filigree on the border. He'd never buy such things for himself. She'd never seen him purchase anything other than food or beer. Once, a toothbrush at Comercial Mexicana.

A few birds chased each other in the dark rafters. Above, the recessed shops spilled over with t-shirts and silver statuettes, cheap toys and imprinted coffee mugs. Shoppers leaned on the metal railing.

"Naranjas, platanos, kiwi, limón," Bartolo listed from Lupe's scrawled note.

She saluted him. "Sí, señor." He moved towards a nearby vegetable stall, politely examining the lettuce. A sullen teenage girl in tight jeans reached under the counter for a damp cardboard box full of leafy greens.

The woman working at the fruit stand wore a dingy smock over her purple print dress. She swept her eyes up and down Carey's body: sneakers, jeans, long-sleeved running shirt and hasty ponytail. The shirt had cost forty-five dollars at Indy Running Co. back home. Her running shoes were SUVs compared to the modest, utilitarian tennis shoes Mexicans wore to run in the park. Her jeans were factory-faded in a specific, battered configuration to the tune of ninety dollars.

A few feet away, Bartolo held his slim body erect, shoulders back, as he pondered lettuce, tomatoes, and onions. The woman barked a command to the teenage girl in such a familiar tone, hard-edged and quick, that Carey knew she was her mother. The girl cast her eyes down and reached for a cilantro bunch. Water droplets flew as she handed it shyly to Bartolo. The girl asked her mother for permission to go to the bathroom.

"Put on some lipstick," the woman yelled after the girl, grinning at Bartolo. Some things were universal.

His dark, pockmarked face was immobile. He wore a plain beige polo shirt, tucked into stiff blue jeans held up by a narrow black belt, plus the shined black loafers he almost always wore. Next to him Carey felt underdressed in her expensive outfit. Mexicans dressed presentably, even if their clothes were cheaper than what Americans wore for exercise.

A young man with thick silver chains around his neck stacked the stall's empty wooden crates. His white t-shirt reminded Carey of Ben. He saw her watching.

"Cuanto cuesta?" he asked.

"Perdonéme?" Carey asked.

He stooped down to examine her feet. "Cuanto para los zapatos?" How much for the shoes?

They were fine shoes. A thick, springy sole, with gel in a clear plastic casing. Cleanly white, even though she'd had them a few months. The laces threaded in tight coils with a blue stripe. Ben had half-joked that her shoes could've fed a Mexican family of ten for a month. Or a smaller family of immigrants in Indianapolis. "My mom could introduce you," he said. "Her clients would kill for kicks like those." The shoes cost $150; Carey's dad had paid for them. She couldn't say that. The man only wanted to know her price.

"Lo siento," she said, always apologizing, never sorry.

He lifted one of a dozen silver chains off his chest. "Te gusta la plata?"

He unfastened the necklace and held it out. He knelt as if to untie her shoelaces.

"No, gracias," she said, moving her foot out of reach and kicking a crate of melons. Bartolo glanced up. He shooed the silver vendor away with one hand.

"Get out of here," Bartolo told him in Spanish.

The teenager backed a couple feet away. He wasn't going any further. "Joto," he muttered. "Pinche cabrón."

Bartolo's pitted skin flushed purple and he pretended not to hear, but Carey knew those words. Fag, bastard. You always learned the curse words first. The kid, Bartolo told her, came by the jewelry shop every month. Trying to make trades with fake silver. She touched the St. Christopher medallion Bartolo had given her and knew it was real.

The fruit vendor sucked on her teeth, rearranging oranges. When she spoke, she addressed Bartolo rather than Carey. "Que tipo," she droned. The silver vendor sat on an upended box, glowering over a comic book.

Carey brushed a strand of hair behind her ear, heat rising in her cheeks. She cleared her throat loudly and began naming all the fruit Lupe had asked for. Naranja, limón—what else? A bird's call echoed and bounced around the large room. When Carey motioned Bartolo closer, he stepped swiftly to her, ready to translate, problem-solve. Always at the ready. Carey laid a hand on his arm and tilted her head to look up at him.

"Que más?" she asked him, gesturing to the fruit. She squeezed his bicep and stared right at the woman and smiled like a shark. She wanted the silver vendor to see. But he read his comic, idly playing with the chains around his neck.

Bartolo pointed to the kiwi and bananas, but his eyes were on Carey's hand. She knew he was blushing without having to look.

She selected the rest of the fruit with both hands. Flies buzzed around the kiwi, and she made a face and searched beneath. The vendor jotted prices on a pad. Carey slowly counted and handed over Lupe's money. She slung the canvas sack of fruit on her shoulder, which Bartolo gently removed. She did not reply when the woman thanked her.

"Vamonos," Carey said.

She'd tried and failed at polite. Something clearly was lost in the translation. Her freedom as an outsider, if she wasn't going to be accepted: she didn't have to follow custom, even niceties. She could leave. She was no different than any average American tourist, wanting to be untroubled by the cultural differences she'd traveled miles to experience.

The market was growing more crowded. In the blinking daylight, when Carey glanced at Bartolo over her shoulder on the narrow sidewalk, a smile played on his lips. There was a look on his face Carey deliberately ignored. At the car, Bartolo asked her if she was eating dinner with the family later. She nodded.

"Y más tarde?"

She had no plans, other than what Ben might have planned.

"Probablemente ir al café con mis amigos. Conoces Ben?" She smiled at his name.

He nodded, no longer smiling. He placed the two canvas bags of produce in the backseat, and stepped out of her way. He did not close her car door for her. In the driver's seat he stared straight ahead. Carey asked, overly cheerful, about Bartolo's plans. Not an invitation to join her.

He shrugged. For the second time that day, Carey put her hand on Bartolo's arm.

"Are you mad?" she asked in Spanish. "What's the problem?"

He downshifted, concentrating on maneuvering around a white delivery truck, then chugged up the cobblestone hill before answering.

"You come to Mexico to be with Americans. You tell me the problem."

The house was quiet that evening. She closed her book and carried her laptop to the parlor. After plugging in the phone jack, it took ten tries to log on. But she kept clicking. Connect. Connect. Connect.

Date: Sunday, Sept. 24 1995 4:45 a.m.
To: Carey Halpern <chalpern@intercambio.edu>
From: Ben Williamson <bwilliamson@intercambio.edu>
Subject: hey

C—

Thanks for keeping me out all night. I haven't felt that alive in a long time. Partly from the mountain air & stars. Mostly from you.
—B

With one hand she gathered her hair into a ponytail, remembering the pins-and-needles feeling at the base of her skull, Ben's fingers raking through her hair.

Hector cursed from the kitchen. Alicia flew into the parlor.

"Mi papá necesita el teléfono," she accused. "Es muy caro."

Carey quickly removed the phone jack. She hadn't considered the Alarcóns' bill for dial-up service. "Lo siento," she called down the hall.

Hector said nothing. A moment later, they heard his calm phone voice.

Alicia perched on the arm of the brocaded sofa. Her arms and legs were wiry, her middle soft. She'd been playing soccer in the park and came home in her shiny uniform shirt, shorts and shin guards, but had since changed into jeans and a pink long-sleeved T-shirt with a dark pink heart stitched in the middle. She grinned at Carey.

"How was Pastel?" she asked in Spanish. "Did you dance with anyone?"

Carey stifled a yawn and told Alicia she left early.

"Then where did you go next?" Alicia asked. Her braces shone. "Because you didn't get home 'til veeery late." *Muy* tarde.

"You weren't asleep?" Finally, someone knew she'd been out all night. Proof it had happened.

Alicia giggled, shook her head. "Only pretending."

Carey held one finger to her lips. Alicia nodded, delighted to be Carey's accomplice.

Hector appeared in the doorway. "Estás lista?" he asked his daughter.

"Can she come, Papa? We're going to Mass, Carey. Come with."

Hector shrugged. "Si quieres," he said. If you want. The Alarcóns went to Mass every Sunday evening at the Basilica. Carey, a non-practicing Methodist, had never been invited to the Catholic ceremony. But she wanted to go. Not for religious purposes, or to spend more time with the Alarcóns. She wanted to be out.

•

She'd been to the Basilica once as a tourist, trying to take unobtrusive pictures on a weekday. The walls and altar were heavily ornamented in gold, and great crystal chandeliers hung from the high, rounded ceiling. Chant-like music played over the speakers. Around her men and women on their lunch breaks kneeled to pray, lips moving silently. When they finished, they crossed themselves multiple times, touching a closed hand to their lips at the end. The ritual moved her.

The Alarcón family sat close together, ten rows back. On Carey's right was a young couple with a swaddled infant. He fussed, and the mother leaned down and murmured "chuh." The baby quieted.

The priest walked down the aisle swinging a heavy gold pot from a chain, and smoke rose into the air. The incense layered over the parishioners. Carey stifled the urge to cough. She knew enough to be quiet in church. The Halperns had rarely gone when Carey was younger. Her mother thought religion was "small town." She had grown up on the outskirts of a tiny Indiana farming community. She was done with that life, done with religion.

The large church's wooden pews were packed, and parishioners leaned against the walls. Some of the faces looked familiar—the same people she'd seen in the Jardín Unión, or the café, or working in the cafeteria of Intercambio's dining hall. Guanajuato was shrinking into familiarity. Over Alicia's head she caught Bartolo watching her and smiled at him. He smiled back. She should've asked him to join her plans earlier, even though she had no plans.

The organ music stopped and the priest began his echoing intonations, doubly unfamiliar to Carey. She followed along with the thin paper program. His homily was about forgiveness. There are three things to know in life, the priest said:

Perdón.

Perdón.

Perdón.

The same word people used when the bumped into you in the club or on the street. When she'd first arrived, Carey had said "Lo siento," I'm sorry, and received puzzled looks. She'd needed not to apologize but to ask forgiveness. The lesson eluded her.

When it came time to give the sign of peace, Alicia reached first for Carey's hand. They shook heartily. Carey wondered if she might regret telling Alicia anything. She hadn't said much. She could've been a better role model, but Alicia wasn't her real sister, she wouldn't follow her back home. Carey was a stranger here who could do what she wanted. Mexico was a theater stage: costumes, hot lights, heavy red velvet curtains. Reality was somewhere else, in the wings, backstage, unglamorous without makeup.

Bartolo stuck out his hand, flushing to the tips of his ears as they said "La paz" to each other. It echoed in strong whispers throughout the church: peace, peace. When she shook Bartolo's hand, she didn't mean to look over his shoulder. But the eyes reveal you far earlier to others than to yourself.

Across the aisle stood Alejandro. He looked only slightly more presentable than the day of the fire show. He wore clean gray slacks and a brown sweater, though his hair remained greasy and his face stubbled with whiskers. He, too, shook hands with people, reaching back two rows. His lips formed the words, "La paz," and the hand he'd been shaking was connected to an arm in a long-sleeved burgundy shirt. Unmistakable hair, Ben's long wingspan. Her heart skipped like a stone across a calm, clear lake. She didn't know he went to Mass at the Basilica. And church was the last place she expected to see Alejandro.

Ben and Mike never explained about Alejandro. She could still hear Mike's voice, oddly affectionate: "El Viejo," he'd called him. "We've known him forever," Ben said. "He's like a grandpa." And Mike had replied, "Maybe *your* grandpa."

Bartolo gave her hand an extra squeeze. He asked without speaking: Are you all right? She smiled to show him she was fine. Briefly puzzled that Bartolo looked into her face and felt concern. He'd seen an emotion she had yet to put a name to.

Outside on the steps, it was dusky, cooler. At home it would still be Indian summer, but here in the mountain evenings fall hung over their heads. The emptying church crowd gathered in pockets, and the Alarcóns walked slowly down the steps, Hector and Lupe stopping every few feet to greet people. In public Hector became a sociable ambassador. Alicia trailed a few feet behind. Bartolo waved over Luis, who surprised Carey with a kiss on one cheek.

"Que bailadora, ella," Luis told Bartolo. What a dancer, this one. He mimed a brief salsa, holding his lit cigarette in the air like a partner's hand.

Bartolo whistled like he was impressed. "De veras?"

"Claro que sí."

Relieved, Carey thanked Luis.

Luis spoke quick and slurry Spanish. He told Bartolo, "See what you missed? You ought to come to the disco." *Dees-co.*

"Tal vez," Bartolo said. Maybe.

Luis pointed behind Carey. "Tu novio," he said. Polite, respectful, even. Ben leaned down to introduce himself to Lupe and Hector.

Ben put his hand at the small of her back. He was charming, fluent, polite, ingratiating. How old is Alicia? And where does she go to school? She's your image exactly, Señora. Your bank is a good place to change money. The jewelry shop is close to school, right? Mucho gusto. Mucho gusto. Encantado.

She beamed, radiant, bright and reflective enough to believe her host family beamed back.

"Would it be all right to take Carey out?" Ben asked Hector in Spanish. The suitor routine would be comical if she weren't so flattered by it. He couldn't be serious. This was a guy who refused to iron his clothes, who went so long without brushing his hair that he once had to cut the tangles out. Played *The Doors* and moved his hips to the music like the long-dead singer Jim Morrison, dead longer than Ben had been alive, and longer than he would live.

Ben clearly knew what he was doing with the Alarcóns. Hector, pleased to be consulted, gave his blessing to take Carey out, and smiled at Lupe and Bartolo rather than the American couple. Ben shook their hands, even Alicia's. Carey failed to register the wariness in Lupe's eyes, or how Bartolo turned away and quickly spoke to Alicia, who stared after them. Details to remember later. Like seeing a movie for the second time and picking up complicit glances between characters that give away the plot. Only once you know how it ends.

"A dónde vamos?" Carey asked Ben.

When they were out of earshot, Ben whispered, "Sorry, I didn't mean right now."

She bit her lip. "Why not?"

He waved vaguely to the foot of the steps, where Alejandro stood waiting, docile and unhurried. "I've got to meet Mike. I promised someone a favor."

Someone. He touched her hip with one hand. Tentatively. "Did you get my email?"

She nodded.

"I meant it. We'll go out soon. Just not tonight."

She believed him.

She'd fantasized about being closer to Ben, and now she was. Guanajuato, a capital city of some seventy thousand people, seemed to curl inward the longer she lived there. Ben had never been more accessible. She had his email address. She knew his name and how to find him. Yet he kept moving out of reach.

Carey waited until Alicia was asleep. Like a stealthy sleepwalker, she rose from the bed and slipped on jeans and a t-shirt, and pulled her cross trainers over her bare heels. Her socks were in the top dresser drawer, and Alicia would wake at the squeak of the wood. "We got the bureau, special for you," Alicia had revealed a few weeks back. "My uncle made it." Carey had brought too many clothes to fit in the dresser. The rest spilled from her suitcase under the bed.

Leaving the house was easy enough. The return, unlocking the series of loud deadbolts, would be trickier. In the moonlight, her hand on the gate appeared otherworldly, not her own. Sometimes she imagined stepping outside her body. Like she was watching herself walk downtown, in the direction of Alejandro's, the streets lit in muted yellow. A group of men changing a truck tire, a work crew sweeping the steps of Teatro Juárez with push brooms. They didn't see her; nobody did. She'd planned to go to Ben's dorm. A few minutes later, she spotted Ben and Mike ahead. They turned down the unfamiliar street and Carey sped up.

Mike, now alone, tried to conceal his surprise when Carey approached him on the sidewalk.

"Where's Ben?"

"Nice to see you, too, Miss Manners." His eyes darted around the street. "He's back at the dorm."

"I just saw him," she said.

"Right," Mike said. "Which would explain why I'm alone. You been drinking?" He tipped an imaginary bottle to his lips twice. Even people who spoke the same language, even people who spoke the same *two* languages, talked with their hands in a foreign country. He glanced over his shoulder. "Why are you out so late?"

"I see how it is," she said. "You don't want me to know that you're in the middle of doing someone a 'favor.'"

Just barely, Mike's forehead wrinkled as he shifted gears.

"Look, he'll be back in a few minutes, and I know he'll want to see you," Mike said. "We'll meet you at the café. You can hold down a table. Have a tasty beverage. Another, it would seem."

She pushed his shoulder with her fingertips and turned away. Mike watched her turn the corner, then she wove around the cross street and positioned herself on a darkened stoop behind a parked car. She'd wait them out.

Soon Ben's long leg emerged from a first-floor window. He balanced on the sill and dropped the short distance to the ground. Dangling from his neck, a large black camera on a strap. He and Mike conferred briefly—she couldn't hear. Mike clapped him on the shoulder in congratulation or consolation. Before he turned and darted down the street, Ben glanced about his surroundings. It was too dark; she wasn't visible. Still, out of habit, she ducked.

Mike beat her to the café. He sat alone with a pitcher of beer at one of the indoor tables in the nearly empty room. The old waiter sat with a drink and a cigarette at the bar.

"Good thing you found a seat," Carey said. "This place is *loco*."

"Shaddup. I got sick of waiting on your prince. He never showed."

Your prince. So he knew they'd spent the previous night together. Her face burned. "Mike, I saw him. Both times."

He frowned into his beer. His voice bounced around inside the pint glass: "Oops."

She read his face, so clear and open and unlike Ben's, now clouding.

"If you tell him I told you, I'm dead," he said.

Not "you're dead," or "we're dead." Mike was playing to the assumption she would sympathize with him. She did.

"A guy we know borrowed something. He needed to return it in a more timely fashion. We helped in the matter."

He spoke like a teacher explaining a logic problem. Someone, something, it. If Mike would confirm the details and verify what she saw, she'd gratefully accept Ben as Robin Hood, redistributing wealth. Returning property to its rightful owner. Not a thief who broke into Mexican homes.

"It's drugs, right?" Carey asked. "You guys are dealing. With Alejandro."

Mike laughed. The beer had hit him, softened his eyes and mouth, his entire body relaxing. Less alert.

"Dealing!" he snorted. "Yes, we're a couple of *dealers*. That's the dealy-o. Oh, Carey-Carey-quite-contrary. So con*trary*, Carey."

"Stop rhyming."

"Sorry," he said. Mike did what she asked. "Look. This guy Octavio borrowed Ben's camera. He wanted it back."

She felt her own body relax, certain in her bones that they were in the right.

"What's taking him so long? I should get home."

Mike's face darkened again, his plain features shifting. "He's not coming." He shrugged casually. "Probably visiting a lady friend. Who knows?"

He saw her face. "I mean, you *do* know. Right?"

"Of course," Carey lied. She knew nothing, only what it felt to learn, the night after having everything but sex with the object of long-term affection and desire, after savoring the reality for a day, that she was not first in his mind. At least not tonight. There was always the chance Mike was lying. Greater, as Carey's unchecked emotions decided for her, was the chance she'd been made a fool.

"Of course," she repeated, louder this time. From the kitchen came the sound of breaking glass, followed by the old waiter's heavy sigh.

She'd snuck out without money, or, as it happened, her key. Mike paid for their three pitchers and then boosted her over the wall of the Alarcón house.

"Shhh," she told him, tipsy, though he'd said nothing but a quiet goodnight.

"Carey," he tried tentatively from the other side of the wall. When she didn't answer, his footsteps retreated.

Maria sat out back atop the upside-down wash basin, smoking. It was close to two a.m. She tsk-tsked, then offered Carey a cigarette from her red leather case.

"No, gracias." Back then she'd been haughty about her lungs.

"You're locked out," the maid announced in stern Spanish.

"Un accidente," Carey slurred. After Mike told her Ben wasn't coming, she'd refilled her glass, losing count.

"Un acci*den*te, bah!" Maria scoffed.

"Let's not tell Lupe, huh?"

From the open upstairs window, Bartolo poked his head out, alarmed. "What are you doing outside?"

Carey motioned to the wash basin and asked Maria, "Permítelo?"

The older woman stood stiffly, obliged to the houseguest. She wouldn't tell Lupe about the night, but for months afterwards, she'd look at Carey slyly, as if she were waiting to call in a favor. She never did.

Carey stood on the basin and hoisted herself up to the flat roof. She came through his window headfirst and landed on the bed.

"There," she said.

"Estás loca." He moved to the foot of the bed. His pajamas

consisted of dark sweatpants and a white undershirt.

"Sí," she agreed.

The moon lit up Bartolo's bedroom, which she'd never entered, though she'd peeked inside once while he was at work. Like him, the place was unadorned, neat. Her brown hair fanned over the pillow of his single bed. A crucifix on the wall. A wooden dresser and matching bedside table, all of the same dark wood. He stifled a yawn but did not ask her to leave.

"So, big brother, aren't you going to ask me where I've been?"

Even in moonlight, she could see the change in his scarred skin, the rising blush.

"Que?" he asked, because she'd been speaking to him in English. That dumb adrenaline flooded her veins, along with remorse. She'd been speaking English all night with Mike. Bartolo had been shut out in his own home.

"Lo siento," she apologized.

"Perdóneme," he corrected her, and she repeated him.

She didn't translate her question or even ask it again. Without planning or purpose, she leaned over, nearly losing her balance as she grabbed his face with both hands and kissed him on the mouth. His lips were dry but soft, like cotton.

He gently pushed her away. His hand on her arm shook slightly. "You are drunk."

"I know," she said. "It's fine." She moved to kiss him again; he turned his pitted cheek.

She realized her mistake. She jumped up, muttering goodnight, and went to her room. Later, he would lecture her about going out alone. She would accept his admonishments. Grateful that his shyness prevented him from mentioning the kiss.

She hadn't wanted Bartolo, hadn't wanted to kiss him or even be in his bed. He was a person she'd come across while wishing for another. He was a body, a placeholder, in a place too close to where she lived.

CHAPTER 9

SHE SAT IN HER car Sunday evening, her head thick and slow, waiting to meet Mike. The hangover dulled her nicely, took the edge off.

That morning, she'd woken with a gritty mouth and a pulsing headache behind her eyes, thinking about Juan and Roberto. She knew from eavesdropping that they budgeted for two drinks apiece, a game of pool, then sent the remaining money home to Dolores Hidalgo.

A springtime mist hung in the dusky air. She'd parked across the street and waited, not wanting to arrive first, which gave her a perfect view of Mike Gibley coming down the sidewalk in a black trenchcoat. He appeared to be talking to himself. He paced half a block and stopped at the dog-treat bakery's storefront, closed but backlit so the display of dog bones in tin buckets glowed like teeth. He returned to the bar, one hand on the door. He turned away and headed toward the street.

Carey went to him without thinking. She said his name, she held out her hand, she erased time.

"Carey?" Mike said, as if their meeting was unplanned. They hugged like two people who didn't know how. Her chin smashed awkwardly into his left shoulder. Her black slicker sleeve slid along his upper back.

"Is this the right bar?" Mike asked. "I'm bad with names."

"No, this is it. It's still warm out, though. Want to walk?"

"Perfect." He sounded relieved.

The Monon Trail closed at dusk, but a few runners and cyclists passed them, heading south. They faced the narrowing lane of pavement bordered by budding oak trees. They told the requisite lies about how the other hadn't changed a bit. Meant as a compliment. But when you considered the implications, there was no greater insult.

Losing weight made Mike seem taller. Walking with him down a running path in Indianapolis should have been bizarre, dream-like, a slice of film created in her sleeping mind. The normalcy of their stroll, this unexpectedly casual, comfortable walk, felt strange.

"You still run?" he asked, after the fifth spandex-clad athlete sped by. She'd been fumbling in her pocket for her cigarette lighter, but now she stopped.

"Not really."

"Yeah? I figured you'd have a couple marathons under your belt by now." He'd remembered her goals. He'd speculated on her activities.

"I lived in Chicago for a couple years, and I thought about doing the Marathon," she admitted, something nobody knew.

"I'm in Chicago all the time," he said, shaking his head with wonder that a large city had anonymously housed strangers who once knew each other. "What stopped you?"

"Training," she said, pleased when he laughed.

He explained his web startup; the pitch was tomorrow. The company marketed cereal prizes to manufacturers. "Sounds fun," she said, remembering her breakfast treasure hunts for a matchbox car she wouldn't use, or a plastic princess based on a cartoon she did not watch.

"They're for piñatas, too," Mike said, his Spanish inflection still perfect. "Actually, I'm building a bilingual website program."

To talk about Spanish would be to talk about Mexico would be to talk about Ben. "Computers have always been your thing, huh?" she asked.

"What do you mean?" His voice turned sharp.

"Nothing," she backpedaled. "Just an observation."

"No," he softened. "You're right. Ever since high school."

She touched her hair, now damp with mist. A lamp at the bridge glowed on the otherwise dark trail. "We should turn around soon."

"Sure," he said, though they continued forward. She told him about Casa Colmo. He cocked his head and said, "You're full of surprises, huh." Without trying, she'd become someone surprising.

They leaned over the red metal railing of the bridge and watched the water swirl beneath them. The river was high, clogged with branches. Side by side, her sleeve brushing his, she shivered despite the warm spring air. She leaned into him, nudging his arm.

He pulled away and straightened. Coughed unnecessarily. "Did I tell you? I'm getting married. I'm engaged."

"Really," she said.

An electronic jangle split the air: Mike's cell phone played a tune she'd heard on the radio but could not name. Don't answer, she thought; of course he did. "Hi," he spoke into the phone. "I'm still in Indy. Right now? Um. Walking around town."

Mike's exchange evolved somewhat from a strict reporting of GPS coordinates. What he'd eaten for dinner. When he'd next call the caller. A low, quiet, "I love you, too."

She walked, to give him privacy. After he'd finished the call, he caught up quickly. She didn't give him time to apologize, if that was what he'd planned.

"We should celebrate," she said.

The bar was quiet on a Sunday, decorated with colored Christmas lights and leftover St. Patrick's Day paper shamrocks announcing the drink specials. Mike told her about Claudine, his fiancée and boss. Sure we're happy, he said. Hard to keep work out of the condo, but you know how it is. Carey nodded like she knew.

"What's the ring like?" she asked. "When's the wedding?"

He grimaced. "We haven't set a date. We're getting the company up and running first. And Claudine's not the type who wants a ring. She doesn't like jewelry."

"Doubt it."

Mike waved his hand, indicating he was skeptical but willing to hear her out. His hair, now darker, was crisply cut. It suited his navy pants and white button-down. She missed his shaggy blond hair.

Nostalgia: one part comparison and two parts longing. For the familiar, not something better or worse.

"Every woman wants a ring," Carey said. "Doesn't matter if she likes jewelry. It's a symbol. It's from you." This was Gwen Halpern, emerging uninvited.

He raised one eyebrow. "You ever been married? Or close?"

The only other patron was a gray-haired man eating pretzels. He bit each in half and stacked the remainder atop his beer can. "No," Carey admitted, swallowing the last of her gin and tonic. She chased an ice cube with her tongue. Mike watched her. Watched her tongue.

"I saw the Williamsons yesterday," he said abruptly.

She crunched ice. Immediate headache. "How are they?"

"OK, considering." He sighed, and suddenly turned into the Mike she once knew, beleaguered Gibs, underconfident and in the middle of things.

"Mike. Tell me what you know."

His mouth drooped, how he always had shown fear and doubt. The way he watched her hadn't changed: a beat too long and with an intensity she had trouble witnessing.

"Somebody got ahold of his passport somehow," Mike said.

The barroom disappeared for a minute and she was back in Mexico, just before the police discovered Ben's body, when she snuck into his room and took his belongings. She'd brought home his green backpack, and as far as she knew, it still sat high on a closet shelf in a cardboard box, unopened for years. Ben's passport. She hadn't even considered that it could have been inside, and somehow she'd missed it. Had her mother given the items to Goodwill? She had stowed the box in the closet, sealed with clear tape. Surely she would remember Ben's passport, there among the compact discs and clothing and the journal. His passport, she realized, had probably been on his body.

Mike wasn't telling her anything new. The newspapers and TV stations were all over the story. So was the Internet. A bombardment of news, uncovering emotions long swept under the rug, out of sight, out of mind.

What rot, these adages. What wants out, gets out.

"What do you think happened?" she asked.

They had never talked about the possibilities. She had not allowed it. "I don't know," he finally said.

Carey held his gaze a beat too long; Mike dropped his eyes. As if she had seen him in a way he didn't want to be seen. He opened his wallet. She stared at her hands, cupped around an empty glass. They sat, an unofficial moment of silence, before settling the bill.

He walked her down the block to her car. "I'll let you know if I hear anything more," Mike said, his voice clogged with an emotion Carey couldn't categorize. She sensed that Mike watched her drive away. This time, for once, she did not glance back.

CHAPTER 10

AFTER BEN CANCELLED YET another date, Carey went running.

Her legs pumped, muscles lengthening and contracting, as she circled La Plaza de Las Ranas on the edge of town. The stone frog statues squatted and stared, silently observing La Americana, with her ponytail and blue track T-shirt and black mesh shorts, the only woman running, the only white woman. The thick-soled running shoes that the teenage silver vendor tried to buy off her feet sprang upward with every step.

She ran to give herself time to think. All else disappeared. For months she'd jogged up and down crowded, uneven sidewalks, alongside the white-and-green taxis in the narrow bricked streets, dodging shopkeepers hustling to open their tiendas. She'd been gawked at, cat-called, spoken to in English by a few men who called her guera. "Hello," they would say, one of the few English words they knew. "Hello." She pretended not to hear. Harder to ignore were the women, who said nothing. Watched her with suspicion and curiosity. Stared openly at her finely muscled legs, the sweat trickling down her face and ringing her shirt. These women wore their shiny black hair in ponytails, pulled tight and smooth and sleek, stretching their eyebrows into elegant arches. They wore form-fitting jeans or skirts, and stretchy, bright-colored tops, high heels that wobbled on cobblestone, trailing scents of hairspray, Givenchy perfume. Carey smelled like salt, sweat. Running felt pure.

But running in the city, even in the mornings before the streets teemed with people, dirtied her inside and out. The staring. The distraction. The mingling diesel exhaust and pan dulce from the bakery, clogging her nose and lungs. On a busy street corner one day, an old woman told Carey about the park. She mimed running, wiping her dry brow comically with her forearm, dislodging the scarf covering her gray hair.

The park's loop soothed her—she could put her body on autopilot. Medium-fast pace, about a seven-minute mile, shaving off seconds as her mind reeled. She was supposed to be with Ben today. The warm October wind stung her eyes.

She passed two women out for a walk. Track suits, baseball caps pulled low, gold and diamond rings on both hands. The woman on the left raised a hand in greeting, and Carey waved back. *Buenos días,* they said to each other, quick smiles and nods. Their husbands, Carey imagined, did not break dates.

On the other side of the loop, a bicyclist rang his bell, the kind attached to the handlebars and depressed with one thumb. *Cling-cling.* She could follow the sound, be led around the path by the ringing.

She and Ben were almost never alone. In public, crowds of students and strangers surrounded them, swallowed them whole. They carried dripping cones of buttery pine nut ice cream in the Centro Historico, amid hordes of Mexican tourists marveling at the Basilica and Teatro Juárez. They sat on benches beneath Indian laurels in the Jardín Unión, scribbling answers to history and culture homework in spiral notebooks, or more likely avoiding work, politely saying "no" to vendors—women in smocks with their ratty black trays of silver jewelry, the blanket salesmen who wore their serapes like capes, or held them out as if to cocoon tourists. More often than Carey liked, Mike joined them. They trekked from Intercambio to the Centro, usually with a handful of other exchange students, for a meal. Carey had met classmates from California and Wyoming, Iowa and Ohio, who attended colleges across the country. She knew little about them.

She preferred to be with Ben, and even Mike, grudgingly, listening to their shared tales of Madison. They'd nicknamed half the men in their dorm "Rufus," their inside term for "dork." She'd believed that type of meanness to be particular to women; they taught her otherwise. Ben had spent an entire rainy March in a tent outside of the administration building, protesting a janitorial union contract he was not even part of, and Mike delivered his food.

When it was Carey's turn, Ben listened intently to her stories about home and college, as if he were translating. When she said Nicole was her oldest friend, Mike asked if Carey would set him up. "Blonde?" he'd asked. "Enough said."

She ran faster, thinking. Ben had emailed: Meet me on the steps of La Alhóndiga. If you see Mike, make something up. This morning, he emailed again. Sorry. Gibs needs my help moving furniture for someone.

A gap emerged. A disconnect between Ben the person and Ben the writer. The emails may as well have been scrolls sent by carrier pigeon.

On the path, Carey periodically wiped the sweat from her eyes and face with the hem of her T-shirt, exposing her midsection.

Ben had placed his hand on that hip. He'd kissed it. After their night on the rooftop, he'd walked her home. Her running routes taught her navigation. The city belonged to her now. "My house is just around the corner," she'd told him. He'd been willing to walk the rest of the way, but she said no.

He had a way of finding her, picking her out in a classroom or at the long table of students in Restaurante Silvio. He was watching. In those moments, all doubt disappeared. She could not believe there was another woman (women?), and had no proof besides Mike's offhand comment. Mike had his own agenda, sharing a café table with Carey.

Something else she'd learned from running: patience.

"What?" she found herself asking Ben, more than once. Self-conscious in his gaze. Curious, too. Last week, as they'd sat on his bed after classes in his tiny, single dorm room at the college, they'd gone through the motions of homework while listening to his CDs. He was into the American 1960s right then, he said, when people actually gave a shit about civil rights and politics and people. He'd already told her this, more than once. He was quiet and distant for such a long time that it was shocking when he turned, suddenly so near.

"I was just thinking," he said, "that I might like to freeze this moment."

She thought she understood, having mentally catalogued their days together. But he meant literally. He grabbed his camera and aimed. She brushed her hair away from her eyes with one hand, quickly and lightly biting her lower lip to give it color. She smiled in one picture, was serious in another. In both, flattered to be the subject. Next he arranged the camera atop the dresser, set the timer, and jumped next to her on the bed. The Doors' organist soloed while they froze, smiling.

"Nude photography: your thoughts," he'd said after the shutter clicked.

"Depends," she said. "How comfortable are you taking pictures with your clothes off?"

He laughed. "The photographer can be naked. Whatever you desire."

He reset the camera and returned to the bed. Then Mike entered without knocking. Carey turned to look just as the flash went off. Before she left Ben said, "Consider my proposal, all right?" Mike asked for an explanation, but Ben only said, "Carey knows."

Now running had done its job and worn her out. She finished her last lap, drenched and thirsty. After walking half a mile, she caught her breath. The bicyclist's bell sounded again, and behind a copse of trees some thirty yards away came the rider. *Cling-cling.*

He cycled closer. A lion's mane of gray hair fanned back in the wind. Alejandro. El Viejo. He wore a dark blue uniform with a pocket logo. She stopped dead in her tracks, sweat trickling down the sides of her face. He rolled towards her with a sly grin that said he knew her, knew things she didn't know. He rang the bell again and pedaled faster.

"Buenos días," he said, when he was so close Carey could smell him, old sweat and body odor with an inefficient masking of crisp aftershave. And a baser scent, earthy and stinging. She thought "lighter fluid," though that might've been her imagination.

"Sí," she replied, stunned by a mix of confusion and fear—not of Alejandro on his bicycle, pedaling away without even a backwards glance, but of the memory of Alejandro that day in the courtyard garden. The man who swallowed fire whole.

"Wait," she called to him in Spanish. He slowed to a stop. Once both feet were on the ground, he edged the handlebars and front wheel around to face her. Age showed in his deliberate movements.

"You know Ben," she said. "And Mike too." When he didn't answer, her heart sped up as if she'd never cooled down from her run. "Right?"

He lifted his chin and smiled at her. One of his front teeth was slightly chipped and a darker shade of ivory.

"You're a runner," he said. "Very healthy. Strong."

His slurry Spanish was unlike the language she'd learned in high school and college, and unlike the way Intercambio teachers spoke in class.

"Ben works for you," she tried again. "What does he do, exactly?"

"Pardon?" He patted down his thick gray hair as if the act comforted him. He stroked his head with the flat of his palm but watched her with interest.

Carey's nerve fluttered around in her chest awhile, dispersing. Her sweaty mesh shorts and track t-shirt stuck to her skin, clammy, and she pulled at them. "Maybe I'm wrong. I thought he helped you somehow?" The lilt of her question pitched high.

Her Spanish was near-fluent, according to her host family and teachers, but now Alejandro appeared not to understand her.

He finally smiled. "Odd jobs," he said. "I'm an old man. They do my errands."

She sighed with relief. This old man needed help. Kind Ben had obliged. Ben saw him as a grandfatherly type, laughing over Carey's misgivings. "You're just sheltered," he told her, when they'd bumped into Alejandro on the street. Later, she'd told Ben he set off her creep-o-meter. "It's good you finally got away from home."

Alejandro was harmless, then.

"By any chance," Carey asked, "did Ben and Mike help you move some furniture?"

Confusion appeared in his dark eyes for a flash before a curtain of confidence fell over his expression. Again, she chalked this up to miscommunication.

He smiled, and she focused on the chipped tooth once more. It looked like an upside-down glacier.

"Sure," Alejandro said. "Furniture. The boys are a big help to me."

On certain afternoons she went to Ben's dorm, surprising him. She remained in bed when he'd get up to use the bathroom. Beneath the scratchy wool blanket and rough white sheet she stretched luxuriantly. Pointed her toes, arching her permanently blistered and callused feet. Reached her arms overhead, imagining she was being pulled in two directions. Her body lengthened, grew taller, when she stretched flat on her back on his twin bed. They shared a single pillow, which took on the apple scent of her shampoo. The first time they made love was during the lunch hour, in Ben's bed, a place she loved to be. Once they'd started having sex it was as if they'd always been having sex. She covered up immediately after, at least a shirt and underwear.

These days the sun grew weak earlier. She felt brighter. While he was down the hall she would sit up and sneak a look at herself in the mirror. Faraway eyes like a magazine model's. When she wore her hair piled on top of her head, it formed a tangled, flattened knot in back. Make-out hair, Nicole called it. Pliant strands pressed against a pillow, stretching and breaking under pressure. If she happened to put on make-up in the morning, as she did more regularly, by the time she'd rise from Ben's bed it smeared around her eyes and mouth. She didn't mind.

Often, Ben would return to the room from his dining hall shift with his hair still tangled and mussed like hers, and she liked that he hadn't noticed or cared. Once, he had come back to bed and grabbed her foot, thumbs digging into the thick pads.

"I can feel your calluses through the blanket," he said.

"Sexy."

"It is. You are." But he was smirking, that one-dimpled half-smile, thinking of something else. He shifted his eyes to the window. They never bothered to close the curtains. Nearby, invisibly high, came the crows of O.J. the rooster, day and night.

A couple of afternoons, Ben had called in sick to the dining hall. Carey had told Lupe she was trying out for Intercambio's winter play. An unnecessary lie; Lupe would still be working at the clothing store. Perhaps Carey told her so Bartolo would know. He said nothing about the night she'd tumbled through his window, but watched her from the corner of his eye, lingering in doorways.

Those afternoons when Carey allegedly attended play practice and Ben played sick, they holed up. She didn't know what he did, other days. He evaded her awkward attempts to find out. She'd tried to discern the nature of their relationship, if they were together or merely having sex. But if she was bad at asking direct questions, he was worse at giving straight answers. He took advantage of her lack of nerve and switched subjects, trying to impress and distract her. Half-truths, exaggerations, harmless lies: "When I was hacking through the Panamanian jungle with my machete, I discovered a new tribe of people. They wear puffy down jackets they found in a plane wreck, but no pants." Or: "Me and the guys used to sneak onto the roof of the high school at night. Once, the nuns caught us. But we didn't get in trouble. They invited us inside the convent. Sister Mary Margaret's a swimmer. Real young, nice body? Very smooth skin."

"Whatever."

"You don't believe me?" When he grinned he looked about eight years old rather than twenty-three. "I happen to know," he'd said, "about certain identifying birthmarks."

"That'll be helpful," she'd said. "If you ever have to identify her body."

"Oh, I've identified it." He gave himself away, telling these stories, with a burst of laughter. "So, I don't suppose you'll believe that I dated Andrea Cunningham. Mike, too. Our first summer here."

"Nope." Carey had been resolute.

"Too bad." He didn't laugh. "It's a good story."

He told her another one. "One night last spring, driving home from work, I swear I saw a ghost in the backseat of my car."

"A girl ghost," he'd added, pausing. "In fact, she looked a little like you."

Maybe he'd been trying to tell her, I know you followed me. Trailing me home from the mall, so close you could've been in my backseat. Memorizing my University of Wisconsin bumper sticker, watching me drive Molly home from school. Weren't you relieved when I put her in a headlock on our front lawn. You rough-house with a sister, not a girlfriend.

Carey decided that he didn't know, and she wouldn't tell. Her anonymity protected her. The past belonged to Carey alone. The more time she spent with Ben, the less she remembered who she was without him. He withheld from her. So she found one thing to keep from him. As if she were saving a sliver of herself for an unspecified later.

Besides The Doors he played her Led Zeppelin and occasionally something softer like Cowboy Junkies. He took her picture, freezing her in time. He offered her cans of mango juice from the supply that always sat on his dresser, though she didn't care for mango and never accepted. He convinced her, with little coaxing, that it was fine to ditch class or dinner with her host family. Not irresponsible: *living your life*. He disappeared and reappeared on a whim, doing favors, running errands. (But he never *bought* anything, she'd think.) He pushed towards her and pulled away. The push and pull appealed to her as much as anything physical about him—the green eyes, the dimpled smile, the lean, pale-skinned back around which she had wrapped her legs. The memory of him, sometimes better than being with him.

She wanted to stay in bed and he'd want to get dressed and go out. She feared being left behind. Once, she'd gone slack in the bed, dead weight, as he attempted to dress her prone body. He was hungry. He pulled her jeans to her knees, and she kept her narrow hips on the mattress. He gave up and yanked socks on her feet. He didn't massage them this time.

"You're the only boy brave enough to touch my feet," she said.

He didn't ask about the boys who refused. "I'll add it to my résumé," he said. He joked regularly about his nonexistent work prospects after graduation in the spring. Sometimes he talked about staying in Mexico to teach, or working with immigrants in Indianapolis, like his mother. Sometimes he shrugged, saying maybe he'd disappear for awhile—the Panamanian jungle, it's a beautiful place to get lost.

The day he'd tried unsuccessfully to dress her, he finally tickled her foot and she yelped, cursed him in Spanish. A voice in the hall told them to be quiet.

"Chinga tu madre," Ben hissed toward the hallway. Fuck your mother.

He hauled Carey up by the armpits. She squealed in a girlish pitch, unrecognizable to her own ears. "I'm opening the door in five seconds. You want the dorm to see your green panties?"

"Hell, yes," she said. "Do it. I dare you." She posed there, defiant with her jeans around her ankles, but chickened out as soon as his hand was on the doorknob. He watched, half-smiling as she pulled up her pants, zipping and buttoning hastily.

One November day, it rained so hard that the teachers talked of Guanajuato's great flood of centuries before. Throughout the city, men carried sandbags up the twisting stone steps of the callejones. The scene reminded Carey of news footage from natural disaster sites, though the placid residents shored up their homes by rote. They adapted. Even if downpours usually came in summer.

Ben acted surprised when Carey knocked on his door after classes, though they'd fallen into an unspecified routine.

"I was just heading out to meet Gibs," he said. He hadn't even opened the door completely.

"We should stay in." Carey tried not to sound disappointed. Her walk home would be long and wet.

"I wish I could," Ben said, though his face told her otherwise. "I promised Mike. I haven't seen him much lately."

Implied: *Because of you*. She nodded like she understood, though she didn't, not then.

"Aren't you coming?" Ben directed the question towards her back, tempering his impatience with a softer tone.

The café had closed early because of the weather, so the three of them walked a few blocks to a brightly-lit cafeteria. They could've eaten cafeteria food at the dorm. Instead Carey's socks and pant cuffs were soaked, her hair plastered to her head.

Mike hustled ahead of them, moving through the line and selecting a table in the near-empty restaurant. Ben loaded his tray with two of everything. He ate like a teenager. Never gained weight.

The young man working the register waved Ben through without ringing him up. When Carey reached for her wallet, the cashier clucked his tongue. He shook his head. His close-buzzed hair made visible a few bony bumps of skull, and his sunken eyes were ringed with circles, as if he hadn't slept in days. He could've been fifteen or thirty.

"Está pagado," he said. It's paid.

Ben had not paid for his own meal, let alone hers.

"Seguro?" she asked.

"Claro que sí." He winked. "Para la novia de Ben, claro que sí."

Of course, he said. For Ben's girlfriend, of course.

She beamed. Someone she'd never met could see they were together. At the table Mike took in the large piece of chocolate cake on Carey's tray and whistled, jokey and loud.

"That is one big-ass piece of cake," he said. "Hope you ran some extra miles today."

"Shut up," she said. Trying to laugh it off, but it came out sharply. The rain drummed on the hoods of parked cars.

Ben nudged Mike with an elbow; they were conspirators. "She gets plenty of exercise."

The flush crept up her neck and into her cheeks. Of course he meant sex. He'd been talking to Mike as he always had, about what they had always talked about. Mike appeared delighted and cocked his head to one side, considering Ben, refusing to look at Carey.

Too late, Ben realized his mistake and tried to change course. "She's a fast girl," he said. "A fast runner!" He ran his hand along his smooth jaw, his eyes telling her he was sorry. But he couldn't stop smiling.

"You're making it worse," she observed. "Abandon ship."

Mike's blond hair had grown longer, shaggier, over the last couple months; he hadn't had a haircut since he left home. Damp strands fell in his eyes as he shook his head. "No, continue. This is entertaining."

Carey shot Ben a glance. She'd been embarrassed, but part of her liked what he said. It was true. Ben's comment somehow validated their coupling. And her subconscious registered that it also described two people fucking for sport.

Mike shoved a slab of yellow bread in his mouth. "Seriously. Welcome to Cake Mountain. Did they charge extra?"

She shrugged.

Now Ben appeared amused. He raised his eyebrows, equally curious. Answer, his expression said. He widened his eyes. Mike had this effect on him. Everything turned into a set-up for some great punch-line. She was a bystander watching two sidewalk performers. They'd pull her into the routine, a set-up for humiliation.

"I don't know," she said. "Ask the cashier."

"This was compliments of the house," Ben told Mike.

"What?"

Ben's right shoulder rose and fell. "Who cares? You get free meals sometimes."

But tonight Mike had paid. "I'm going to have a word with Octavio," he said.

Ben forked in mounds of spicy rice; he winked at Carey and kept eating. "Thanks for putting up with us," he said. "God, you're adorable when you blush."

When Mike returned Ben changed the subject, like the last five minutes had been erased.

"Want to go out later?" Mike asked. "Octavio gave me a flyer."

"Cool," Ben said. "Where at?"

Carey was supposed to go back to Ben's room after dinner. Rarely did she return to the Alarcón's before nine, and she'd begun to feel a greater curtness from Hector, a chill from Lupe. They hadn't said anything directly about her lack of family involvement.

Ben smiled hopefully at Carey. "This band's good. Octavio plays guitar."

"It's nasty out. It's only going to get worse." She knew she was shutting doors Ben wanted to prop open, attempting to construct her own indoor climate.

Ben laughed. "That's right. The sky's falling. All the more reason to live it up." He often said things like this. Of course, he had been right.

She tried silently to communicate to Ben the benefits of giving up a night out. Mike's glare morphed into a smile when Octavio joined them.

"Qué onda?" Ben asked the cashier. They bumped fists.

"You working tonight?" Octavio asked in Spanish. "Alejandro wants you."

Ben grinned widely. "Too bad," he said. "I'm missing my camera. Damn, where could it be?"

"You can use my camera," Carey offered immediately, then remembered Ben's lanky body emerging from a window, the boxy black camera on a strap around his neck.

Ben ignored her. Octavio, with pursed lips, seemed to be deciding if he was angry or if he'd accept the joke. You could see it spreading down his face, the wrinkles relaxing in his forehead, the sunken eyes crinkling. He forced a laugh and clapped Ben's shoulder.

"So it was you," he said. "I knew it, guey."

Octavio gave Carey a long, appreciative look. To Ben he said, "Now I know why you stopped calling my sister."

"Hey, man," Ben said. He was actually blushing. "No hard feelings, right?"

The manager called Octavio's name, and he returned to the counter without answering the question. Later, when the Americans left the restaurant, Octavio waved pleasantly. At the door, Carey tripped on the nearly invisible step as she led them outside. "Careful," Octavio called, to any or all of them.

•

After dinner, Ben closed his dorm room curtains against the night sky and turned on the radio. The music was slow, mournful, Mexican.

A salsa band played somewhere in Guanajuato. Carey couldn't salsa; Luis had been kind when he told Bartolo she was a good dancer. She knew how to be led.

"Want to smoke up?" Ben asked, in the same tone he would use to ask if she wanted to go for ice cream. The lack of intonation served to disguise his resentment. If they stayed in, he'd blow a little pot smoke into her climate-controlled life.

She knew people in college who were occasional marijuana users, though she'd never tried it. In high school they had team policies against drugs, and pot was absent from any party she attended. At her school, those who smoked were hard-core partiers. Eighteen- and nineteen-year-olds who could pass for twenty-seven.

At Intercambio, the exchange students had been warned repeatedly not to bring drugs into the country or buy them once they arrived. She wondered which Ben had done. The penalties, Don Hernando had intoned, were stiff. Carey liked her clean track record. Nancy Reagan would be proud to know someone had listened to the "Just Say No" campaign. Runners needed healthy lungs. She heard Don Hernando in her head, saw him standing in his guyabera at the podium at that first assembly, which seemed like years before.

"Sure," she said.

The first hit made her cough. The second and third she managed just fine. By the fourth she was squinting through smoke, listening hard to the radio's melancholy guitars. Surprisingly, she had no urge to fly out the window or eat her weight in Cheetos, as some of the anti-drug ads had warned. So this was being high. Nice. OK. Why had she waited?

"How can it be," Ben asked, "that we both lived in the same city our whole lives and never knew each other?" They sat on the hard tile floor with their backs against the bed. Stretched out next to his, her own long leg was ridiculously shorter.

"I know," she told him. Thinking of Prisanti's, his hands wrapped around pizza dough. Ben at the wheel of a red sedan, plainly watching as she ran along 56th Street. But not remembering. Or not knowing who she was. How she'd watched him, an unbroken spell of wanting and not wanting to meet him. This was the kind of thing you revealed later, when you were inextricably bound and laughing over your bumbling beginnings. Even now, stoned, she understood they were not at that stage.

"I guess we were supposed to meet," he said.

For weeks she'd tried to coax this kind of sentimentality from him; now it tasted synthetically sweet. She'd forced the moment, engineered it through spying and plotting. It was a scene, the predictable next frame in a movie she'd watched obsessively in her head. She scratched a bug bite on her thigh through the material of her jeans. Fingernails scraping loud as maracas.

Part of her wanted to go out—Just not now, she told herself, because of the weather. The joint glowed briefly at Ben's mouth, and he exhaled towards the open window. Cool air filtered into the room. "Fate, karma, whatever you want to call it," he said. "In some religions, they'd say we have lessons to pass on to one other."

"Which religions?" Was she thinking in her head or speaking out loud?

"Eastern ones," he said. She either had spoken or he could read her thoughts.

The rooster kept at it. Ben kneeled on the desk and stuck his face to the window. "O.J.!" he yelled through the rain. His voice echoed off the buildings. A moment of quiet, then the rooster began again.

She leaned over to change the radio. The sad yelps of the Mexican cantador made her itch. All that emotion on the surface. It wasn't for her. She spun the dial until she landed on an oldies station playing "American Woman." The singer grunted long and low, making them laugh for five minutes straight; no, ten. Maybe just a few seconds.

"Why O.J.?" Carey leaned back and closed her eyes.

"Gibs named him," Ben said. "His dad's from Buffalo. Orenthal James Simpson is his all-time favorite football player. So Mike, the Bills." He waved his hand, a *voila* gesture. "You know that question? If-you-could-invite-five-people-to-dinner? He always picks O.J. He wouldn't ask about murdering his wife, he'd talk yards rushing. You gotta give Gibs credit."

No, I don't, Carey thought. She wondered whether she'd said it aloud.

"What other four people would Mike invite to dinner, then?" Carey asked.

Ben's head seemed to swing and loll on his neck as he turned to her. His mouth opened briefly and he licked his lips. She hoped he would kiss her, but his head righted and he stared straight ahead.

"No clue," he said. "Ask him yourself sometime."

Carey suggested that after tonight, Mike would be too angry to talk to her.

"He'll deal. He can afford dinner. Mr. Scholarship gets a stipend but likes to pretend he's broke."

Carey didn't know about Mike's scholarship. Ben stubbed out the joint without offering her another hit. She could tell by the way he avoided her eyes, by the distance he created when he moved to the bed, that they weren't going to have sex. At about eight he checked his black plastic wristwatch and stood.

"Want me to walk you home?" His begrudging company, worse than going without. She said no and shrugged on her jacket, hoping she didn't smell like pot. Would Lupe and Hector, or more likely Bartolo, recognize the scent? The Alarcóns were temporary in Carey's life, their opinion of her irrelevant once school ended and she returned to Indiana. But a shred of guilt nagged her like a hangnail she couldn't help but touch.

"It's on my way," he said.

"On your way where?" she asked. "It's pouring out."

He slowly smiled a half-smile, the single dimple sinking into his right cheek.

"The rain doesn't bother me," he said. "I'm meeting Gibs."

CHAPTER 11

CAREY LAY DOWN ALONE in the backseat of her Mazda. Her parents didn't notice when she walked out the front door around eight p.m. and camped out in her car, which was parked in the driveway. She still wore her restaurant uniform. The red Casa Colmo shirt and black pants were stained with margarita mix, grease spatters and dried white cheese. The stale aroma of beans and fried tortillas clung to her hair. Her mother quietly loathed Carey's appearance and scent at the end of the day. Her mother, a woman who came home well past the middle of the night, who dangled from ropes at a climbing wall.

It was the day after she'd met Mike. She'd stayed up half the night rifling through Ben's backpack: the burgundy shirt that still held traces of his smell, the piney scent of his cologne. She had not expected a weak, seven-year-old aroma to make her eyes burn. She'd long since opened and played the cds she knew he'd meant to give her, PJ Harvey and Pearl Jam, and inside the bag were the long cardboard sleeves of the discs' packaging. A waste.

His textbooks had been in the backpack, and she ignored them, just as she'd once ignored her own. She sought his journal. She'd gone over each line, obsessively, repeatedly. For clues about him, and herself. She flipped the pages, canvassing the territory, this map of her past that she did not know how to read.

The journal was filled not with stories and details but with dates and numbers: when he came back to Mexico for the full year after working his way through—Prisanti's on breaks, bar-backing in Madison, then Intercambio's dining hall. And there were several pages of initials, followed by the names of towns she'd never heard of, in Nevada and Illinois and North Carolina and even Indiana. Other pages of what must have been his wages: calculated hours multiplied by a rate, like an old-fashioned accountant's ledger. Carey had woken before dawn with a kink in her neck, the waffle-weave of Ben's shirt imprinting her cheek. She'd fallen asleep on her closet floor. It was the first time she could recall being bored by Ben.

She crouched in the car, cramped, tapping her foot against the door. After a half-hour, she saw the light go on in her father's study, and the faint glow of the computer. The light dimmed; he'd closed the blinds. He would be seated at his desk, reviewing legal briefs or playing solitaire. He sat for hours at the computer each evening.

Carey shifted in the backseat and considered moving outside to the lawn when the garage door rumbled upwards. Nine-twenty-two. He had to hear the noise. Where did she tell him she was going? A minute later her mother piloted the Jetta out of the driveway, and Carey watched for lights to sweep the corner before climbing into her own driver's seat. At the second cross street, the Jetta's taillights turned into a wooded, private drive about a half-mile down the road. She wasn't even leaving the neighborhood. Her mother was going to the Finebaker's.

Judy Finebaker and Gwen Halpern had been friends for years, volunteering on school committees. Carey had been a grade below twerpy Andrew Finebaker at Township High, whose engagement announcement was posted on the Halpern's refrigerator. Judy, an importer, spent lots of time in her mother's shop, helping set up displays of African masks, bamboo boxes, delicate porcelain she'd gotten for a song. Finer Things also carried carved wooden fish from Mexico, though they were pieces Gwen Halpern had selected from a catalog. When Carey was preparing to leave for Guanajuato, Judy Finebaker had asked her to scope out the local handicrafts. "To be honest," she'd told Carey, "I haven't had much luck with Mexico."

"She means they make crap," her mother had offered. Judy tried to smooth the awkward moment: "Maybe Carey will uncover the secret stash," she said.

The Jetta rolled down the long private drive, past the Finebaker's. Deeper into the forested neighborhood, where the reclusive rich lived in architectural dream homes that were featured in *Indianapolis Monthly* photo spreads. The unlit road jogged around the woods, turning to one lane across the creek bridge. Carey had run that road before.

If she followed, she'd be seen. There were no other cars on the street. Gwen accelerated into a driveway without using her turn signal.

Carey parked. The drive where Gwen had disappeared was about three-quarters of a mile away. In her pocket was a crumpled cigarette pack from the restaurant kitchen. She pulled out a slightly bent cigarette and lit a match from a Casa Colmo matchbook. The first drag was always the best—lightheadedness and a rush that felt like elation, invincibility.

When she reached the driveway, she stood there a while longer, smoking. The black metal mailbox rested on a wooden post; reflective stickers spelled out "Elliot." The name was unfamiliar. A metal sign advertising Circle City Landscaping sprouted from the lawn. She saw the company's trucks across town, the pickup beds filled with Mexican migrant workers.

The few parts of the ultra-modern house that weren't glass or steel were painted white. Carey sat on a numbingly cold white marble bench near a small, empty carp pond.

When the man walked into the living room carrying a long-stemmed wine glass, she recognized him from the climbing wall. It was like watching a play. Before her was the stage, and she, the hidden audience. In the high-ceilinged room the man appeared diminutive. He was older than her mother. Salt-and-pepper hair, his face tanned like a hide. He wore jeans and a fitted black sweater. His mouth moved with words she could not hear.

When Gwen Halpern entered the room, alone, Carey saw someone other than her mother. She had changed from work clothes into khaki pants and a gray zip-up sweatshirt. She held a glass filled with red wine, and stood languidly by the window. Gwen saw her own reflection in the glass and played to it.

Only one cigarette remained. Carey lit the end and dropped the match onto the stone bench, leaving an ashy trail. She didn't try to mask the glow of the match to the white tip—the two people inside were oblivious. Now Gwen sat on the overstuffed leather chair. He was across from her on a leather couch. Two tall red pillar candles glowed on the glass coffee table, making reflections.

Atop the oak credenza rested the useless silver ball with the hollowed-out cherry base. Unsold for a decade in Finer Things, with a price tag of two grand. Carey already missed the thing, though it had never been hers.

The person inside was and wasn't her mother. Gwen brushed away her longish bangs. Her fingertips rested briefly on her forehead. Carey had seen that gesture before, when her mother was considering how to say something. She looked like she was trying to draw out her thoughts manually. The man nodded, smiled. Cupped his chin in one hand, transfixed. She sloshed her drink, and the man moved to the chair next to hers and handed her a napkin. She clutched it in her hand, worrying it into little pieces. She seemed girlish, almost vulnerable, and Carey's eyes pricked with tears. She missed her mom. This other woman made her furious. As if sensing Carey's agitation, Gwen turned sharply to the window. For a moment, Carey thought she could be seen. But her mother was checking her own reflection.

A few dead leaves sat at the bottom of the empty cement pond. Carey flicked in the cigarette. She didn't know if anyone noticed the smoke from the smoldering leaves. She was long gone, jogging along the driveway for a few paces before the searing pain in her lungs and side kicked in. She resorted to a fast walk that hurt just as much.

The next day, Carey arrived early for her shift. Elena was leaning on the glass case, studying the packets of gum and candy inside. She glanced up and wordlessly took in Carey's stained pants and shirt.

The men were huddled around a table with the day's paper. Fast, loaded whispers: *El pasaporte. You know him? Which, el Americano or el Mexicano?*

She looked over their shoulders. On the color newspaper page, Ben smiled at her in an unfamiliar photo that accompanied a follow-up story. He wore a blazer, a tie, and an artificial expression. The headline read, "Slain Student's Passport Used in Other Cities." Another article. There would be more. She'd been up half the night, the skin beneath her eyes thin and purple. The men conferred, marking their associations. Roberto felt her presence. "*Que pasó, Kah-ree?*" He examined her face. She couldn't take her eyes from the newspaper.

"You're shaking," Elena said. She looked Carey up and down and wrinkled her nose. "*Vamonos.*" She walked to the back room. When Carey didn't follow, she turned impatiently. "Come on," she said, with only the trace of an accent.

How could she work today, with Ben's picture in the paper, hovering over her? Today she could not bear the rudeness of customers, nor how inept she would continue to be at the job. She spilled and spilled: yesterday, a sizzling tray of fajita platters and a pitcher of sangria. Juan only laughed, clapped her on the back. Elena somberly helped clean up.

She picked at the thin crusty layer of food on her short sleeve. Elena led her to the stockroom. A bright, bare bulb lit up the large closet. Sturdy wooden shelves held plastic bags of rice and dried beans, and huge burlap sacks of the stuff were stacked on the floor. Industrial-sized tin cans of tomatoes, chiles, and maraschino cherries perched in neat rows. Elena rooted around until she found the right box. She pulled out a new bright red shirt with the Casa Colmo logo stitched on the left breast, deeply creased from being folded.

"Change your shirt," Elena said, tossing her the red polo. "*Es sucio.*"

Elena never spoke Spanish to Carey. Sucio meant dirty. It sounded dirtier than dirty.

Elena tried to glare around her curiosity. American women wore their shirts two days in a row, even with crusty bean and cheese on the sleeve. "This isn't some wall-hole," she said. "This is my family's restaurant."

Carey's face turned as red as the shirt. "I was too busy to do laundry last night."

Elena shrugged. "So now you have two. One for wash day."

She pictured not the gleaming white appliances in her parents' mud room, but the old metal tub in the back courtyard of the Alarcón house. Wash day in Mexico, when she tried to save Maria from scrubbing her clothes by hand. Maria, who crossed herself in Carey's presence after Ben died. Who told Lupe that La Americana was possessed by diablítos.

"I'm sorry," Carey said, fidgeting with her messy ponytail. "I'll change."

Elena nodded, averting her eyes. She left her alone in the stockroom, and Carey tried to control the tears pricking her eyes. She pulled off the dirty shirt and flung it to the floor. She was glad there was no mirror. She didn't want to see her soft sides, or the thin arms that shook under the weight of a serving tray. A lovely body with changes she could not accept.

The door opened again.

"Momentito." She hurriedly pulled the cotton polo down to her hips. Roberto, in his cook's apron, stood there with a dirty cotton dishrag in one hand. His widened eyes indicated that he'd seen her bare back, the strap of her black bra.

"Ay, disculpe, señorita," he said, shutting the door quickly. From the other side she heard a muffled, nervous laugh. In five minutes she was supposed to be setting up for dinner. She flopped on a stack of twenty-pound rice bags. The grain molded to her shape, held her. Perhaps the maid had been right. She was possessed, filled with espiritus malcriados, and she didn't know how to exorcise them.

Elena knocked softly and poked her head in. "What?" Carey asked crossly. She could never be alone; alone was all she ever was. She kept her head down. Those desperately in need of kindness are the first to reject it. Strung out on pain or the substances used to numb it, they worry about strings-attached.

Elena barely looked at her. "Maybe you could use the bathroom.

Roberto needs lentils for the soup."

Once again Carey had misread someone. But she didn't wipe her wet eyes or apologize. She stared Elena in the face and Elena stared back.

"Give me a minute. If he wants to come in, tell him to come in."

She spoke fast English on purpose, waiting for Elena to ask her to repeat it. She didn't. Instead, she yelled down the hall: "Espérate, Roberto." She sat down across from Carey on another stack of rice bags. Their eyes were level. Carey's red-rimmed, glazed; Elena's dark, fathomless.

"Que pasó?" she asked. Spanish, again. Elena elicited her trust. She was of another atmosphere and geography and language. The mountains, the twisting streets and callejones.

Carey's words came out jumbled, some in English and some in Spanish. Elena listened.

"That was my boyfriend. In the paper today. He was killed down there. Seven years later and nobody can say what happened, but I hear the waiters talking. Back then I went a little crazy. It's not getting better."

Elena nodded. Not agreeing, just encouraging Carey to continue. But she didn't pry. She was maybe a few years older than Carey, with clear skin and shiny black hair. When she walked customers across the restaurant floor to seat them, she appeared to float. Elena made Carey want to put on make-up and style her hair. The kind of woman who made you realize what you weren't.

Elena didn't pat her arm, pass a box of tissues, smile and say it would be OK. She sat and listened, sometimes nodding. When Carey fell silent, exhausted, she looked at the clock. Quarter to six, the dinner hour underway. But Elena made no move to get up. She sighed heavily.

"In our town, we heard about the murder," she said. "Dolores Hidalgo, it is not so big or so far. And Guanajuato es muy tranquilo. We were shocked. Mi papa, Juan, our cousins, they worked at a hotel restaurant in Guanajuato. Our neighbor is a maid in the town. We all knew. It is a tragedy."

Carey nodded.

Elena had grown pensive. "In the papers they gave much attention to the American's death. Yo recuerdo."

Roberto knocked on the door again, asking in fast Spanish for the lentils, por favor. Elena grabbed three bags from a shelf, opening the door no more than a crack to hand them through. She resettled on the sacks of grain, but she didn't let herself sink.

Elena glanced at her watch. She stood and straightened her skirt, and smiled without showing any teeth. Between them was silence, a storeroom floor.

"I remember the American—very handsome, no?"

Carey thought of Ben's green eyes, the color of moss, and how she'd never thought about the loveliness of moss before she saw his eyes up close. His distinct, large nose, the dimples carved into his cheeks. His way of moving did her in—something as simple as the way he unfolded his tall body from a desk.

"He was beautiful," she said. "Even if that's not what you say about a man."

"And what happened?"

She considered her answer. Elena might've heard gossip from people in town. Teachers in the exchange program speculated that Ben knew people who could be trouble. Perhaps Ben himself was trouble—his association with Alejandro, with Octavio. And she could not forget her own anger, after Ben stood her up hours before his death. She'd gone back to Mike's dorm room. She'd woken the next morning hung over, pulled by competing regrets. The police found Ben's body in an alleyway where the two of them had walked.

She told no one that after Ben's body was found, her first fleeting response was relief. She'd loved Mexico, loved Ben, with a fervor that terrified her. She'd opened herself up, her body splayed like a starfish, her heart pinned through like a specimen on a tack board.

Seven years later, she was home. Unpinned.

"I don't know," she said finally. A half-truth, thus a half-lie. "Wrong place at the wrong time."

Elena wore flat pink ballet slippers that clicked on the tile. She walked to the door and kept her back to Carey. "You love him," she said.

Carey had never said so, not to him or anyone else. This, her love for Ben, the silent truth of her life. We all live by such unarticulated truths. Carey's imagined relationship was too real to risk, better than any actuality.

"Yes," Carey said.

"What is his name?" Elena asked.

Carey told her, like speaking a language she made up in a dream. His name circled her brain constantly, safe, protected. Unspoken and unshared. But she told Elena. She said Ben's name out loud and her voice didn't crack.

"I know we prayed for him," Elena said. "On Sundays, when we went to the cemetery for our family. I remember it rained that day. The clouds seem close only because we are in the mountains. The sun came out later."

The image of Elena with Juan and their parents sitting among tombstones and mossy angel statues praying for strangers—praying for Ben—dislocated something inside her. A choked sob escaped Carey's mouth, but Elena didn't notice.

When she finally turned, her face wasn't sad at all but dreamy, like she was remembering the taste of smooth berry ice cream, or the feel of the sun on her face. A deeply pleasurable time that was long ago, but worth remembering. Cherishing.

"When the weather's nice, it's like being in a park," Elena said. "Everyone is there with us. Just like always."

Tears rolled down Carey's cheeks. Elena smiled, her chin bunching up.

"Sometimes," she said, before gently shutting the door behind her, "we stay so long we bring our lunch."

Carey waited tables, zombie-like, for less than an hour before Elena sent her home. In the parking lot she leaned against the dirty back bumper of her Mazda and chain-smoked. The western sky turned the striated clouds fiery orange and red, a sunset Ben would've called an

Indianapollution Special. In Guanajuato he'd theorized that dramatic sunsets were due to burned toxic waste, poison gases, the depleted environment. She'd disputed his claim—she and her parents had admired many such sunsets on their back deck, and all this time they'd been admiring *pollution?* Mike backed Ben up, of course. He'd read an article. With a little research she could have proven them both wrong. She hadn't done any research.

Carey sat on the car's trunk. Midway into her second cigarette, Elena appeared with Roberto in tow.

"Tell her," Elena said, and Carey anticipated an apology for Roberto's earlier laughter as she stood exposed, her shirt over her head. But Roberto stared glumly at his shoes like a child being punished.

"Por qué?" he asked dully. He told Elena, It's a risk. She replied, No, it's safe to talk to her. She reminded Roberto that Carey spoke Spanish. And she's not deaf, Elena added, which pleased Carey.

Elena jerked her thumb towards Roberto like an impatient hitchhiker. "My cousin remembers him," she said. "Tu novio."

Carey's breath caught in her chest, and since she'd just taken a drag, she coughed for a long minute. Roberto's eyes were two pieces of dusty coal, framed by the black curls on his forehead. He stood several inches taller than Carey. His stained white apron was slung around his waist, strings securely knotted below his belt buckle.

"The photographer," he said. "Right?"

Carey nodded, remembering Ben's nickname among a handful of Mexicans who were strangers to her, glimpsed once or twice and never again.

Roberto held her gaze. "You know he took many pictures," Roberto said. "He took my picture."

Carey didn't know. She envied that Roberto had something of Ben's she lacked. The twin gaze of his camera and his eye.

"Sure," she said, feigning politeness.

"Mira," he said, Spanish for "look," but it could also mean "see." He reached into his back pocket, and before she even glimpsed the picture, she knew what he would show her. Her mind had locked on the right flashes of memories, parts of Mexico she'd not conjured in years, let alone combined into a coherent whole. Twined in grief and guilt, Carey had overlooked exactly what Ben meant for her to overlook. She'd kept alive the memories that fit best.

Now she saw perfectly. This was what she had come for. It took three seconds for Roberto to reach into the back pocket of his jeans. One more second to flash the passport picture Ben had taken. And for the weeks' worth of seconds that followed, Carey would wonder why she hadn't seen it coming. Even though she hadn't known Roberto in Mexico, even though she'd never seen the photograph, depicting a blank, unsmiling, much-younger version of the restaurant cook she scarcely knew, even now. The small square photograph was laminated into the fake passport Roberto held before her.

With Ben, she allowed herself to fade away, to be led like a tourist following a guide. He'd pointed out the sights. She trusted and believed. In return, he renamed the landmarks, rearranged them. He taught her to see without seeing.

CHAPTER 12

ONE MORNING IN DECEMBER, Ben and Mike did not arrive for class. Jennifer smiled and waved, choosing a seat across the room. The other students filing in knew to leave two open seats near Carey.

Carey opened her notebook and glanced down at the syllabus. *Choose a significant aspect of the culture in Guanajuato and write 3-5 pages, using methods of primary and secondary research.* The Diego Rivera paper. Due today. She hadn't even started. She had yet to go to Rivera's childhood home and museum, near La Alhóndiga. She'd planned to go last week, but instead joined Mike for quesadillas from a street vendor. They later met Ben for a drink and she didn't get home until midnight. She specifically remembered the time because Hector was parked in front of the television long after his normal bedtime, watching President Zedillo speak to a crowd of cheering supporters. Hector grunted hello and switched off the set, trudging to bed. "Noches," he had said. As usual, he couldn't manage *Buenos* for her. A sign of his indifference, Carey thought, oblivious to the compliment of informal address, his worry.

The paper was not the first assignment Carey had missed. Luisa Maria hummed with exasperation, collecting assignments from the responsible students who would sail from the program with an "A" in every subject. Everyone said exchange program classes were easy; you had to have a pulse and a modicum of interest. Yet there she was, flailing.

She left halfway through class. Outside, the sun warmed the buildings and the street. So bright her eyes saw blue, as if through tinted lenses. Would Ben and Mike be in one of the plazas? Would she find them on a bench, lolling in the sun? The papers said it was warmer than usual for early December. Lately night had carried a deep chill, but days were in the high seventies. She removed her cream-colored woolen sweater and tied it around her waist. At home, the fields had long been harvested, the leaves raked. It was pitch dark by six p.m., and everyone waited for a sign that the sun still existed. Lately home came to her only through Nicole's emails, or her parents' vague, general updates via blue airmail letters. ("Busy at the store. What else is new? Your father says to tell you hello.") She could barely picture Indiana's winter. She now lived in Mexico, in a mountain valley, when December meant no sweater.

She wished she knew where Ben was. Or Mike, who could lead her to Ben. They skipped classes occasionally with no repercussions. If the teachers cared, they looked the other way. "We wrote a proposal," Ben explained once. "We're like teaching assistants. For real, Intercambio made us community liaisons. We ensure that the fine people of Guanajuato adjust to the hordes of Americans storming their castle. As it were."

"Please," Carey had said.

"Andrea loved the idea," Mike said. "Andrea loves *us*."

When they ditched, usually they invited her. Cajoled her, which now took little effort. An independent study with city as classroom. Sometimes she assumed the same arrangement applied to her by proxy. But days like today, when Luisa Maria wanted a paper on Diego Rivera and she had nothing, not even a plausible excuse, she understood she was alone.

She remembered the first day of school, when she'd gone with Ben and Mike to see Alejandro spit fire. "We're teaching class today," Ben had said. Well. Today she would teach her own class. At the Jardín Unión, she sat on the steps of Teatro Juárez and watched a mime perform for a handful of people. He had long, black hair tied in a ponytail, and a white-painted face with an exaggerated red mouth. When the church bells clanged, he startled. A few seconds later when the bells pealed again, he jumped in the air. People laughed, but he made Carey sad. The mime relived the same day, feigning surprise every hour on the hour, and expected a few coins for the effort. She scanned the park benches from her seat on the steps. Recognized no one.

A wreath with pink and purple advent candles perched on an apartment windowsill. Christmas would arrive in weeks, and none of them were going home. She needed to buy and ship gifts. At the market she'd purchase a tacky Jesus keychain for Nicole, a colorful blanket for her father. She had no idea what to get her mother.

She decided to skip afternoon classes, too. Finally she understood kids in high school who seemed willfully to fail. Once you fell in a hole, you had to claw to get out. Why not go about the chosen distraction that sunk you in the first place?

Turning a corner, she entered the first open door, connected to a church, its sign flipped to "Abierto." She descended a short flight of stairs, catching her breath. At the steps' base, a wide, stone cavern gaped, a dark hole.

A few feet in, a bench carved into a small alcove offered a place to rest. An intermittent drip of water echoed, and a shaft of light traveled from the end of the passageway. Signs with arrows indicated more rooms. The air was cool and dry, musty.

She placed both palms against the stone bench, cooling her hands. Leaned back against the wall and closed her eyes. Below ground the temperature fell perhaps twenty degrees, yet Carey remained comfortable. This was infinitely better than sitting in class: a field trip of her own design.

She wished Ben were there. She wanted to introduce something new, to lead for once. In the past few weeks, he'd come by the house to pick her up for actual dates, and despite her protests, he always paid. They'd gone to Restaurante Silvio with its white tablecloths and wide-rimmed goblets, and to the movie theater, where they watched American movies with Spanish subtitles.

Two weeks back, she had been serenaded. It was after midnight, for good luck. Lupe came to wake Carey and Alicia; she wore a long, white nightgown, her face pale without makeup, startling Carey as she leaned over the bed. Lupe and Hector occupied the front bedroom, a place Carey had never seen. In the moonlight she discerned the huge walnut armoire and dresser, and Hector in bed beneath a wooden headboard and a framed picture of the Virgin Mary. He rolled over once but otherwise ignored the event.

"It's tradition," Lupe whispered to the girls, and pointed out the window to the street, where Ben stood in a giant black velvet sombrero. Mike was there, in a cowboy hat, and five or six Mexican men strummed guitars. Carey recognized Octavio, the cashier at the cafeteria. It's paid, he said. For Ben's girlfriend, it's paid. Now he played guitar, engrossed in the music.

They sang three songs she didn't know. She listened with a mix of pleasure and embarrassment, Alicia sighing beside her, Lupe exhibiting a closed-lip smile when she wasn't yawning. At the last chords of the third song, the men bowed and Ben blew her a kiss. Mike tipped his cowboy hat like a rancher, and the women laughed. On her way back to the bedroom and a giddy, sleepless night, Bartolo emerged from the bathroom.

"Young love," he'd said dismissively, and closed his bedroom door behind him.

The memory of his words chilled her. Bartolo, she assumed, took her interest in Ben personally. She did her best to ignore the assumption. Bartolo wasn't that much older, but his offhand remark equated young love with a passing whim. Her feelings for Ben did not ebb and flow. This was a quiet war. Lives magnified on a movie screen. A collapsed star deep inside her chest, swelling with importance because it was hers.

She wended down the cavern's long hallway, her shoes silent on stone. Behind a counter stood a young man, ready to dispense tickets and maps. The small room contained brightly-lit paperboard signs showing diagrams of gems and stones, and a brief explanation of la inundación. The flood. She asked the man how much the museum cost.

He wore thick glasses and had a barrel-shaped torso and fleshy face. "Americana?" he asked. "De dónde?"

She told him.

"Ah!" He mimed steering a race car, the vroom of the engine bubbling from his lips. "The 500," he said in Spanish.

He wanted to shake her hand. He wanted to give her a kiss on the cheek. "Me permite?" he asked. She allowed him, half-expecting a discount. Still she paid fifty pesos, about fifty cents.

She held the small map in one hand and walked through the displays of different rocks and minerals. Some were in glass cases, others were glued to paperboard. The floors were dusty, the exhibit meager. She had no interest in geology but circled the floor like a cat. She was the only one in the underground museum. She'd grown unused to loneliness, so common a feeling growing up that she'd barely noticed it.

The ticket taker appeared from behind the wall. "Me llamo Paco," he offered. She smiled warily and told him her name. She was alone in a stone basement with a man she did not know, who'd already kissed her on the cheek. If Ben were here, she would not worry. She was angry with Ben, and herself, for instinctively conjuring a man's protection. She straightened, then worried that her breasts stuck out. Slouched again.

She pointed to some wooden scaffolding propped against a stone wall and asked what it was. Girls learn early the rules of distraction.

Paco's eyes shone, proud to be a tour guide. "That is old Guanajuato," he said. "This is where the city used to be, before the floods." They were maybe twenty feet underground. He walked to the wall and brushed his hand over the seemingly ancient stonework. It was carved in an intricate design she couldn't make out. His hand moved tenderly, his eyes on her.

"This was the original church," he said. "The one above came second. Muy bonita, no?"

She nodded stiffly.

"After the flood, they built over it." He motioned to her. "It's OK to come closer. Don't be scared. The ceiling won't fall." His knuckles rapped a wooden post wedged into the wall. A dusty trickle of rocks scattered to the ground.

The small room shrunk as the walls seemed to push in, gray and white stones damp with water from an unknown source. Not enough air.

"Perdóneme," she said, and bolted. Up the stairs and out into the street, where she leaned on an iron rail overlooking an underground highway tunnel. The tourists and the shop owners were still there, and so were the small children harassing pigeons in the fountain. She breathed steadily, as if she were running a race in a high school cross country meet. She shouldn't have gone into the museum alone.

"Señorita."

Paco stood before her, offering a glass bottle of Coke. Above ground, he looked like a kid. Several years younger than her. Not thick or large but baby-fat pudgy. He opened the Coke in a quick motion with a key from his keychain, and handed the drink to her with a little bow. At the top of the stairs, he turned and gave a shy wave. She drained the bottle in three gulps, grateful, ashamed. Her instincts, she thought, were useless.

Date: December 5, 1995 2:34 p.m.
To: Ben Williamson <bwilliamson@intercambio.edu>
Cc: Mike Gibley <mgibley@intercambio.edu>
From: Carey Halpern <chalpern@intercambio.edu>
Subject: MIA

Nice of you to skip school and leave me to fend for myself. Got harassed by a rock museum man. Attended a grand total of 1½ classes. Where are you?

Carey

Date: December 5, 1995 3:41 p.m.
To: Carey Halpern <chalpern@intercambio.edu>, Ben Williamson <bensays@freenet.com>
From: Mike Gibley <mgibley@intercambio.edu>
Subject: re: MIA

Maybe you didn't look hard enough. Seems we're easily replaced. Where the hell is this alleged museum? We think you made it up.

Mike

P.S. Nice sweater today. Creamy.

They were baiting her, threading sharp hooks with fat, bloody worms. What they were fishing for she could only guess. But back then, she was hungry, willing to accept that piercing jab.

She bit.

Date: December 5, 1995 4:20 p.m.
To: Ben Williamson <bensays@freenet.com>
Cc: Mike Gibley <mgibley@intercambio.edu>
From: Carey Halpern <chalpern@intercambio.edu>
Subject: re:re:re: MIA

Meet me in the Plaza del Baratillo immediately. Big news. Could affect the rest of your stay, according to Intercambio.

—C

Mike was leaning against the dry blue fountain when she arrived in the Plaza de Baratillo. Its name came from old-time vendors who promoted their goods by yelling "Cheap!" A few people strolled around the brick walkway, or sat on wrought-iron benches, reading newspapers or sipping iced fruit drinks. Mike had been fixated on her when she spotted him, then pretended to examine a storefront display of magazines. She marched within a foot of him.

"Where's Ben?" she asked.

Mike giggled. He actually snorted. Couldn't stop laughing, and had to clutch at his stomach, doubled-over, shaking silently. When he straightened, withheld laughter still causing his lips to tremble, Carey caught a whiff of smoke. Stronger. Rank and sweet. Mike was high.

He couldn't answer, but instead waved for her to follow. They walked side by side on the narrow cobblestone sidewalk, Mike throwing sidelong glances.

"You said you had news," he prompted, a little out of breath.

"I'll tell you both at the same time."

"I should warn you. Ben's a little out of it."

"As out of it as you?" She wanted to be mad. She forgave so easily then, so readily. Chances and chances.

"I'm not that out of it." He wiped his eyes. "Now Ben. Ben is outty-out-out of it. Audi 5000-out-of-it."

They crossed the street in front of Banco Federal's tall white columns. The bank was closed, missing the armed guards who'd stood before it the first day of class. Mike directed her into the alley, and she knew they were going to Alejandro's. No gifts or ceremony this time, just a primer-gray door Mike pushed open, and a courtyard garden that seemed much less beautiful, much less cared for than it had several months before. The apartments surrounding the garden were as decrepit as she remembered.

Up a flight of stairs. Mike knocked in a particular rhythm, a pathetic and small gesture. Like something he'd seen in a bad detective movie. A moment later the door swung open and Alejandro stood before them. Today he looked bookish, with his hair pulled back into a ponytail and small round wireless glasses on his face. His belly stretched the fabric of his dirty gray t-shirt.

"Señorita," he greeted Carey. "We meet again."

He didn't call her Grace Kelly this time. Ben sat on the couch gazing at the television, oblivious to their arrival. The television cast the only light in the room. The apartment smelled like something recently burnt; also, lilies.

Carey's eyes adjusted to the dark room, which the television occasionally illuminated like a strobe. Even without overhead lighting, Carey felt the closeness of the living room. Stacked precariously from floor to ceiling were cardboard boxes, three layers deep and forming new walls. A few of the boxes on the floor spilled open with cheap, plastic-wrapped toys and candy. Hanging from wall hooks were several dozen thin t-shirts on hangers: "Guanajuato" in glittery script with green frogs underneath. White plastic laundry baskets held shot glasses, coffee mugs and brass bells with the city's name. Crumpled newsprint lay all around the recently-unwrapped goods. Alejandro the fire-eater sold souvenirs.

Ben turned his head and saw her. His mouth stretched into a broad grin. A silly, silent, lovesick smile. He opened and closed his hands to say "come here." The Mexican gesture was palms down, American was palms up. His palms were up. She fell next to him on the couch and examined his eyes, dilated and in a far-off place but nonetheless glad to see her. "Oh, my girl," he said, kissing her. "My sweet, true girl."

"Lovers," Alejandro said with quiet approval, gliding silently down the dark hallway.

Mike told them to get a room.

"Why don't *you* get a room?" Ben asked.

Mike grabbed his laptop from the coffee table and settled into the worn green recliner. "Me and my hand have other plans tonight."

"Calm yourselves," Carey said. She stood and opened the drapes a crack. Sure enough, she could see the steps of the theater and the tops of the Indian laurel in the Jardín Unión. They'd spied on her from the window. She couldn't be angry. She knew what it meant, watching from afar. Sometimes you didn't want to break that spell.

On TV, Bill Clinton's head dominated the screen. She translated the graphic: Deficit, closing, 260,000 government employees.

"They're shutting down our government?"

Ben's head wagged. "Been shut down for decades, baby. The latest is just a technicality. That's not our government, anyway. We belong to Mexico now."

"Yeah, where've you been the last four months?" Mike's fingers clattered across the keyboard. "Damn. That is some head of state. Look at that hair. So thick!"

Mike hadn't asked again about her alleged important information. Stoned, Ben and Mike's repartee took on a silly, looping quality, only a shade different than usual. It obscured and connected them, leaving her out.

"When does it close?" Carey wondered. "Do they flip a sign on the door?"

"As we speak," Mike said, turning an imaginary sign. "Attention American shoppers: your nation is now closed. At least the immigrants get a day off work."

Ben exhaled, slow and measured. "Mexicans don't get how fucked-up the U.S. is," he said. "They risk their lives crossing over for crap jobs. Then people like my mom process their Burger King applications, or for some chain-gang landscaping crew."

Ben didn't mention his father, who mowed lawns at Trinity Academy. Carey said nothing. Alejandro returned wearing what looked like a woman's cardigan sweater, cranberry-colored. He offered her a can of Tecate, already opened. She accepted.

"You here to work?" he asked her in Spanish.

"No," Ben said. "She's here to do whatever she wants."

"What kind of work?" she asked, ignoring Ben. Alejandro pulled a folding chair next to the couch and sat down, clasping his hands together like a gun, index fingers to his lips.

"What are your skills?"

Mike snorted. "Ask Ben."

"Fuck off," Carey replied in English.

"That's my girl."

She turned politely to her host and pointed to the glassware and ceramics in the laundry basket. "Do you need help?" She pitied Alejandro, one more vendor trying to live off tourists.

"Si quieres," Alejandro said. If you want.

She reached inside one of the cardboard boxes. The newsprint came off on her hands as she opened the parcel. Inside, a collection of small, hand-painted ceramic frogs stared up at her, bright green with black eyes and red mouths. Painted on each glossy back was "Guanajuato." She knew from class—she had learned something after all—that the city's name emerged from the indigenous tongue. It meant "Place of Frogs." She turned one over in her palm. "Made in

China" read the sticker.

Alejandro gently nudged her knee with his knuckles. He held another can of beer in his hand. She had drained the first, barely paying attention; he'd already opened the new can.

"Gracias," she said.

When she rose to use the bathroom she saw Mike's computer screen, where he fiddled with margins on a document. Red letterhead stated "P&K Energy." He lowered the laptop's lid, his eyes hooding over.

"Quit spying," he said.

"You should talk." Their bickering shaded with flirtatious undertones.

The bathroom was surprisingly clean. A neat stash of girlie magazines sat on the floor between the freestanding shower and toilet. No medicine cabinet. No soap dish or toothbrush on the sink, no razor. No towels hanging over the shower rod.

On her way back to the living room, she peeked in one of the bedrooms. It was mostly an office. Instead of a bed, a sleeping bag was tossed atop a cot. A small desk lamp had been left on in the curtained room, and a table served as the desk. It held a large printer but no computer. Clipped to a string on the wall were photo ID badges; she could make out Alejandro's gray hair in two of the dozen thumbnail pictures. Stacks of booklets and papers rose from the desk in neat rows. She took a step inside. The blue booklets carried gold embossing on the covers, official-looking stamps and seals.

"Carey?" Ben whispered. She tried not to jump. Failed. "Come back to the living room, huh?"

"What's this?" she asked, though she knew. She was too far away to read the script, but she'd produced her own blue book numerous times in travel, and at Hector's bank, cashing traveler's cheques. She knew what an American passport looked like. But she asked Ben anyway. She wanted to know that he understood.

"I don't know," he said. "His work stuff. It's private." Ben squinted, eyes moving to the floor. He asked her without asking, *Don't ask*.

He held up the beer she'd left on the coffee table, next to the green Guanajuato frogs that had been made in China. His eyes were still hazy but she could see Ben inside, somewhere. She took a long sip. Gave the can back and let him finish.

They would return to the living room, spending another hour unwrapping souvenirs, newsprint-swaddled tokens nobody wanted. But first she glanced over her shoulder. In the far corner of the room, a camera rested on a tripod, a large flash attached to the top. A black, boxy camera identical to the one Ben had climbed in a window to retrieve.

The photographer, a Mexican would say on the street. Once at the café, another time at Pastel. "I've become known for my touristic impulses," he told Carey, who recognized but did not question the lie. Because of Ben, she'd become so self-conscious taking pictures that she stopped after the first month. Live, he'd said, don't constantly record. Experience this and you'll have it in your head forever. Ben already had the place in his head. He probably had hundreds of prints from his first year, while she had hastily shot a couple rolls of film, practically nothing.

He'd lied to her. Omitted the truth. Taking photos for fake passports, ID badges, God knows what else. This wasn't altruism—he'd been paid.

And he was wrong about memory, Carey thought. A photo could offer proof, but a memory changed at will. You could turn a thought in your head into anything you wanted.

CHAPTER 13

THE NEWSPAPER CREATED A special graphic for the coverage of Ben's passport resurfacing: an airplane circling the globe, with the bolded words, TROUBLE ABROAD. Ben was now a logo, a headline: Murdered Local Man's Passport Found.

Her parents had taken note of Ben's reappearance in the news in a way that showed how gravely they failed to understand, then and now, what Ben meant to her. They had seen her come home from Mexico with stinking, unwashed hair, with a blank expression, with fits of sobbing that sounded like choking and elicited a frantic knocking at her bedroom door. Her father handled this by asking if she wanted to go out for pizza. Her mother's tactic: disparaging Ben, as if she could minimize the loss by minimizing him. She did it again now.

"That boy from your program had to have been mixed up in something awful," her mother said. "He kind of looked like a deadbeat, sorry to say. That hair." Carey wanted to defend him. Didn't. Couldn't.

The latest news coverage bordered on the obsessive, and the paper's website linked to past stories about the Williamson case. Given the story's renewed interest, they'd dredged up everything, even the obituary. Carey searched and clicked. She had still been in Mexico when the first articles ran. She hadn't had the stomach to seek them out.

Now she couldn't stop reading.

BENJAMIN C. WILLIAMSON

Benjamin Curtis Williamson, Indianapolis, died February 25 in Guanajuato, Mexico, where he was a student in the Futuro Real exchange program. Survivors: mother Lida and father Andrew, sister Molly, and a paternal grandmother.

Williamson was a senior at University of Wisconsin and a graduate of Trinity Catholic Academy. Funeral mass, 3 p.m. March 4, Trinity Catholic Church, 5459 E. 87th St., Indianapolis. Private burial in family plot, Fortville.

Accompanying articles shouted headlines and speculation. "ARE AMERICANS SAFE ABROAD?" The *Star* sent a reporter to Mexico for the memorial service. The one she had not attended, when she'd stayed in her room at the Alarcón's, balled up on the bed like a fist.

She'd had no contact with the Alarcóns since returning to the States. First she was miffed that they did not care enough to reach her. Then she was ashamed that she had not offered an apology for consorting solely with Americans and ignoring her new family. In addition to the letter of apology she owed a thank-you note, for the care they'd shown her when she was incapacitated. And an additional, regular thank-you note with a gift, for feeding and housing her. And an explanation why she'd waited to contact them. The list of owed correspondence grew. She did nothing.

Was it active or passive, reading words on a screen, traveling backwards? She clicked the mouse twice, three times, waiting for the opening.

LEARNING TRIP TURNS DEADLY
By Patrick Thomas
March 5, 1996

GUANAJUATO, MEXICO—In an ornate, 16th century basilica, some 200 students, teachers and community members gathered to mourn the loss of an Indianapolis man killed in this peaceful capital city.

Benjamin C. Williamson, 23, was shot in the early morning hours of February 25. Mexican police have no suspects. The shooting, Guanajuato's first murder in 10 months and the first in the history of the Futuro Real exchange program, has raised questions among U.S. universities about the safety of study-abroad programs.

"We will continue to investigate," Guanajuato Police Captain Eduardo Saiz said through a translator. "There is very little trouble here but perhaps this young man stumbled through it."

Williamson was a University of Wisconsin senior and Spanish major. He minored in business. The Trinity Catholic Academy graduate led his high school soccer team to a sectional victory in 1992. Williamson was buried last week after a funeral mass in Indianapolis.

During the Mexico service, many of the shocked students studying at Guanajuato's Universidad Intercambio wept openly.

Williamson's only sibling, Molly, an 18-year-old Trinity Academy senior, accompanied her parents, Lida and Andrew, to the service in Mexico.

"It's important to us, to be where he was," she said.

Lida Williamson, a social worker who counsels new immigrants in Indianapolis, and Andrew Williamson, head of Trinity's buildings and grounds crew, declined to be interviewed.

"There are no easy explanations," said Don Francisco Hernando, the exchange program's director, in his eulogy. "We have to support and comfort each other. We have to honor Ben by living."

Andrea Cunningham, Intercambio's American student coordinator, knew Williamson for several years. He had previously traveled to Mexico with Intercambio's summer program.

"He always tested the limits," she told the mourners. "He pushed himself. On a trip to Dolores Hidalgo, while the rest of us spent the day shopping, he snuck off to hike in the hills."

She pointed to the collage. "That's Ben," she said, her voice cracking. "That's how I want to remember Ben."

As the service drew to a close, Michael Gibley, also a Wisconsin exchange student and Williamson's best friend, presented a picture collage to the family. The collage included a picture of Williamson, Gibley, and a few other students crowded around a nightclub table, celebrating student Jennifer Trinder's birthday. All grinned for the picture.

"Ben and Mike were like brothers," Trinder said. "Best friends. We all loved Ben."

Mike and Jennifer had been there. Perhaps Mike had told the Williamsons what happened the night their son died. That Carey and Mike had been drunk. That they'd done things they couldn't take back. Even after the police found Ben's body, after Carey trashed Mike's dorm room and threw his laptop out the window, after Mike tried to soothe her.

She would never forget the article's description of the service she should have attended, the grieving she now understood she should have performed. The way Mike and Jennifer had performed, and Andrea Cunningham and Don Hernando and the Williamsons, even stoic Molly, the family ambassador. They played their roles.

Curled up on that twin bed in her host sister's room, so had she.

Carey balanced a large, round tray of steaming plates on her shoulder and crossed the restaurant floor. Elena watched her move about the restaurant, and Carey surreptitiously checked her shirt to confirm its cleanliness. After Carey confided in her, Elena shared secrets of her own: Roberto was one of the few men at the restaurant with a false passport; the rest had no identification at all. "Too expensive," she'd said. "Maybe later, we get the real ones."

"What if you get caught?" Carey asked.

Elena had smiled. "Like my brother says, no problem. Free trip home."

When Carey passed close to the hostess station, Elena pulled her aside.

"What are you doing tonight?" she asked in Spanish.

Friday. Carey had been thinking about the Williamsons all day. Mike had left two messages this week; she did not return them.

"Nada," Carey said.

Elena smiled. "Good. You're coming with us to the dance."

"Like a high school dance."

"No. A Mexican dance."

Carey was flattered. "I'll think about it."

"But we want you to go," Elena pouted. "We need you to go."

It turned out they needed her car. The transmission on Roberto's old Dart was shot. When the last customer left just before ten, Elena locked the door. She actually giggled as she applied thick eyeliner to Carey's eyes in the bathroom, slicked back Carey's ponytail more tightly. She loaned a blue rayon scoop-neck top that showed off Carey's delicate collarbone. Above the toilet was the same picture she'd seen the first day at the restaurant: the Sleeping Woman, a mountain relief awash in bright sunshine. Like another life.

Carey followed Elena's directions and drove them to the dance. The scent of cologne filled the car. In the backseat, Juan, Pedro, and Roberto passed a flask. The men sipped casually and talked about a girl who might show up. She came last time, Roberto said, slapping his heart with a wide hand. She said she'd be back. Ay. Face of an angel, body of a devil. His curly hair looped over his dark eyes. Carey could see how a girl would come back for Roberto.

"Nos entendemos, Kah-ree?" Roberto asked. Do you understand us?

"Claro," she said, and the men burst out laughing.

The dance was in a warehouse on Michigan Road. The large parking lot already formed a sea of cars. Loud salsa music poured out the door. The bouncer patted them down for weapons.

Carey paid the five dollar cover charge and walked in. Juan caught up with her and stuffed a bill into her hand. "Thank you for driving," he said. She protested, but he wouldn't take back the crumpled ten dollar bill.

Inside, the conversations of a few hundred people competed with the music. Couples danced salsa and meringue across the warehouse's cement floor, boots and heels clacking. A disc jockey in baggy jeans stood on a platform, holding headphones to one ear as he danced. At the makeshift bar, customers lined up ten deep.

Roberto passed her the silver flask. The music was too loud, so she raised her eyebrows. He mouthed, Tequila. She took a gulp and handed the flask to Elena, who swigged even longer. The fiery liquid had to burn going down, but Elena didn't flinch. She smiled. Flipped her loose hair over one shoulder, looking around.

Dancers spun by to the pumping music. Carey's shoulders loosened and fell, her body warm and liquid. The warehouse sat squarely on an open field on the Westside of Indianapolis, but it could have been Mexico. Even bigger than Pastel. A giant plastic curtain separated the dance floor from gleaming rows of green and yellow tractors, intermittently lit up by the strobe lights. She grabbed the flask from Roberto's hand and took another swig. He egged her on.

"Chupale," he said. Suck it. Something ordinarily said among men, drinking.

Men in hats, men without hats, men with thickly waxed mustaches, men who were clean shaven. A warehouse full of Mexicans, except for her. There were women, Mexican women, but Carey only paid attention to the men, letting herself be passed from dance partner to dance partner. She'd let a man buy her a drink and then accept the next offer. If her drink was unfinished, she'd suck it down. Chupale, Roberto had said. Plenty of time to sober up and drive home.

She turned down no one. Once she passed by Elena, who twirled out from the long arm of a tall, thin man. She shouted to Elena the first word that came to mind: "Amiga!" Elena laughed, returning to her dance partner. Seamless, quick moves like a zipper.

The men became a blur, a composite. Carey wasn't sure who she was dancing with, until it was Roberto who held her, held her up, who had cut in on her last partner, an electrician from Juárez. Roberto's hair kept falling in his eyes. He looked confident and unconcerned, his white shirt crisp and fresh, the top three buttons undone, his chest smooth and hairless.

"Where's your devil?" she asked in Spanish.

"Dancing with someone else," he said. "She'll be back."

"I'll bet." The music was just as loud for slower numbers, sung by emotional women with astounding vocal range. The word "amor" repeated like a skipped disc. His hand crept down her back, spider-like, not quite landing in an inappropriate position. Roberto maintained a poker face. On her way to the bathroom earlier, she'd seen couples moving through the fringe of plastic curtain, lost in the dark. Roberto increased the pressure as he turned her. She reached back and grabbed his hand, moving it lower. That palm, the one Roberto had thumped against his chest in the car while describing another girl, stayed where she'd put it. His eyes focused over Carey's head.

The silver flask in his shirt pocket bumped against her breast. Chupale, he'd said. All she needed was another sign, and she'd invite him on a walk. To the dark side of the warehouse, or out to the car. There were hours before she had to drive. But when the song ended he removed his hand and led her back to the fringe. He deposited her with Elena and disappeared.

She and Elena leaned against the cool, stubbly cement wall. Carey asked Juan for a drink, and he returned with water. He handed them each cigarettes and lit them. The flashing colored lights bounced dully against the plastic curtain across the room. Juan moved back across the floor, to a pack of men she didn't know. He'd only sipped from Roberto's flask once or twice.

"Listen," Carey whispered to Elena.

Elena watched the dancers. "Mmm."

Carey followed her gaze and located the man Elena had danced with, the tall thin one who'd spun Elena out and reeled her back in. He danced now with a much shorter woman.

"I found some articles online," Carey said. "About Ben. Mi novio."

Now she had Elena's attention. "What did they say? Did you learn what happened?"

"Not exactly."

Elena shrugged, and Carey sulked. Her dry mouth wanted the water, which hit her stomach like a heavy stone. She closed her eyes briefly, and saw Lida and Andrew and Molly Williamson, a trio walking down the aisle of the Basilica. No. She imagined Ben instead. She'd seen that hiking picture of him in the khaki shorts with all the pockets, his T-shirt hanging from the waistband, his bare chest vulnerable-looking with its small, hard muscles. She knew that look on his face, even if he wasn't standing on a hill. She smiled to herself, almost forgetting the couples on the other side of the curtain, a place where pairs were admitted secretly.

The music still pulsed. Below the beat, she heard rustling, flapping, like a flock of birds taking off. Elena jostled Carey, who opened her eyes. Someone screamed.

The first thing she saw was people running, the movement of the crowd. A small circle had formed near the dance floor, like a setup, a television dance-off: two rivals surrounded by cheering fans. So absurd she almost laughed. Then an object flew into the air, glinting: the jagged end of a broken liquor bottle.

Carey couldn't see the circle anymore; the crowd pushed to fill in. Elena didn't yell or scream. What came out of her mouth was more like a growl. She began running towards the floor, Carey still holding up the wall.

Later, Carey would wonder how Elena had recognized her brother Juan, whose entire face was swollen and cut, his hair clumpy and matted with blood. Roberto pulled Juan up by the armpits and dragged him across the floor. Juan didn't move. His head lolled at an odd angle. Carey ran to them.

"Oh my God, oh my God," Carey repeated, a mantra.

Elena, shaking, still spoke with a businesslike voice. "Get the car."

Carey was transfixed by Juan's black-and-blue face. "He needs an ambulance," she said. She'd been drinking all night.

Elena pushed Carey's shoulder, hard.

"Ahorita! Rápido!"

Carey ran.

She shouldn't have been driving. Elena and Roberto sat in back with Juan, who moaned.

"Que pasó?" Pedro asked over and over, swiveling in the passenger seat.

Roberto's white shirt was soaked in Juan's blood. His face formed a stony profile in the rearview mirror. Juan breathed in shallow fits and gasps.

Carey peeled out of the parking lot and headed north on Michigan Road. The nearest hospital was St. Vincent's. Heading in the other direction were three police cruisers, sirens blaring and lights flashing. None of the cars turned to follow them.

CHAPTER 14

THE FLAT ROOFTOP IN daylight: whitewashed stone, a waist-high cement wall, the same straw broom propped in the same corner, the surface covered in city grit. Specks of gray chimney ash danced in a gentle breeze; the larger pieces fell apart when touched. In the dark, it would've been difficult to see the two lovers lying together on the hard stone, their bodies pressed together, faces inches apart, whispering to each other. Or quiet, locked in a staring contest. A view available only to the sky: the boy and girl half-dressed, soaking up moonlight.

But now the sun beat down, and the other boxy stone houses seemed closer, the roof lower, the retaining wall shorter. Anyone with a good pair of binoculars could make out the intertwined legs, the brown hairs on Ben's calves, Carey's unpainted, cracked toenails. She squinted up at Ben, exposed. It was Friday afternoon, sunny. The feeling of weightlessness and flight. The school play, the one she'd lied to Lupe about, was in progress. They lay on white towels he had filched from the dorm laundry service.

He moved so his shadow covered her face. "Better?"

She smiled. He somehow felt light on top of her. Propped up on his elbows. He balanced on one arm and reached down to unzip his pants. His fumbling knuckles grazed her pelvic bone. The feeling was neither painful nor pleasant. She always sucked in her breath when he first pushed inside her. And then: pleasurable. Carey still wore her white V-neck, her denim skirt bunched around her waist. Shirtless, Ben moved on top of her, his green fatigue shorts unbuttoned and unzipped but still hanging on his hips, covering him.

He was sweating now, small drops falling on her shirt, and his arm muscles tensed as he lowered himself and moved one hand to cup Carey's head. His fingers pulled through her hair at the base of her skull, her body a pincushion, tingling to her own fingertips. They tried to keep quiet, but the breathing was hard to control.

Right before he came, he pressed his lips to her ear.

"God, I love—" He caught himself. "This."

They rolled onto their sides, laughing, both surprised by what he almost said.

Her cheeks ached from smiling. "I love this, too," she said. The things you said without saying them.

Ben fastened his shorts. Carey fanned the skirt from its accordion folds. The sun still bearing down, a witness. Ben sat up, but she remained stretched out on the stone. His backpack sat against the wall a few feet away. His arm like a crane, reaching and retrieving. He pulled out a pack of gum and handed her a piece. Spearmint Chiclets, the kind the shaggy-haired Indian children sold for a few cents in the park. Where were their parents? Carey always wondered. She'd never bought their gum. Next time, she would buy an entire box.

Since Alejandro's, they'd talked little about what had happened, how she'd glanced through the open bedroom door and seen the stacks of American passports and laminated ID badges. Mike with his laptop, designing a bill. Ben told her, Look, don't sweat it. Mike's got a side gig. He never tells me anything. Ben had glanced away, and Carey knew he was lying.

A bedroom door accidentally left open, and she'd peered inside. Later she would come to realize that Ben was just like Alejandro's apartment: some doors were open, others closed. But she did not press the issue, either. She could've placed her palm flat against any door she chose and pushed. She didn't.

"Ben?"

"Carey?"

She loved the way he said her name. Slowly, as if he enjoyed lingering over the first syllable. Cautiously, as if her name were breakable.

"It's nice to be alone for a change," she said.

He smiled, both dimples carving his cheeks, and held up his hand to shield his eyes. His expression difficult to discern in the near-white sunlight. He whistled the bars of a tune she didn't recognize, and she asked what it was.

"When we get back home," he said, "I'm going to make you a mix."

This was the first time he'd acknowledged the two of them together in Indianapolis. Her heart bungee-jumped off the roof and sprung back up again.

"Really," she said. He wasn't particularly good at follow-through. He hadn't even told her the name of the song, and wouldn't.

"Two, three mix tapes at least," he said. "Mexican pop, blues, the Doors, the Stones, '80s. Pearl Jam. How about Nirvana?"

"Definitely," she said, far more enthusiastic than she really felt, wanting to be someone he'd want.

He reached in the bag for his journal. "I'm going to make a list of songs," he said. He began writing, though he wouldn't let her see. "Any particular thoughts on Chicago?"

Now she sat up and ran a hand through her mussed hair. "Nicole and I are moving there after graduation. We haven't ruled out summer."

"I meant the band," he laughed. "But it's a hardworking city, Chicago. Lots of Mexicans."

His approval buoyed her. She was trying out versions of a personality, like clothes she could model. Watching him for a reaction. Her hopes for Ben, inextricably tied to who she hoped to be. He was her audience, even in absentia.

"I might end up on one of the coasts," she added. "Anywhere but Indiana. There's no culture, not like here."

"Estás loca," he said, not meanly. "Every place has culture."

"Culture of hicks," she said. "Culture of corn."

"Careful. This is one of my soapbox topics: Indiana ingrates.

What about the whole month of May, before the race? It's bacchanalia. Drunken, pagan good times. Or the underground music scene. The Art Museum. Great hiking in Bloomington, and—"

"Culture of malls," Carey interjected.

He'd already thought about this. "Indy's spread out. Malls—bullshit commerce aside—are just community centers. How many times have you run into people you know at the mall?" She glanced away at his challenge, wondering what he knew.

"You can't see culture when you're part of it," he said. He wrote something else in his journal. "New York and L.A. think they're the cultural bookends of a nation. Want to know my theory? The Midwest is pushing them out to sea."

She laughed. "All right."

"Chicago's not too far from home," he said, absorbed again in his writing.

"How will you get me this supposed mix?" she fished. "You're from the Northside, and I'm a Westsider." She arranged her fingers in an arthritic "W" like the gang wannabes in school. "Different zip codes. Practically different cities."

He glanced up from the journal and held her eyes. Reassuring, yet so intense that she wanted to look away and couldn't. This was real. She had not imagined it or misremembered.

"I'll find you," he said. His expression softened. He smoothed a strand of hair from her face. "Don't you know that yet, Carey?"

Later they walked the streets. Ben's body outlined against the sun, his height reflected in the surprise of much-shorter Mexicans who stared at him wherever he went. Carey and Ben were relaxed, arms around one another's waists. No. They wouldn't have had room to walk arm in arm. The sidewalks were too narrow. Perhaps they had held hands, moving aside to make room for other people.

Or had she imagined they'd been touching? Maybe they walked single file like ducklings, and she ran to catch up to Ben's longer strides. As for the sun, she could not say if a cloud formation passed through the mountains that day, and Ben hadn't been outlined at all—they could've walked under an overcast sky.

Maybe.

She was forgetting.

But what was clear in her memory: they'd descended the roof staircase and walked aimlessly. Friday rambling, when the whole city seemed to stroll with the life of a thousand Mexican tourists, like extras in a movie who'd just arrived on set. Ice cream cones in hand, family arguments in progress—where to eat dinner, whether to walk the steps to El Pípila or take a taxi. When night fell, the youthful callejoneadas in their black and purple robes would be singing, playing tambourines and guitars, leading packs of travelers from San Luis Potosí and Michoacán and Guadalajara into the alleyways on guided tours.

A few of Bartolo's friends were callejoneadas. She once asked him why he didn't participate, and he gave her a look. The singers were his age, some still students, and they sang and danced and flirted with women who sat on the stone church steps during performances. Those were things he didn't do.

It was not yet night. The callejoneadas had not yet come out to sing. Carey and Ben were across the street from Bartolo's jewelry shop on Calle Positos. "I want to show you something," Ben said, pushing her towards the shop.

And the thought popped into her head, accompanied by a ferocious nausea: It's an engagement ring.

Her eyes darted around the street as if looking for an escape. Surprised by her own sudden panic, emotions like muddy water she tried and failed to sift through.

A proposal was for later. She was twenty-one, her hands light as birds. She wasn't ready. Maybe she was having a premonition. In a matter of weeks he'd be dead. She needn't have worried about the ring, though those thirty seconds of distress would eat at her for months, years.

Inside, Bartolo greeted them. Perhaps he'd seen them coming from the L-shaped glass counter, filled with silver and gold necklaces, watches, and rings. A few small mirrors hung from the wall for customers to admire themselves. Behind the counter, Bartolo's tiny jewelry tools and large gem polisher rested on a workbench. On the wall behind the cash register hung a framed photo of Bartolo's late father, Juan, from whom Bartolo had inherited the shop. An uncle ran the business until Bartolo was old enough to take over. Juan's portrait showed him a few years younger than Bartolo was now. Hair slicked back, eyes dark as his son's. Peeking through the serious expression: mirth. Carey had never seen Bartolo resemble his father in that way.

Bartolo pulled a small square box from the locked compartment under the scratched glass counter and handed it to Ben. Clearly not a ring box. Carey relaxed, disconcerted by the largeness of her relief.

Ben's parcel held a Swiss army knife. It was red, like every other Swiss army knife she'd seen. Ben flipped the knife over and ran his thumb over the inscription: BWC. It reminded Carey of the codename she and Nicole concocted for Ben before they knew his name. HPC. Hot Preppy Catholic. Naming him gave her some power, control, where otherwise she had none.

"Wait," Ben said in perfectly accented Spanish, though Bartolo already waited patiently. "You messed up. My last name starts with 'W.'"

Bartolo explained that was how monograms worked. The last name initial went in the center. Ben's face colored; the relaxed mood he and Carey had shared on the roof and in the street vaporized inside Bartolo's small shop. After Ben feigned a yawn, Carey knew he was embarrassed to be corrected by Bartolo.

"I know it makes no sense, but that's actually right," Carey said quickly. She didn't tell him about her designer monogrammed purse, the one sitting in her closet back home. Her mother probably paid two hundred dollars for the bag, even though Carey disliked carrying purses. Her own monogram, CHB, announcing Carey Beth Halpern had entered the room. Ben would have been outraged. That she owned such an expensive item, first of all. But also that she didn't use it.

Bartolo demonstrated the knife's various tools, unfolding and folding the blade, the tiny fork, the nail file. She wondered, why now, why a knife? Ben didn't even buy the newspaper. He'd borrow Mike's or browse at the newsstand. Her first thought was that he needed protection. Then she blanketed that instinct and admired the knife's utility, its tiny practical features. "Very nice," she said. "It's your color." And both men smiled, Ben at his new toy, Bartolo at Carey.

Ben asked her to look around and pick out something for herself. Instinctively she reached to touch the St. Christopher medallion she'd worn since Bartolo gave her the gift that first night in Guanajuato. The necklace was gone.

"Oh, no," she said. Probably it was on the roof. Probably it was under Ben's pillow. She couldn't remember the last time she'd noticed the silver dime-sized disc resting at her collarbone.

"Que pasó?" Bartolo asked.

Sometimes the first thing to pop into your head is a lie. And sometimes it comes out of your mouth.

"The necklace you gave me? It broke."

Bartolo clicked his tongue. "No me digas," he said. You don't say. Andrea's all-purpose expression, the one Mike imitated in a high falsetto to amuse Carey. Bartolo's inflection made it mean something else: Don't tell me that.

"Let me fix it," Bartolo offered, holding out his hand.

"The thing is," Carey prattled, "I'm not sure where it broke. It might be at home. So I have to look. But definitely, if you can fix it, that would be good."

Ben rubbed the back of Carey's neck, where the silver chain usually lay. For once she did not want his touch. She had no idea where the medallion might be.

"You'll never find it," Ben said. "I'll buy you another one." He leaned over the counters, scouring the silver. "There," he pointed inside the case at an unadorned thick disc on a chain with heavy links. Bartolo frowned.

"It's a little big," Carey said.

Bartolo walked down the counter and searched through the glass briefly. In a second he plucked out a necklace similar to the one he'd first given her. A delicate chain, a tiny saint embossed on a tiny medallion. For luck, Bartolo had said back in August; St. Christopher watched over travelers. Who was the patron saint of lost causes? That was who she needed around her neck.

"Like this?" Bartolo laid the necklace on the counter; he didn't consult Ben. Bartolo picked his cuticles and wouldn't look up. Her lie had been unconvincing. Ben stared out the plate-glass window into the street. He'd made his offer: a thick necklace she'd never wear.

"Take it, free of charge," Bartolo told nobody in particular. Gratis. It could still be a gift from Ben to Carey. Bartolo's acne-scarred skin flushed. Perhaps he was considering the kiss, so many weeks ago, with his own idea of how Carey's lips felt. What it was like to have a drunk woman climb through his bedroom window.

She knew enough to decline the offer. For Bartolo's sake, and Ben's. She knew nobody would be pleased with her decision, the only thing she could think of doing.

"Let me look for my old necklace first," she said. "I bet it's at home."

It wasn't. Carey spent hours searching. She went back to the roof, which had been newly swept. If she'd lost the chain there, someone else had claimed it. She combed Ben's dorm room, even lifting the mattress. At the house, Alicia helped Carey search their shared bedroom. Nada.

A few days later, Hector was in his study with Bartolo, going over jewelry shop receipts. Hector bragged that he could add figures faster than anyone at the bank. Bartolo and Hector grouped register tape in small piles and secured rubber bands around sheaves of bank statements. Carey stood in the doorway and cleared her throat. Hector continued penciling marks in a ledger.

"Bartolo, I've searched everywhere, and I can't find my St. Christopher," she said. "I'm so sorry I lost it. I feel terrible."

"It is no problem," he told her, and returned to the papers. When she didn't walk away, he slowly raised his head. Irritation creased his forehead.

"I was just hoping," she stammered. "The replacement? That you showed me in the shop? I'd still like to have it."

Bartolo shot a quick glance at Hector and back to Carey. Hector continued to frown at the papers. Like a schoolboy, his tongue stuck out as he worked.

"Of course," Bartolo said. He smiled slowly, so easy to win over that guilt stabbed Carey in the stomach.

"I'll pay for it," she offered.

Bartolo waved his hand dismissively as if erasing a chalkboard. But the movement was quick, intentionally easy to miss.

Perhaps it was the motion that drew Hector's attention. Or he'd been listening all along, waiting for an opening. He shook his head, the close-cropped black hairs perfectly in place.

"She'll pay for the necklace," Hector said. He motioned to the papers in front of him. "Do you know you're running a business?"

An awkward silence followed. Down the hall, the noises of Lupe turning the page of a novel, setting her coffee cup on the table. All Carey could think to say was, "Oh."

Bartolo's face flushed as it had in the jewelry store a few days earlier. His neck a canvas of red splotches. "I offered to replace the necklace, Hector," he said. "And I will."

Hector marked the ledger with his pencil, the sharp rasps filling the quiet room. Then he slammed the pencil down on the desk. Carey jumped. Lupe grew still in the other room.

"Then you are a fool," Hector said, belying his angry gesture with a slow, quiet voice. He gazed wearily at his stepson. "Do you think she cannot afford your cheap jewelry? Of course she can. Or her American boyfriend can. Don't you see? We're a bunch of lazy Mexicans, giving our lives away for free. This is business, Bartolo. Your father's business. It's a wonder you haven't run it into the ground. Lord knows Juan nearly did."

Bartolo stood and towered above Hector. Tears sprung to his eyes. "You did not know my father," he cried. *Mi papa.*

Lupe stood at the open door and pushed Carey aside. "Stop it, both of you," Lupe said, wedging herself between her son and her husband.

Hector reached around Lupe and cuffed Bartolo's ear. "Your son does not like to hear the truth."

"Insulting my father is not the truth," Bartolo said. He swiveled out of his mother's grasp and to the door, swiping at the neat stacks of receipts. The papers dropped to the floor, graceless as a shot bird.

Lupe questioned Hector: what had he said about Juan? Didn't he know Juan was her first love? Didn't Hector know whose house this was? You do not disrespect a man in his own home. Even—especially—if he is dead.

Carey tried to lay a hand on Bartolo's arm, but he walked a wide circle around her and out the door.

Lupe and Hector engaged in a heated argument. Hector pleaded in a pained voice, Mi Lupita, por favor. Lupe shouted that she was tired of listening. Carey imagined explaining that she wanted nothing for free. She knew they were hard workers. Her first night in Mexico rang her head, when Hector asked what Americans thought of Mexicans. She'd said "lazy" when she meant to say "laid back." Trying to explain her mistake later had gotten her nowhere.

Bartolo. That was who she needed to find. She caught up and led him to El Centro. They drank beers in a café that still wore its Christmas decorations, and talked until he calmed down. Bartolo knew Carey didn't fit Hector's description, which mattered more than she expected.

This is what a sister does, she thought, hearing about Bartolo's father, who smoked incessantly and died of lung cancer when Bartolo was six. She didn't have a grief remotely comparable to his, not yet. But she listened. And she knew, at least that one time when she decided to go after her sort-of brother, that she'd made the right choice. Finally. Like most things, it seemed obvious in retrospect. But she was grateful to have known in the moment.

CHAPTER 15

THE HOSPITAL SMELLED LIKE old flowers and industrial-grade floor cleaner. Overhead a television played a twenty-four hour news program, and they sat below in metal-framed chairs upholstered in orange wool. Construction paper Easter eggs were taped to the wall. Roberto slept. Elena's immobile face was trained on the television. Occasionally she moved her lips in prayer. Across from them, Pedro read the newspaper. He spoke little English but wanted to learn. Pedro was not family. Since he stayed in the waiting room, Carey stayed.

Juan had been stabbed in the stomach with the broken edge of a liquor bottle. A piece of glass was lodged in the muscle of his intestinal wall. The doctor, now operating, had explained about anesthesia. None of them mentioned to the doctor that Juan had slipped in and out of consciousness in the car on the drive to St. Vincent's. Nobody had asked. There had not been time. They rushed him to the emergency room and he'd been whisked away, his slender body prone on a stretcher, large feet in polished black Oxfords splayed in a vee. The nurses and doctors moved methodically, ignoring everyone but Juan.

"How will you pay?" Roberto asked Elena quietly.

"Stop asking questions," Elena replied, though he had only asked one.

The earlier hours filled Carey's head like a weird dream. Swigging tequila and holding up a wall and dancing with the world. With Roberto, moving his hand on her back. Lower. Driving to the hospital was a blur, either from alcohol or adrenaline. She'd sobered considerably. Next to her, Roberto breathed heavily, still in the once-white, once-crisp shirt, now caked with the rusty amoeba pattern of Juan's dried blood.

A police officer had briefly interviewed Roberto and Pedro in the waiting room, and took down their names and phone numbers. The men glanced at each other before speaking. She had thought Roberto's last name was Gutierrez—she'd seen it handwritten on the tissue-thin airmail envelopes that arrived at the restaurant—but he told the cop it was Perez. Roberto and Pedro said Juan got in the way of a fight. He didn't have grudges or enemies, he wasn't in a gang, he barely knew anybody here besides his family. The cop, a young man built like a linebacker, asked, "You sure about gangs, then? Because ordinarily you all stick together. Where do you people come from?" Pedro told him Texas. He pronounced it *Tay*-hass. The cop raised his eyebrows. He closed his small black notebook, glanced at Carey, and asked if she was OK. She nodded, a slight lift of the chin. The way the restaurant cooks and waiters greeted one another. "You sure?" His gaze lingered uncomfortably, until finally he tucked the notebook in his belt holster and left.

They weren't talking about the fight. The men shrugged and held up their hands. She suspected they knew more than they told the cop, more than they would tell Carey and Elena.

Carey offered her car keys, but Elena shook her head. Her long, dark hair looked dull and dirty under the fluorescent light. Her black eye makeup had settled in small half-moons beneath her eyes.

"I will not leave my brother," she said.

Carey didn't want to leave, either. It seemed important that she stay, even to remain in the waiting room, ineffectual and hung over, still in her black pants and Elena's blue shirt.

"Can Pedro take your car?" Elena asked. "He can call our parents from the restaurant."

Relief flooded Carey's body. Of course, she said, handing Pedro the keys.

Carey's parents probably wondered where she was. Her mother

might not have come home last night, either. Juan should've been on her mind. Thin, boyish Juan, with the butterfly-wing ears and jutting nose.

If Juan died, would they bury him in Indianapolis or Dolores Hidalgo? Ben had been buried in a family plot. That's what the newspaper obituary said. In Fortville. Home of the martini-swilling pink elephant. Carey once had taken its picture. She hadn't been back.

"Where's the doctor?" Elena asked. "It's been too long."

Eventually Carey drifted into an uncomfortable sleep in the metal chair. She woke to Elena's elbow nudging her arm, a smeary face inches from her own. Roberto now wore a bright blue Indianapolis Colts t-shirt someone must've given him.

"The doctor says we can see him," Elena said. Relief rose from her shoulders, the muscles unbunching like flower petals in bloom. Carey blinked and jumped up.

"It is just family," Elena said. Matter-of-fact, unapologetic, eager to be with Juan.

Roberto briefly touched her shoulder before following Elena down the hall.

"Gracias, querida Kah-ree." Thank you, dear Carey.

"De nada," she said, blinded by sudden tears.

Alone, she wandered the building. The hospital walls pulsed with urgent energy that had nothing to do with her. The cafeteria glowed by the light of the vending machines: coffee, snacks, soda. Hidden in a small vestibule as if ashamed, a cigarette machine. She fed the five-dollar bill from her pocket into the slot, receiving a small green and white package in return. Outside, around the building's edge, the floodlights were less harsh. The unusually warm pre-dawn air reminded her of being a kid, waiting for the bus. She'd had the feeling one other time: arriving in Mexico.

Now she perched on the pebbled curb, unwrapping the plastic from the pack. She wanted to be anywhere but the hospital. Home was at least ten miles away. At one point in her life she ran that distance twice over in a week. She could call somebody to pick her up. There was Nicole. There were her parents. The hospital probably fell on the bus route, but Carey had never ridden a city bus. A fact that struck her as odd, sad, considering that she'd navigated places like Mexico and Chicago, each time feeling that she was somewhere important, based on its newness. Indianapolis was so familiar she could no longer see it; familiarity bred contempt. But Indianapolis was not the problem.

Roberto pushed open the glass door. He smiled through a face sagging with exhaustion. "He is asking for his parents. He is speaking. This is good, the doctor says. Come—it is fine now."

Moments before she'd contemplated her escape. Now her relief and guilt were so thick they felt painted on top of her skin, a Halloween mask. She began to cry; her throat tight and raw. Roberto rubbed her back briefly, as if she were a baby. He soothed her with a small Spanish *chuh*. It will be fine, he said quietly. Roberto pressed his white handkerchief into her hand. After everything, he still carried a clean handkerchief. He gestured that her makeup had run down her face. She'd noticed Elena's smeared makeup, not considering her own.

"There are others coming," he told her at the door of Juan's room. "A translator, and somebody from the state." El estado, he said.

"I could've been your translator," she said.

Across the room Juan asked for water, and Elena told him to eat the ice chips. Roberto joked about his flask and Elena shut him down.

Juan lifted two fingers in greeting. Elena walked around the bed and hugged Carey. Roberto leaned back in a chair, balancing on two legs.

"Regresó Pedro?" Elena asked, and Carey said no.

"Mis padres…" Juan said hoarsely.

"No te preocupes," Elena said. Don't worry about our parents, she told him. Pedro will call them. Just get some sleep. Juan closed his eyes. Elena would do the worrying for the family. Juan would not die, and their parents would not even see him as he had appeared that night, bloodied and pale and slight on the hospital gurney.

A nurse in pink polka-dot scrubs came in to take vitals; she smiled grimly at all of them, looking Carey up and down as she pumped Juan's blood pressure cuff full of air. Juan winced.

Standing in the doorway holding a cardboard tray of coffees was

Mike Gibley, wearing a red sweatshirt and jeans. The thin skin beneath his eyes bore delicate purple half-moons, marking hours of missed sleep. An apparition, at once startling and comforting.

"Carey?" He straightened.

"You're still here?" Carey asked, as if he were a hologram.

"I'm staying a couple extra days," he said. "Lida's downstairs, registering."

"What?" Carey thought she might need the blood pressure cuff. A shower and change of clothes also wouldn't hurt.

"She's a social worker with the state. Got called in, and I decided to tag along. What are *you* doing here?"

Juan, Elena and Roberto all turned to her. Mike, holding all that coffee. The useful people. The needed people.

Carey moved toward the door, and it was like stepping away from a bonfire in a dewy backyard, and shaking with the sudden chill. Roberto beckoned to Carey. Lida Williamson was downstairs, arriving any moment.

What are *you* doing here? She heard it like an echo, and the only answer was a repeated question.

CHAPTER 16

CÉSAR DIDN'T RECOGNIZE CAREY. He'd driven the exchange students from the Mexico City airport to Guanajuato six months ago, and now he commandeered a local city tour bus to the Mummy Museum on the city's northwest corner. To Carey alone he'd given the view of the volcano Ixtaccihuatl, the Sleeping Woman. Now it was early February, and she smiled secretively when he announced their stop outside the museum with "Ho-kay." Remembering how he'd assured Andrea Cunningham, "Ees OK," when the bus door opened unintentionally, that rare, clear day when he had deliberately driven them in the wrong direction so they could see the volcanoes.

The Mummy Museum stood squat and flat-roofed like a prison. Nearby, children's voices whooped and a soccer ball bounced on pavement. Mike wore dark sunglasses and a beige fisherman's hat he bought at Mercado Hidalgo. Sick of being blond in such a dark-haired country.

"La vida," he sighed. "It is so hard for a gringo."

"Excellent disguise, Mr. Obvious," Ben said.

Mike pretended to listen to an imaginary earpiece, like a Secret Service agent or bodyguard. "Shh," he said.

Ben knocked Mike's hat off with the flat of his palm, then retrieved it from the parking lot blacktop and stuck it on Carey's head. Mike snatched it back, pulling Carey's brown hair. Children at play despite technical adulthood. All three stuck in place, an emotional limbo of looking back and ahead. Also known as the present.

Nearby, a young mother herded three small girls close to her waist. She wore a gray wool poncho over acid-washed jeans, and one child stuck her head under the poncho. The woman could've been trying to keep the children out of the Americans' way. Or keeping them away from the Americans.

Carey gave Mike the finger before remembering the little girls watching.

"Children, behave," Ben said. And they did.

Guanajuato's Museo de las Momias, a collection of preserved corpses in glass display cases, was one of the city's most popular tourist attractions. No archaeological find, these graves were reopened deliberately. Local bodies, regular people whose families couldn't pay the cemetery tax a hundred years ago. Unearthed from their alleged final rest to make room for the newly dead. The mummification had to do with the mineral properties of the area's water. People drank from the Guanajuato water supply for a lifetime, then their dead bodies somehow remained intact underground. No one knew why.

For months Carey had planned to go, but she'd been busy. Weekends spent with Ben and Mike, who'd already seen the mummies. When she suggested it, they'd told her the attraction was nothing special—a bunch of dirt-brown dead bodies lying behind glass. Ben and Mike had already been, numerous times and without her, during other summers.

She needed to get out of the Alarcón house. Tempers had cooled since the fight about the necklace, though Bartolo hadn't given Carey the replacement and she couldn't ask again. On weekends, she created errands. Or she'd walk the city alone for hours at a time. But she didn't want to go to the mummy museum alone.

That day, they paid admission and spun through the metal turnstiles. The dry air stifled their conversation. In some ways the museum seemed as cave-like as the rock and gem gallery Carey had visited. A smooth stone floor, the low ceiling, dark corridors, and displays under glaring fluorescent lights.

They'd barely crossed over the threshold before reaching the first body. Raisin-withered in its glass box, the remains of hair like steel wool perched atop her dark forehead. You could tell it was a she by the pelvis. Butterfly wings pointing at the ceiling. A tattered, manila-colored garment bunched around her neck like a clown collar, the rest of her body unclothed.

"Disgusting," Carey marveled.

"Reminds me of Rachel," Mike said, and Ben smirked.

"Who's Rachel?" Carey asked with as little curiosity as possible.

No one spoke. Finally Mike asked Ben, "She doesn't know about Rachel? Oh." Mike drifted, feigning interest in the rows of corpses he'd visited before.

Ben scratched his temple beneath the bandana. "She's just someone I used to know," he said. "We dated. Mike wasn't a fan."

Carey was silent. In front of her, a tiny baby mummy lay on its back, its mouth open as if poised for a bottle. It was one of the few that bore a sign, and she translated: "The Smallest Mummy in the World." A creature both endearing and repugnant. Carey walked along the cases and examined the other bodies. The display coffins touched end-to-end like train cars. Some were stacked on top of each other. The dead in bunk beds, a gruesome sleepover. Nearby, a Mexican family in matching Cancun vacation t-shirts snapped pictures.

Ben touched Carey lightly at the base of her neck. He knew her well enough by now to know she was upset. She rarely showed anger.

Ben steered her down the hall and whispered in her ear.

"You know Mike's an asshole," he said. "You know that, right? He doesn't know what he's talking about."

Carey hadn't been thinking about Mike. She'd been thinking about Rachel, a person she'd never known, a living, breathing woman, her looks compared to death. And then she thought how easily Ben would betray his friend: *You know Mike's an asshole.*

But in that betrayal, a gift. Un regalo para ti. An open door he ushered her through. Complicity. Information meant only for her. Carey and Ben versus Mike, or versus everyone else.

"I've noticed that," Carey finally said. "Must be why you love him so much."

The peeping, rolled "r" voices of the tourist children bent around the corner. Ben eyed her. The green of his irises glinted, unsure. What had she felt in that moment? Seven years later she could still feel Ben's hand at her nape, but she could not recreate the right mix of emotion. Everything tinged by what came after.

She kissed him there among the corpses, then continued down the long hallway of the dead. Ben followed, for once.

A few yards away, Mike snapped a picture of one of the mummies. "Look," he pointed. "No glare."

The glass case bore a small, half-moon hole through which Mike aimed his lens. The male body wore old fashioned woolen trousers and thick black overshoes. Eye sockets dark and empty.

"You broke the glass?" Carey asked. "Jesus, Mike."

Mike shook his head, shaggy blond hair falling in his eyes. "Do you see broken glass?"

It was true; the brokenness had happened before.

Ben whistled. "I bet you could touch his leg if you reached," he said to Mike. A sinewy ankle like dirty rope exposed itself between the corpse's trouser cuff and shoe. A hundred years earlier, those legs probably had walked the same cobblestone streets as the three of them.

Ben and Mike dared one another. Touch the leg, they taunted. It's just an old man's old leg. The exchange heightened, and she could see the languid, unhurried enjoyment in both their faces. Mike raised an eyebrow, so Ben raised two. Ben scratched his nose, and Mike repeated the gesture. In the absence of glass, we are each other's mirrors.

"He looks like beef jerky," Ben said.

Carey pushed past and stood before the missing piece of glass. "Here," she said, like clearing her throat. She reached through the jagged hole, careful not to scratch her wrist. Taking over a dare no one offered her.

"Holy shit," Mike said.

Her fingers grazed whatever was left of the man's tendon and bone. Not rope or beef jerky or even human flesh. It felt like dirt. Like dust. Something that once carried weight but could float away at any minute.

She pulled her hand back. Ben stared, disbelieving. Mike uttered a string of fucks, showing she'd impressed him.

"Who wants to hold my hand?" she asked sweetly.

They both refused, suddenly squeamish. Insisted she go to the ladies' room and wash vigorously—Use hot water, they'd joked, trying to hide their seriousness. The bathroom, like many of the public facilities she'd encountered in Mexico, had no soap, paper towels, or even toilet paper. The water dribbled from the tap, lukewarm. She rinsed her hands and shook them like a wet dog shakes and smiled at herself in the waxy mirror above the sink, practically laughing out loud at what she'd done. At how they reacted.

They'd all made light of the unnaturally posed corpses, the mummies' clothes and hair. But only she stepped forward to reach through the hole. Brave, bold Ben—that's how she'd seen him for months in Mexico, and for years earlier in Indianapolis. But when her hand maneuvered through the broken glass, Ben's face clouded, unmistakably, with fear. That's what she would think of later: He was capable of fear. Scared of death. It was the first time he'd showed her. She couldn't stop seeing.

They'd blown through the small museum and the tour bus wasn't due for another half-hour. Outside, they sampled tamales from a vendor's cart. Carey paid.

"Gotta make a pit stop," Ben said, his Indianapolis vernacular, disappearing down a stone staircase. She and Mike sat on the edge of the retaining wall, listening to the children playing soccer in the parking lot below. Lines painted on blacktop, bright-yellow goals without nets, rubble underfoot, power lines crisscrossing overhead. Parents and siblings sat on car bumpers, cheering.

They chewed the tamales in silence until Mike pointed to her corn husk. "You're not supposed to eat that part," he said. Always correcting her.

"That's how we do it in Indiana," she lied.

"Really?" He was genuinely curious. He believed her. Whatever she wanted to tell him. Something, anything.

She shook her head and smiled at him then. Softened those brown eyes, a look she'd often given herself in the mirror, as practice. Again she had the sense of watching herself act a role. Disconnecting self from actions.

"I was going to say," he laughed. "Eating that can't be good for you."

Carey wadded up the rest of her tamale in a napkin and tossed it into an overflowing trash can. Mike watched its arc. Had she been sitting with Ben, she would have asked if he wanted to finish it.

"So you dating anyone these days, Gibsy?" Carey asked casually. She knew he wasn't. The last time they'd tried to set him up was months ago. Jennifer had been Carey's suggestion, because Jennifer still asked Ben about Madison and the homework on page fifty-two and what was everybody doing, later? Jennifer conjured a boyfriend back home in Illinois, seemingly at whim. Like when she didn't want to be set up with Mike.

Mike had dated no one in Mexico. Carey wanted to remind him that he was alone. He could needle Carey, and conjure Ben's former loves like ghosts, and attempt to repossess his best friend. But Mike? He was worse off than her. After the murder, she needed this inhospitable comfort, to know she wasn't *that* bad, not as bad as Mike.

Mike stretched his arms overhead. He still wore the fisherman's hat but had removed the sunglasses. "You trying to set me up again?" he said. "I'm keeping my options open."

"My friend Nicole says that's code for 'No prospects.'"

"I'm liking this Nicole more and more." Mike's tone indicated the opposite. He ducked his head, examining his ragged, bitten fingernails. "Sophomore year of college, visiting my mom in Buffalo, she tried to set me up with one of her dental hygienist friends. A double-date with my mom. It was fucked up."

Mike saw her face and backtracked. "I didn't go. My parents got divorced when I was seven, but my dad still would've killed me."

"That was two years ago. You haven't dated anyone since?"

He massaged his own jaw with one hand as if to wipe off his slow grin. "Dating—it sounds so formal," he said. "I'm fond of the cheaper date. So to speak."

"Hooking up in bars," Carey supplied. She'd participated in her share of collegiate rituals: keg parties in dank basements, sloppy kissing on the sidewalk at two a.m. But she'd never gone home with a stranger.

"And of course there's the safest sex of all," he said. "Online."

"You actually meet up with people?" In 1996, the Internet seemed new. Was new.

"I was supposed to once. Didn't go."

"Why not?" She pictured a bespectacled Internet girl stood up by Mike Gibley.

He watched the soccer game below. "Let's say I was less than forthright about myself. She didn't need that disappointment."

"How pathetic," she said, though she was impressed. She didn't know Mike had it in him. Carey waited for another comeback, but none came. Below, the soccer ball thunked off the wall and a girl cried, Give me the ball! *Dame la pelota.*

Carey regretted her words. She and Mike competed for Ben's attention, bickering. But Mike was a friend. For all his faults, she knew he considered her a friend, too.

"I'm only asking because I care," she said, swooping to peer at his face under the hat. His eyes, blank as blue sky. "I need to know who to be jealous of."

His mouth slackened. She hadn't meant for him to take her seriously. But what *were* her intentions, considering the small spark she felt hearing about Mike's sex life? What did she want, considering what came later? The day Ben stood her up and she and Mike spent the night together. Maybe she had wanted Mike to name what bounced between them. She began to have a sense of her own power, the high it gave her. She wouldn't control it. Why should she? Men didn't.

Mike's already ruddy skin deepened in shade. His cheeks and forehead flushed red as agave seeds, eyes shining with an emotion she ignored. Hope.

Ben's holler came from the parking lot below. A distinctive cry that meant excitement or danger or love or hate. Impossible to tell. Carey and Mike swiveled to see. So used to the whoop that it no longer held meaning. Thank God for Ben, saving them from the silences erupting between them.

But Ben hadn't been trying to get their attention. He'd joined the game. This was his battle cry. He ran the length of the blacktop soccer field. Boys and girls no older than ten ducked and wove around the white man who towered several feet above them. Mike told her that Ben had tried out for Wisconsin's varsity soccer team as a freshman and was cut. Besides, Mike said, the captain already wore Ben's jersey number, nineteen. Now Ben played on both teams, neither, or maybe just for himself. He balanced the black-and-white ball on his foot and considered his options.

One of the dark-haired girls waved her arms. She shrieked, "Cristian Castro! Cristian Castro!" The parent spectators laughed at the impossibility of a Mexican pop star descending on their neighborhood soccer park. Ben bore a passing resemblance to clean-cut, light-eyed Cristian, but only at a certain angle. The red bandanna restraining Ben's hair made his green eyes stand out more than normal. His face was tanned almost the same color as Cristian's skin.

"No-oo-ooo," Ben teased. "Sabes los Doors? Los Puertos?" Clearly the girl didn't know The Doors, and she was losing patience. She was the only one wearing shin guards and a jersey: red, white and green stripes. The rest of the kids wore street clothes.

"La pelota!" she hollered. Ben passed her the ball, jogging downfield. Down-parking-lot.

He spun. He alternately bounced the ball off his knee and head. His long, muscled calves grew lines with each step, smoothing out while at rest. When he breathed heavily, hands on his hips, the knobby bones of his shoulders danced. He moved as smoothly as a marionette twirling on strings, utterly coordinated.

Watching him, Carey wished that Ben could see her running, when she felt most like herself and truly lived in her body. When strength radiated from the soles of her feet to her sweaty ponytail. He'd have to see her by accident. She'd never ask anyone to watch her run, though having an audience made her run faster.

Below, Ben had grabbed the ball with two hands and lifted it high. The children jumped in vain to reach the round prize.

Ben didn't give it to the kids, not yet. He kissed the dirty leather like some emotional Maradona, then hurled it to where Carey and Mike sat. A child grabbed at Ben's arm, and the retaining wall was too high, too far away. The soccer ball hit several feet below Carey and Mike, then dribbled back to the parking lot. Ben shrugged his bony shoulders and grinned anyway.

One of the fathers stood, eyeing Ben's slow extrication from the young swarm. The man crossed his arms over his buttoned suit vest. Ben tried to get the game back on track.

"Whose ball?" Ben asked.

Carey and Mike kept their eyes forward and watched Ben play. Now he showed the players how to knock in a header. He adjusted the red bandana. Every once in awhile, he squinted at Carey and Mike, who sat above, silent as mimes.

Carey sighed unconsciously, audibly. Next to her, Mike shifted position, hanging his legs over the wall for a better view of the game. His calves and thighs were thicker, less exercised than Ben's. Muscles gone slack, covered in a layer of beer fat. When he finally spoke, his voice sounded tinny as an old phonograph recording.

"I know who to be jealous of," he said. A mutter, loud enough to be heard. Facing away, the silly fisherman's hat shielding his eyes.

Carey wasn't listening. She continued to imagine the way her own legs flexed when she ran. When Mike's words finally sunk in, too much time had passed for a proper response. She convinced herself he had offered a platonic compliment, an olive branch. Yet once she'd finally heard him, a smile took over her face. She had not been able to look at him. She didn't need to; her gaze focused inward, lingering over the sway she held.

Her memory's tape looped endlessly; time had diluted nothing. Not the withered baby in a glass coffin, its mouth an 'O' of surprise, nor the corpse leg she touched, that few seconds' contact with the inevitable. She rewound and replayed this film, depicting Ben alive among mummies. The ropy clench of his calf muscle as he ran the length of a blacktop soccer game, playing with ten-year-olds who would turn eleven. This one day out of her past foretold her future. She and Mike left behind, alone with the space between them.

CHAPTER 17

CAREY BACKED OUT OF Juan's hospital room with a string of excuses, everyone watching her with knitted eyebrows. She jogged down the sterile corridor, which looked like every other corridor. Only after passing the nurse's station three times did she realize she was running laps, in boots and black pants and Elena's blue shirt. She collapsed into the push-handle of a beige steel door marked EXIT.

Hands on her knees, she tried to catch her breath. Smoking had done her lungs no favors. Mike caught up to her in the stairwell before the heavy door sighed shut.

"Come back," he said. "They're asking about you."

"No," she wheezed. She began descending the stairs, her vision blurry. "I have to get out of here. Can you get me out of here?"

He didn't ask questions. In the car, he spoke only to ask directions to a restaurant where they could get coffee, strong coffee. The spotless gray interior of his black sedan held nothing, not a stray leaf, fast-food wrapper, or hastily-folded map.

They passed the Casa Colmo strip mall, where Carey's red Mazda was parked. Already, cardboard had been taped over the restaurant's front door. Glass glittered along the sidewalk in the early-morning sun, and it would have been pretty as diamonds were it not the remains of something whole. The intricate etching of the Dolores Hidalgo church spires, shattered. She knew it was not accidental. The fight at the dance:

had the door had been smashed as retribution? For what? Juan had been the one hurt, sent to surgery. She turned her head.

Edna's buzzed with the regulars' Saturday morning gossip, bells jingling as customers picked up pink boxes of donuts. Carey and Mike were the only white people in the room. Five Hispanic men in coveralls dug into eggs and sausage; black men in khaki pants and thin pastel sweaters studied blueprints at one table. Couples dotted the other booths. Two small boys and a girl lined up at the counter stools with their harried mother, a twenty-something woman reading the menu, twirling a braid around one finger.

Derek arrived with menus and his signature grin. "Hey, Ms. Carey," he said. "Please tell me you're having the strawberry pancakes today. I beg of you."

He knew her name. Carey couldn't help but smile. "Just coffee," she said. She doused it with cream and sugar. Mike drank his black.

"I'll try those pancakes," Mike offered.

Derek pointed his index finger at Mike, thumb sticking straight up like a gun. "There's the man," he said. "That's what I like to hear."

Behind Mike's back Derek gave Carey two thumbs-up. He assumed they were a couple; he approved. The coffee exacerbated the high-pitched tremble of her body's sleep-deprivation. And Mike's proximity. She'd tried to escape him. She had.

"You want to talk," Carey ventured.

He cocked his head to the left. "If you do. You were upset last week, at the bar."

She shook her head. "I needed to think about things."

He nodded, still waiting. Mike had always been patient, at least with her.

"The men from my restaurant, they seem worried," she said. "Not just about Juan, but before. The day the news ran the photo of the guy who used—his passport."

She couldn't say Ben's name. Not to Mike, who fidgeted with his knife and fork, clinking the utensils against his plate without taking a bite of his food. Derek had shaped the stack of pancakes like giant hearts.

"You didn't recognize him, then," Mike said. "It was Octavio in the picture."

Octavio. The cashier at the cafeteria, so thin he'd appeared skeletal. In the paper, he was fat. He had borrowed Ben's camera, and Ben had taken it back. The night she was serenaded outside the Alarcón's window, Octavio stood behind Ben, strumming a guitar.

Carey stared at Mike's pancakes, suddenly ravenous. Which brain circuit tripped to make her reactions to bad news uniformly inappropriate? She knew enough to look at Mike's face, to ignore the untouched pancakes, dotted with strawberries, hearts cut into halves.

"He killed him," she said.

"They don't know that. Octavio was competitive, but not like that. He didn't even have a gun. Like the police said down in Mexico, maybe Ben interrupted a robbery. Octavio could've been involved. But I don't think he did it."

"Come on. Why else would he have his passport, Mike? It had to be him."

"Maybe," Mike shrugged, drumming his fingers on the table. "Can't say for sure. Somehow he got the passport, and now he's gone. That's all there is."

She watched him. "You know something."

"No. How could I?"

She pictured Roberto in his apron and jeans, pulling the blue booklet from his back pocket. Information she could not hold. Like her overloaded serving tray at the restaurant, glasses so full her only option was to spill.

"One of the cooks has a fake passport," Carey said. "I know Ben took the picture. You were there too, at Alejandro's, with your laptop."

"The one you threw out the window." Mike tried to smile. "Most likely I was playing solitaire."

"You were there, Mike. At Alejandro's. What was your job?"

"Carey," he warned. "Ben kept us out of it. He kept us in the dark."

"No."

"Ben told me nothing," Mike said, his voice cracking, sharp as ice on a thawing lake. "Nothing. Part of his charm, remember? You remember. He kept us out of it."

They were sitting in silence when Derek brought coffee refills.

"Something wrong with the food?" he asked, worry lines denting his forehead.

Mike glanced at the heart-shaped pancakes before him, the fork and knife beside the plate. Carey reached across the table. She dug into the pancakes, her fingers sinking up to the knuckles. Grainy dough lodged beneath her fingernails as she grabbed a clump from the stack. She brought the sloppy mess to her mouth, widening her jaw until it clicked, her hand sticky and red with strawberry juice.

"Delicious," she said around the wad of food, chewing hugely.

Derek laughed. "Man, your girl can eat. You're lucky, having a girl who appreciates the finer things."

Nobody corrected him.

Mike made arrangements with Lida on his cell phone; her husband would pick her up. Carey had not called to check on Juan, or Elena. She could've borrowed Mike's phone and called the hospital, but she didn't know if, like the cooks, Juan had given a false name.

When Mike clicked his phone closed, he suggested that Carey show him the city. He'd been staying with the Williamsons and needed air. "I've been reliving 'Life with Ben' for three days straight. 'He said he liked the food. What did he eat? Where did he go to Mass?' Molly still lives at home. She just stares at me, waiting for my answers. How the hell do I know what he ate seven years ago, or whether he was a good Catholic boy?"

Carey knew, or thought she did. She could've told them.

She drove Mike's car. They idled around downtown. On the Circle, a wedding party posed on the Soldiers & Sailors Monument steps. The bridesmaids wore light blue satin, their hair in elaborate geometric configurations, and they fanned around the grinning bride, hooped and corseted into her white gown. Six tuxedoed men stood at the foot of the steps, the buzz-cut groom blindfolded with a pink lace garter.

"Must be before the wedding," Carey said. She glanced at the dashboard clock. Ten-forty-two.

"Why?"

"It's bad luck to see the bride in her dress beforehand. Remember that."

Mike snorted. "I've already seen Claudine's dress. She made me go to her fitting."

Like I said, Carey thought but did not say: Bad luck. Carey's hands mechanically signaled turns and spun the steering wheel. She sought out tourist attractions. She passed through Speedway to show Mike the racetrack, glimpsed through the wide slats of the grandstand's metal bleachers. An empty bowl. Checkered flags hung from light poles and mailboxes, and she turned down a neighborhood street where box-ranch homes grew patchy dirt lawns.

"Booming parking industry, at least next month," Carey said.

"I know," he said, sounding like the old Mike. "He invited me down, back in college. We drank for thirteen hours straight."

Even in her own city, Mike had a claim to Ben that she did not. She hadn't been to the race since she was a child. The air full of gasoline fumes and burnt rubber. Families like her own, dodging sun-seared drunks. The May she turned twelve, allowed to wander the grounds with a friend: three shirtless men with squirt guns, perched atop a camper in the infield, aiming at her crotch. Soaking the back of her cut-offs when she ran away, shrieking. Horrified and ashamed and, yes, pleased, though she didn't know why.

"I don't want to go home yet," Carey said. "Do you mind?"

At Eagle Creek Park she paid the attendant with Mike's money and left the window down, letting in fresh, warm air. The calls of robins and cardinals, the hammering song of woodpeckers. The newly-leafing trees were green as crayons. On an open field, clusters of children hunted for Easter eggs. Carey and Mike drove by signs for trail heads.

"Do you want to walk some?" Mike asked. He fished around in the glove compartment and pulled out a small paper bag.

Carey still wore her heeled boots. "The trails are too muddy."

At the marina, the gravel parking lot crunched under the sedan's tires, then under their feet. Mike wore scuffed hiking boots identical to the ones Ben had owned. Ask if they're his, she thought. Ask him. But she didn't.

They reached the grassy shore, where the sun rested on the water's smooth surface like butter on a knife. Two herons and a flock of geese floated, placid and undisturbed.

Mike handed her the bag. "I found this while cleaning out junk from my dad's basement," he said. "I thought you might want it."

Inside was an oblong package wrapped in brown paper. Careful handwriting spelled out Carey's name, and INDIANA USA. She opened it to find a white cardboard jewelry box, with a gold-embossed address on the lid: Positos #35, Guanajuato. A yellowed slip of paper nested inside. In Spanish, the small note read:

I want to return what you have lost.
With much affection,
Bartolo

Beneath the note, on a bed of cotton, was her St. Christopher medallion. She knew it was hers, not a replacement, by the small nicks on the underside of the medal. Mike, proud of himself, mistook her tears.

"After they shipped you off, your host brother asked me to track you down. He was a little embarrassed at not knowing your address."

Carey had thought the Alarcóns had dismissed her; maybe by now they had. But years ago, Bartolo had remembered. He sent her a message she desperately needed, which had moldered in a Milwaukee basement, forgotten.

"What took you so long?" Her voice shook. "This was mine."

Mike held up both hands. "I tried emailing for your address, I tried calling," he said. "You told me to stop writing. You said, 'I can't help you.' Like I was some door-to-door salesman. Or a shill for Jerry's Kids. I didn't need help. I needed to know you were OK."

"Stop. Can you just stop?"

"It's already stopped. It's history. Over and done. What happened to Ben was not our fault."

She squinted against the sun, against his words. "You really believe that?" Her voice dropped low, a gathering storm. He didn't know to take cover.

"I do." He'd moved claustrophobically close. He reached a tentative hand to her hair, smoothing a piece from her face.

"He knew what he was doing," he said. "We can't blame ourselves."

She stepped away. "I blame us."

He continued to stare at her face, memorizing her. A familiar look, entirely unsettling.

"What?" she asked.

"Something about your hair in this light," he said. "It reminds me of Mexico."

"You're shameless," she said.

He grinned, angering her all the more. "It's this auburn color," he said. "I'd forgotten how your hair changed in the sun."

"You'd say that in front of your fiancée? Go ahead, call her."

"She wouldn't care." He spoke too quickly. "God. You never could take a compliment. You and me, we're the same. Claudine wouldn't care. At all."

"Let's call her up, Mike. I'd be happy to explain how you're in a park with someone you once slept with, giving jewelry that's not yours to give. You want to be the hero. You know what? Don't save me. Save yourself."

She relished the possibility of his anger. But his face wore only resignation. "We're not the same," she said. "No. Because I understand that we did something wrong. I think about it all the time and want to vomit. I want to purge that whole night. I blame myself. And you. You know what? I even blame Ben."

Mike flinched. "Don't," he said.

She was gaining momentum, volume. "I never would have gone home with you if Ben had shown up. You know that, right?"

Somewhere in the distance came the propeller-flap of birds' wings, startled into flight. Mike might've been trying not to cry. Maybe that was her.

"I would not have gone with you," she said. "If he'd shown up in the park that day, he'd be alive and you'd be invisible. He said four o'clock, 'Just you.' Just *me*."

She slapped her chest with an open palm, so hard her red handprint would be visible for an hour. The same gesture Roberto had made last night, referring to another girl. *Where's your devil?* An event in the foggy distance, mere hours old.

Mike kneaded his temples with one hand. He pinched the bridge of his nose, eyes screwed shut. His ruddy face looked like an infant's before a wail. Finally he opened his eyes, bloodshot and tired.

"Ben didn't email you, Carey," he said.

"Of course he did. I saved it." She waved one hand, magician-like, as if a computer screen might appear as proof.

"What you saved," Mike said, "was an email from me. I told you four o'clock. I said 'Just you.'"

The stirrings of fear pricked her hair follicles. She shook her head. "The email was from Ben. It had his name on it."

The pins-and-needles now took over her whole body. When she and Mike had slept together, he'd cupped the back of her head and stroked her hair, massaged her scalp. Don't, she'd told him. Even drunk, she imagined how Ben had cradled her head with both hands, protecting her skull from the hard cement roof. Mike hadn't heard or wasn't listening and she had to repeat: Don't. And then he stopped. In the months that followed she'd scraped that spot raw, picking off scab after scab. The wound, unhealed, lay hidden beneath her hair.

"Ben never knew about the email," Mike said. "I created that account. Using his name."

The jolt down her spine made her understand what people meant by "out-of-body experience." For a second, she floated away from herself and stood on the grass among two people she once recognized.

After Ben died, she'd destroyed Mike's clothes, spilling ink, throwing his laptop out the dorm window. Now her fury surpassed that day. She could've pitched his car keys in the reservoir. She could've gouged his eye with the key ring. Instead, she handed him the keys. He accepted.

"I don't believe you," she said calmly.

"Carey," Mike said. "I'm sorry."

She turned and crunched down the gravel path. He let her go.

The wooded trails were muddy but walkable. She trudged in what she thought was the direction of 56th Street. A half-hour later, two hikers, a man and a woman in brightly colored athletic apparel, approached from the other direction. They wore multi-strapped backpacks.

"Are you OK?" the woman asked, taking in Carey's clothes and heeled boots. She tilted her head and her blonde ponytail wagged like a tail. "You lost?"

"I've never been better," Carey said too loudly.

The man smiled agreeably. "Beautiful morning," he said.

"That's so true," Carey said. "Where's the street?"

Wordlessly, the woman pointed in the direction Carey was headed.

At home she slept dreamlessly, erasing time. She had the uneasy sensation of being watched, and she opened one unrested eye. Her mother stood in the doorway, peeking in.

"Are you sick?"

Carey shook her head, tears filling her eyes. *I want my Mom.* But which version? There was never a guarantee.

"Can I come in?"

"Sure."

Her mother opened the curtains and glanced outside. "I want to talk to you about something."

She maneuvered around the heap of Carey's clothes from the night before.

Her mother began tentatively. "I've been making some changes in my life that I'm proud of, and I'm ready to share them with you."

"Okay." Carey drew the word out cautiously.

"Well, first of all, this is a big step being able to tell you: I'm in therapy. My sessions with Dr. Elliot are helping me come to terms with how I live my life. How I want to live my life."

Elliot. The name on the mailbox, the glass house deep in the woods where she'd spied on her mother's late-night rendezvous. Therapy. At night, in a private home, with a glass of wine.

"I was thinking," her mother continued, "that you might benefit from a session or two. It doesn't have to be with him, though he is wonderful. Absolutely wonderful."

"I don't think so," Carey said.

"Carey, sweetheart." Her mother turned honey-eyed. "I know moving back here hasn't been easy for you. It hasn't been easy for me, either. And your father, well. He seems to think everything's just fine, including you, but we know better. These are transition times. Natural, confusing, scary. What helps is working through the transition."

She sounded like a voice on a self-help tape. Carey's problems predated moving home. An emptiness that consumed her, a contradiction in terms. But her mother had been converted; there would be no reasoning.

"No, thanks, but I'll keep it in mind," Carey said politely, as if dismissing a telemarketer.

"Good! Open mind, open heart!" Sadness over her mother's beaming enthusiasm washed over Carey like a scalding shower.

"Dad knows already?"

"Of course." She stood. "He will. I'm telling him now. You came first."

Her mother had put Carey before her marriage, and was asking something in return.

"Mom?" Carey asked, and her mother stopped. "He's just your therapist. That's all. Right?"

Her mother's shoulders tensed. She sat at Carey's desk. The computer hummed quietly, and Gwen put her hand on the laptop lid as if taking an oath.

"One person can't be everything to another person," she began. "You can't expect that. Do you understand what I'm saying?" She didn't give Carey time to respond. "You have to count on yourself first. Don't lean too heavily on one person. Finding the person who can accept even some of your weight, well, it's a challenge."

"So he's more than just your therapist," Carey said.

Her mother sighed. "I feel like you didn't quite hear me, Carey."

"Mom."

Gwen faced her daughter, then cast her eyes to the carpet. "*More* is hard to define."

"Are you having sex?"

"None of your business," her mother said, flushing deeply, which told Carey all she needed to know. "I'm going to go talk to your father now."

She exited, head remarkably high for the conversation they'd nearly had.

Carey sank back into the pillows. One person can't be everything to another person. It was a variation of Gwen's dating advice that Carey never followed: don't put all your eggs in one basket. But Carey was born with just one basket.

Now too agitated for rest, she paced to the window, pulling the curtains closed. She stalked to the closet. The green backpack mocked her from its place on the shelf. Stashed away like a treasure, a basket for dozens of eggs, when it was just a bag.

She removed the journal and tossed it against the wall. A solid thwack, the pages rustling. She dumped the rest of the bag's contents on the floor, scooping up Ben's burgundy long-sleeve T-shirt, the one she'd worn home after the Cervantino festival, and wadded it tightly into a ball. The trajectory of cotton, far less satisfying than that of the heavier journal. His school notebooks she hurled like Frisbees, loose pages spilling out and dropping to the carpet, lazy as fall leaves. She gripped the front and back covers of the hardcover history textbook, unsuccessfully trying to pull the book apart. Something sharp and thick fell from the pages and hit her bare feet, biting into thin skin.

She looked down.

On the floor lay handfuls of small square photographs. They were headshots of Mexican men, staring up at her. Passport photos.

She stared back.

Uneven scissor marks outlined the pictures. Octavio watched her with his blank stare. So did the face of a man she recognized from the streets of Guanajuato. He often said hello, only when she was with Ben.

The pictures had been there all along. She'd never opened the textbook.

On the backs of the photos were small letters in blue ballpoint ink. She retrieved the journal from across the room. She finally understood that the book, with its pages of initials, towns and states, was a legend to the map scattered in front of her. Raleigh, Charlotte, Atlanta. She kneeled among the glossy photos and opened the journal, matching up the initials, comparing faces. GF, Boise, Idaho, wore a mirthful expression. PR slicked his hair back. His passport's lie was Texas.

And there was sunken-eyed Octavio, the thin, unmistakable version. Ben had helped him, and in return he had helped himself to Ben's passport. Next to his initials in the journal was one word: Chicago. A city he and Carey might have shared.

If only a picture of Ben had fallen to the floor. Because in that moment she could not envision what he looked like, nor imagine who he was. He was lost and unknown to her, this version of Ben she'd come to understand in recent weeks.

She flipped through the textbook. In the back were tissue-thin receipts from Western Union. She could read enough of the faded ink to see that Ben had wired money to people in eight different cities in the United States.

Still, she justified. He had been paid, but he'd also kept track. This evidence proved he was concerned about where his customers wound up and how they got settled. She imagined he'd planned to check on them. Using the journal, he could construct a route across the country. Sightseeing in the America he'd helped populate. She still had hopes for him, for the things he would never say and actions he would never perform.

Sorting the pictures, her brain crept around that morning's conversation with Mike. He kept us in the dark, Mike said. Then she'd hurt Mike, told him he was a poor second choice. He retaliated by claiming to write Ben's emails. He merely parroted her: Four o'clock. Just you.

A strange feeling hit, like the time years back when she was running in the park and knew, seconds before it happened, that she would sprain her ankle on the log she'd jumped over dozens of times. She walked gingerly to the desk, her legs cramped from kneeling. The laptop lid felt heavy as a stone.

There was the message from the dead she'd been waiting for. Only now she understood. The signals had gotten crossed.

To: Carey Halpern <la_mujer@freenet.com>
From: Ben Williamson <bensays@freenet.com>
Date: April 19, 2003 8:08 p.m.
Subject: (no subject)

Carey,

I'm sitting in Ben's old room listening to dusty Velvet Underground tapes. Lida's down the hall, swallowing Cadbury Crème Eggs whole and worried that I'm tampering with the shrine. Burn the shrine, Lida. Don't erect the shrine in the first place.

I've kept this account all these years, and for what? For this. Anyone can sit in a room and pretend to be someone he's not. No special talent required. I'm sorry I hurt you. I'm sorry Ben died. But I'm not sorry for anything else.

I don't have the answers you want. Ben walked through life like he had everything. But he didn't have money, and Alejandro had money. Ben worked for him, did whatever needed doing. I got involved because Ben was doing it, not because I had to work. I was lazy. Ben busted his ass for this guy. Passport and ID photos, crappy t-shirts, deliveries— maybe drugs, prescription painkillers, we didn't ask. Let's say Ben got in over his head. Got aggressive, took business from guys who might've needed it more. Let's say I was designing fake documents to go with the fake documents, proof-of-residence utility bills, because why not, who cares, it's not like this matters, long-term. We thought we were helping people get better lives. Like we knew what that meant.

And we were going home. We were supposed to be going home together, the three of us, but then I was the only one left. First Ben. Then you were gone, and when you wouldn't talk to me it was like you were gone twice. I thought about you all the time. Let's say that after the funeral, Alejandro pressed three hundred U.S. dollars into my hand and told me he was sorry for my loss. He also said to stay away for awhile until it's safe, and if I said anything about his business to the police, it would never be safe. Not in Mexico, not back home. I didn't even want to see Alejandro on the street. I thought I'd be next.

Let's say I came home from Mexico and tried to forget everything that happened. Let's say it's all I ever think about. Why am I even telling you this? I don't know. Probably because some part of this matters as much to you as it does to me. Even if it's not the right part.

Seeing you has rattled me more than I expected. Claudine knows; I told her tonight on the phone. She has suggested I need some space. That *we* need some space. For fuck's sake. It's the Midwest. We've got enough space.

So that's that. It's your turn, again. I'd like to pretend I won't wait for you.

—Mike

CHAPTER 18

THE DAY BEN DIED, Carey woke before sunrise. A gap in the white curtains, the sun not yet over the mountains. Purple-gray sky morning, the city of Guanajuato steeped in its bath of pre-dawn light. Coloring everything colorless, blending shades into sameness.

She hardly ever woke that early, and never without an alarm.

Alicia snored in the adjacent twin bed, a small stuffed giraffe tucked under her chin. Sweet Alicia whom Carey had learned to ignore, who had stopped inviting Carey to her soccer games. You can't make everybody happy, Carey told herself, catching Alicia's pout from the corner of her eye. You only have so many hours in a day.

Carey yawned, listening to the splatter of the bathroom shower. Lupe preparing for work, her part-time job at the clothing store, or Bartolo rising to open the jewelry shop. He went early on Saturdays to complete custom orders. Monograms like the one on Ben's Swiss army knife.

Warm beneath the faded blue-stitched quilt, Carey mapped her day: a run, a shower, lunch with Ben. Parlayed into an afternoon together, stretching into her open evening. Streaks of light appeared in the small slit between the curtains, the sky like orange and raspberry sherbet. She could get up now, run, and track down Ben earlier than planned.

Instead she rolled over, contented, and burrowed into the thin pillow. She had plenty of time. She could sleep another hour or even two and still hit Mercado Hidalgo before lunch. Buy the leather journal for Ben, the one she'd seen months ago.

She drifted, dozing. Pleased to have arranged a day with so little obligation. She would oversleep but still go for her run. The leather journal, with its burnt curlicues decorating the leather cover, remained unpurchased at Mercado Hidalgo. Unless someone else bought it.

Here was lunch, an outdoor table in the Plazuela de San Fernando, at a restaurant with no sign. The last time she saw Ben. Not just the last time she saw him alive. The last time she saw him, ever. She did not know if, at the memorial service, the casket stood open like a clam, or if a small silver urn held his remains.

They ate hamburguesas and papas fritas. The oblivious condemned man ate a last meal of burgers and fries. He probably ate dinner, a late bite after his shift in the dining hall, but this was his last meal with her.

Side by side at the outdoor table, observing the passersby. Warm Mexico February, jeans and t-shirts, Carey in her sneakers and Ben with a Trinity Academy baseball cap. Two tanned Americans in casual American gear eating American food under a sun that belonged to anyone.

Since that day, she'd recalled their meaningless conversation countless times, hunting for lost sentiment. She wished she'd memorized the sound of Ben's voice, measured the depth of his dimples, the length of a hair's curl pulled straight.

"Pass the ketchup," she said. Hungry after her run, and thirsty, too. Her burger gone in five bites. The waiter brought more water. She usually drank bottled, and never accepted the glass of proffered ice. One of the first pieces of tourist advice she received. The restaurant sold no bottled water. It was Coke or from the tap, and she wanted water.

A young Mexican father in expensive leather shoes meandered around the small plaza after his two children, a toddling boy and a Kindergarten-aged girl. The little ones chased pigeons, tossing tiny handfuls of birdseed at their gnarled claws. On a park bench in front of the restaurant, his pregnant wife lounged and chatted with a friend. Maybe her sister. Poking out of the diaper bag next to her on the bench: a city map, the free ones the tourism office provided.

"Turístas," Carey said. A note of disdain in her voice.

"Que lástima," Ben replied. What a shame.

More often, they conversed with just a few words. They translated the actions of strangers and tourists, possessive of a place they did not own. They decided what they owned. Laughed at inside jokes, pointing out Mexican strangers who resembled Americans. Celebrities or people they both knew, that was the rule of their game, and they voted on the selection's authenticity.

"Mexican Gibs," Ben said.

Carey followed Ben's gaze across the plaza to a small kiosk loaded with braided bracelets and rainbow-hued purses. A man of Mike's height and build sat on a stool in front of the cart and read a newspaper. He was at least forty, dark-haired and dark-complected. Mike was blond and his skin burnt in the sun ("I glow like Chernobyl," he'd say after a nasty sunburn.) The point wasn't an exact match—just a resemblance.

"Viejo," Carey said. "Doesn't count."

"You'll see," Ben promised. He was obsessed with finding a Mexican version of Mike. His selections were patently ridiculous—a young boy, an old woman. Ben claimed there was something in each that reminded him of Mike. She couldn't see it.

Carey fed Ben a French fry smeared in ketchup, and he thanked her by tipping his grungy baseball cap. A yellow sweat stain ran around the brim. He opened his mouth like a baby bird for another. This time she dabbed his chin with ketchup first. When he couldn't reach the red splotch with his tongue, he jutted his chin in her direction. She kissed the ketchup off with a loud smack.

The women on the park bench watched Carey and Ben, smiling privately at each other. A glance between sisters. They had to be. The same aquiline nose.

The vendor reached a finger to his cheek, eventually walking it over to his nose. He inserted an index finger into one nostril, digging. Ben broke up laughing, pulling his hat brim over his face.

"Mike doesn't pick his nose," Carey scolded. "That's mean."

Ben peeked out from under the cap. The raised blue letters of "Trinity Academy" still fresh, despite the hat's dirty surface.

"Yet funny," Ben said. She thought of the day at the Mummy Museum, when Ben so effortlessly sold out his friend. *You know Mike's an asshole.* She had disliked this about Ben, though it took years to remember. Admit. In death he could do no wrong. Sometimes, later, his flaws flashed in her mind as if projected on a movie screen. She would close her eyes but still see him insulting his best friend, shaking hands with Alejandro in the courtyard, breaking dates and telling her comeheregoaway, all in a glance, all in the length of his stride down the sidewalk. She wondered if she'd known him at all. If she had the right to grieve for a stranger.

One of them called for the check. In Mexico you had to ask. Not like the States, not like Casa Colmo, where you expected the bill soon after your last bite. In Mexico, no one rushed you. Carey and Ben could have sat all day if they wanted.

But one of them called for the check. She had. She remembered because she had said "cuento," instead of "cuenta." She always got that wrong.

And Ben teased, "Would you like the waiter to tell you a story?"

"Such mastery of the language," she said.

"Someday you'll catch up," he said.

She tossed her hair over one shoulder. "I'm closer than you think."

"Is that a fact."

"Nice day to spend on a rooftop," she said. "I've got the afternoon free." Partly true. She'd considered going to campus to address some long-neglected homework.

"Now, little mama, you know I'd like to," he said. "But I'm playing a game in an hour. Across town, just locals."

He'd never called her "mama" before. By the downward, guilty shift of his expression, he seemed to realize his mistake. Someone else was called by that name, not her. The laces of his cleats were tied to one backpack strap.

"I've asked you to the rooftop," she stated flatly, "and you'd rather play soccer."

He thoughtfully munched the last fry from his plate. "Fútbol," he said.

"Fine," she said. Trying to balance indifference and anger in one small syllable.

"Fine," he repeated, mocking her.

Their parting words, because she was too angry for goodbye. A word born of stubbornness, hurt, withholding. The last thing she told him was "Fine," the biggest lie she knew.

He stood, his cleats hanging from the backpack. She slung her black bag across her chest. They kissed. A standing-on-the-sidewalk peck. Not bittersweet or emotional or dramatic. Almost perfunctory. She thought she remembered that kiss. She tried to give it romance, though their fight changed the mood. Thinking back, she'd imagine herself in the brown shirt, instead of the Mini-Marathon T-shirt she'd actually worn. Or her hair was up instead of down. Or it was raining when she knew the sun had been out that day.

Each time, she was forced to remember: she didn't remember. Not exactly.

Ben was supposed to be playing soccer, but a few hours later she got the email. In the nearly-deserted Intercambio library, she had grudgingly begun research for a literature paper on Cervantes. Soon she'd become engrossed, typing a page and then two, the keyboard steadily clacking and her mind whirring, even though she still hadn't finished *Don Quixote*, not in Spanish. She'd been to Guanajuato's Cervantino festival in the fall, and the Cervantes museum twice. She particularly liked the painting of Don Quixote and Sancho Panza looking over Cervantes' shoulder, bossing him around.

Despite her interest in the subject and her rare eloquence on the author, she opened her email account. Nothing compelled her to log on, she just did. A habit. She expected no new messages. The modem screeched and cackled, connecting her after three tries. The Cervantes paper was forgotten. She closed the word processing program and ejected the square floppy disk. She and Ben had just seen each other a few hours ago, but there was his message.

No. Mike's message. But how could she have known?

Date: Saturday, February 24, 1996 2:07 p.m.
To: Carey Halpern <chalpern@intercambio.edu>
From: Ben Williamson <bensays@freenet.com>
Subject: vete aqui

I want to see you again.
Meet me in the Jardín. 4 p.m. Just you.

—B

An unexpected date. Vete aqui meant "come here." The Jardín, at the center of town, was only a few minutes' walk from campus, but she hustled home first, out of her way. Ben wanted to meet her. She would shake out her hair in the bathroom mirror. Step into her favorite skirt, the gauzy purple one that made her legs look even longer, more tanned. From under the bed she pulled out the suitcase that held her clothes overflow. The brown cotton shirt was soft as velvet. She smoothed out the wrinkles in clothes that would wind up on Mike's dorm room floor.

No one else was home, and she left no note. She barely remembered running from the house to the park, but she remembered perfectly the details of the next several hours. The things you wished you could forget trailed after you like a stray dog, mangy and odorous and nipping at your cross trainers. No matter how fast you ran, that dog kept pace.

She'd sat on the bench with *Don Quixote* on her lap. Not reading, just flipping pages. Thinking Ben's shadow might loom over her shoulder at any moment.

Then right in front of her was Gibs, Mike Gibley, feigning surprise when he exited the newsstand with his *Wired* magazine and bottle of Coke. "Oh, hey," he said, and joined her on the bench. He hadn't seen Ben. They waited another half-hour, Carey's request, before walking to the café. Down a narrow street where they could sit at a sidewalk table, watching the blanket salesmen and wandering packs of preteens from a safe distance.

She wasn't hungry. Her lunch, the hamburger and fries, still sat heavy in her stomach. Thirsty still, always, this time she wanted beer. She'd downed two pints before Mike had finished his first. The old waiter didn't bat an eye.

She lifted the third round to her lips. "What's Ben's problem?"

Mike shrugged. "You can slow down," he said. "That beer's not going anywhere."

The streetlamps switched on. "Who needs him?" she asked. "I don't. We don't. You and I can stay here all night and tell stories about our terrible love lives."

"Oh, God."

"You first. You never finished the story about your Internet girlfriend." She settled back in her chair, giving him a flirtatious, encouraging smile. Mike sighed. He had not agreed to this. Still, he complied.

"There's not much to say. She went to Marquette. I drove home to Milwaukee one weekend to see her. Nothing happened."

"You met? Face-to-face?"

"Yes, Barnaby Jones," he said. "More or less. I think she saw me. It was through the window of a bar. She was pretty and all. I just didn't go in."

She'd never seen Mike so somber, almost forlorn.

"You're a great guy, Mike," she said, her body draped over the tabletop, her tan arms stretched forward luxuriantly. "You've got to let people see the real you."

He looked her in the eye and this time didn't look away. "Thank you," he said.

Now both were embarrassed. She was drunk, sincere and

moist-eyed, edging closer to Mike across the table. Inches from his face, as if she were about to kiss him. With hot beer breath she asked, "Now tell me another story: What's *wrong* with me?" And she crumpled back into her seat. Drained the quarter-inch of liquid from the glass. She could blame her behavior on the beer, but she was the one doing the drinking. Still her.

She meant, What's wrong with me that Ben doesn't want to be with me at every opportunity? Even if she still wanted time to go running, or to email Nicole, or to lounge in bed until eleven a.m. on a Saturday. She wanted to be wanted consistently.

Mike licked beer foam from his lips, and his mouth twitched. He was nervous.

"Absolutely nothing is wrong with you, Carey," Mike said. "Nothing. You're perfect."

She could not suppress a smile. Didn't want to.

Mike turned redder than usual. Added a hasty qualifier: "In a fucked up, crazy-girl kind of way."

But the compliment was on the table. She drank it in.

They slammed another round at the café. Tumbled into the street and through the swinging doors of a poorly-lit cantina. Three men sat at the bar, nursing drinks. Carey, the only woman, accepted shots of tequila from the nearest patron, a retired waiter who told them he once served Gary Cooper.

"Cuchillo," the elderly man slurred, his shaking hand spilling liquid from the tall shot glass as the three of them toasted. "En ingles, es *knife*."

A ceramic urinal was attached to the wall at one end of the bar. The heavyset bouncer relieved himself without interrupting his conversation with the bartender, who watched Mexican soccer on the television.

"Fútbol, bah," Carey said scornfully. Nobody paid attention.

"Cuchara," the old man said. "Es *spoon*, verdad? Verdad?"

Carey tottered in her sandals. The night had grown too chilly for a flimsy skirt. The bartender, an unassuming man in glasses, sized up her legs. Her legs struck poses of their own accord; she observed them, too. Mike laid an arm around Carey's shoulder.

"You're shivering," he said. "We should go."

"But I want another drink." She had accepted two tequila shots from Gary Cooper's one-time waiter and anticipated a third.

"We'll go somewhere else," he whispered. He nodded towards the bartender. "I don't like how that guy's looking at you."

She nodded her flattered assent.

They bought two bottles of wine from a bodega and took them back to Mike's room. Their plastic cups thudded dully as they toasted to anything they could think of.

"To Gary Cooper!"

"To Diego Rivera, RIP!"

"To Ben, wherever he is!"

Halfway through the first bottle, she decided they should email Ben. Or Mike decided. Or they both did. She'd show Benjamin Williamson a thing or two about missing her company. She had catching up to do. Fast as she could run, he was always several steps ahead.

She reread Ben's message from earlier. Unlike her mind, the message was sobering. She'd been stood up. She clicked "reply" and slid the laptop to Mike.

"There's a rooftop on the other side of town," she said.

"Too vague. Which one?"

"He'll know," she said confidently, in a way meant to hurt Mike. To remind him of his impermanence. Even though they'd been together all night, even though it was becoming clear that the night was far from over. Everything ended eventually.

"Just say 'the rooftop.' No. Say 'our rooftop.'"

Mike's cheek twitched. He typed the words.

"Read it over," he said. "Does it look OK?"

Carey nodded. She deserved better, and Ben deserved this. Why hadn't revenge occurred to her earlier? (Why did it have to occur to her at all?)

"Copy it to his other email," she said. "We'll double our chances."

He typed in Ben's Intercambio email address. His only real account. But she didn't know that then.

They'd send Ben out into the night and into the path of an armed robber—maybe Octavio, who had played guitar during her serenade. They'd drink more wine. They'd have awkward but somehow freeing sex. Days later she'd throw Mike's computer out the window. For years she would shoulder sackfuls of guilt and blame. Even once she learned Mike had tricked her with the fake email, even though she was devastated, even though part of her, her own inner spy and plotter, understood.

It was true that Mike, not Ben, had told her the park: Four o'clock, just you. But she had suggested sending the email to both accounts. Send Ben out to a rooftop where she was supposed to be, where she'd been before.

"You do the honors," Mike said.

"With pleasure." She clicked the mouse. Send.

The sharp edges of Mike's face blurred. Mike Gibley. Gibs. He needed a haircut in a sort of endearing way, he laughed and opened up like a flower to her sun, he escorted her from a cantina where a man leered at her legs. In the past she'd been occupied with Mike's meddling, jealous of his closeness to Ben. She'd never admitted how much she liked his mouth. A thick lower lip, deep red. Right then she wanted to kiss that mouth. To thank him.

Now Ben would know her humiliation, she thought, waiting for him when he never showed. He didn't own a computer, so he would have used the computer lab. Was Ben down the hall in his room when she strode through Mike's door, tipsy and filled with purpose?

Sometimes she imagined that Ben never received the email. That he'd been out on his own, drinking with Mexican futbolistas. Or searching for Alejandro, or some pot. Even someone other than her, some little mama. But she couldn't ignore the facts. The police found his body along the curving hillside alley the two of them had walked, that led to the rooftop. Their rooftop. Where they'd connected the dots, turning stars into words they couldn't speak aloud.

The computer dinged and a box popped onto the screen: Your message has been sent.

She exhaled and closed her eyes. It was too soon for regret. She still had other mistakes to make. The wine swished in the bottle as Mike tilted it to his mouth. He licked his lips with a purple-stained tongue.

Eyes wide open, she tilted her head and pressed her open lips full against Mike's mouth. Their front teeth bumped, triggering a nerve that rang painfully and made her want to sneeze.

She didn't sneeze. She didn't even flinch. She kissed Mike and bit his lip, hard. He opened his eyes in surprise.

"Ouch," he said, grinning. Licked his lightly bleeding lip with his purple tongue, leaning his wrestler's torso into her. Carey let herself fall. Her face still smarted.

That pain, it was nothing.

She'd done much worse.

CHAPTER 19

THE WILLIAMSON'S FRONT DOOR—panes of glass with no curtain—revealed a tall terra cotta flower pot holding a duck-handled umbrella. Atop a scratched wooden bench sat a stack of paperback library books. A round mirror hung on the wall next to a bronze crucifix with still-green palm leaves crisscrossed behind it.

Carey had already rung the doorbell. In the mirror, her reflection parceled itself out into pieces, made neat and square by the front door's wood and glass. The green backpack hung from her shoulder. A moment later the mirror revealed Andrew Williamson, Ben's father, turning the corner to the hallway. The angle gave Carey a second to observe him. Andrew was as tall as Ben, but stoop-shouldered, heavier. More muscular. Thinning hair that receded inches back from his forehead. Skin leathery from years of working in the sun, managing the grounds at Trinity Academy. The doorknob clicked loudly and then there was nothing between them.

"Hi," she said. "I'm Carey."

The man's eyes shone. Tears pooled but did not spill. He hugged her, tight, and she almost cried with relief. He could crush her and it still would be better than anticipated. She tried to let go. He held on.

They sat in the front room, Andrew Williamson across from her in a worn green recliner, Carey on a chaise. She attempted to keep her eyes on Ben's father, to focus on their nothing conversation, but atop the scratched, stand-up piano were a dozen framed photographs of Ben's childhood. And behind the pictures, leaning against the wall, was the faded memorial service collage described in the newspaper article. There in the group photograph from Jennifer's birthday, Carey sat squarely between Ben and Mike, grinning. Ben's long arm draped around her, his hand resting on Mike's shoulder. The anxiety of that night was not evident in the photograph. Only their collective, exaggerated youth, their posed happiness.

He noticed her looking at the pictures and pointed to a frame in front. "That one's from when Ben was real little. He played goalie. Before they made him a forward." The soccer photo showed a boy already tall for his age, in a too-big jersey and gigantic shin guards, smiling the gap-toothed smile universal among seven-year-olds.

There was a color photograph of a soybean field, a red barn and white farmhouse in the foreground. "The family farm where I grew up," Andrew said. "Cemetery's a half-mile from the grain silo. That's where he is. Where he's buried, I mean."

They were silent for a moment, then from somewhere in the house came the quiet, muffled noise of a CD: guitar riffs laced over hard drum beats. "Is Mike still here?" she asked. Four days had passed since she'd seen him at the reservoir. His sleek black car was not in the Williamson's driveway.

Ben's father shook his head. "Not presently. He's in town, but not home now."

Lida Williamson descended the carpeted staircase and interrupted their attempts at conversation. Carey would have known she was Ben's mother at twenty paces. The length of her neck, the long, loose-limbed manner. Dark hair, curly and hopelessly mussed. She wore a pair of baggy white sweatpants cinched at the waist with a drawstring, and a loose black t-shirt.

Carey didn't know what else to do but extend her hand. They shook, and Lida Williamson gripped tightly and searched Carey's eyes. Traces of Ben: the singularity of her vision, how she stared and held you and kept you in sight. Her eyes were green, too, the kind of green that changed shade, dark as a forest, or light as a cat's eye. Ben's eyes had sparkled, glinted. Looking into Ben's eyes, Carey had felt his energy reflected back to her. She had felt alive. His mother's eyes were deep caverns, dull, crinkled at the edges.

"It's you," Lida Williamson said. A pointed statement of fact.

Carey hadn't called ahead, but the Williamsons seemed unsurprised. Gwen Halpern would have bustled about, preparing a tray of cheese and crackers, opening a bottle of white in the middle of the afternoon, silently cursing the guest who'd put her out. But the Williamsons sat and stared at Carey. One of the last people to know their son. Perhaps she was one in a long line of women to visit their Northside home after Ben's death. She was only seven years late.

"Has your friend been discharged from the hospital yet?" Lida Williamson asked. "How is he?"

"He's better," Carey said. "He's home." She'd visited Juan the day before. Elena scrambled to clear a seat for Carey in their boxlike apartment, which was simultaneously crammed and bare. They apologized for the mess, for the trouble she must've gone through. Pedro, who'd disappeared with her car, had later taken it to a detail shop to clean the blood from the upholstery. Elena fussed over the flowers Carey had brought, a bouquet of purple tulips the florist recommended. She complimented the St. Christopher medallion Carey now wore religiously, though religion had never been a factor. Carey offered to cover Juan's shifts until he recovered. Truthfully, she didn't want to return to work. She made a terrible waitress. And something about the restaurant now struck her as ominous. But quitting now would be disloyal. She'd earn extra money covering for Juan, she thought, touching the silver necklace at the hollow of her throat, mentally calculating hours and wages, converting them into airfare. She counted dates on the calendar, estimating how long it would take to renew her passport.

Lida Williamson reached across her husband's lap and covered his hand so he'd stop fidgeting. She tried to smile. Her stretched-out dimples made long lines, like folds in paper. Her eyes were flat as buttons. Carey had not caused this damage, nor alleviated it.

"What brings you today?" she asked Carey. "Mike said you were at the hospital. Momentarily."

In the Williamson's front room, the silence bore down. Carey asked for a glass of water and Andrew stood. She regretted her request, which left her alone with Lida.

She had wanted to tell Lida Williamson. To admit that she and Mike had written an email that sent Ben out on a false search. She wanted Lida to know that Ben's death, while not Carey's fault, could have been prevented. That Mike, the replacement son staying in their basement, carried some of the blame. She didn't know why she had thought this information would help. Lida had coped, was still coping; she would have her own forms of support. A therapy group, a church network. Television appearances, extolling the virtues of forgiveness. Perhaps she had meditatively walked the curving streets of Guanajuato the weekend of the memorial service, wanting to see what her son saw, to be where he had been.

Carey said nothing. Chickened out. She could almost hear the dumb-cluck crow of O.J. the rooster, mocking her. Amid Andrew's teary, clenching hug and Lida's silence, her admissions grew unimportant. She knew now that Ben had, in part, contributed to his own death. But she'd planned to take ownership, to reinforce the Williamsons' belief in their son's goodness, even though her own faith now wavered.

The backpack sat at Carey's feet. She'd brought Ben's belongings, most of them: Ben's long-sleeved maroon shirt, his notebooks and the history textbook. After some debate she'd removed the passport pictures and Western Union receipts. She made copies for herself, and placed the originals and Ben's journal in a manila envelope. She planned to give the package to Molly, who could decide what to do with the information. This was Carey's way of protecting the Williamsons, Ben included. Maybe a part of her did believe in his goodness.

She'd photocopied pages of the journal for herself, too, and kept the CDs. She imagined him singing to her through PJ Harvey and Pearl Jam, music that held them in place.

"You heard about the passport, I take it," Lida said.

"It's awful," Carey said. "And the killer got away."

"Oh, I don't know. Those things get passed around, passports do.

It doesn't mean anything. In a way I'm glad somebody got some use from it. A Mexican. Ben would've appreciated that, don't you think? Or didn't you know him well?"

It could've been an innocent question. It could've been something else. Carey looked Lida Williamson in the eye and sat up straighter.

"I knew him," she said. "Very well. We were close. I should've come sooner."

Lida turned her gaze to the framed collage on the piano and shrugged. "People need time," she said. "The services were quite nice. From what I remember. That year is a little blurry."

Andrew returned with two glasses of ice water and handed one to each woman. Lida took a sip, tilting her head as if downing a pill.

"I have his backpack," Carey finally said.

Andrew examined the bag on the floor. "That's Ben's?" he asked. Lida mouthed words without making a sound.

"In Mexico, well. I wanted to have something of his," Carey said. "It's not mine. You should have it."

Carey placed it at their feet. Her idea of sacrifice.

"Thank you," Andrew finally said.

Carey asked to get in touch with Molly. "We could have her call you," Andrew said doubtfully. Carey thought of Ben's tanned features, his smooth skin, her hand brushing against his always-shaved cheek. "She went off with Mike earlier."

The rock music still played from deep within the house. They were making excuses. Carey rose from the couch.

Lida shook Carey's hand formally. Thanked her for the visit. For one second, the flatness in her eyes evolved and Carey saw a glimmer in the green Ben had inherited. Something like a chance. Carey took it.

"I loved him," she said.

Lida nodded, tearing up. "Then you know how awful this is."

"Yes."

"Well," Lida said, heading upstairs, "then we have that in common, don't we."

Andrew walked her to the paned glass door. He hugged her, speaking softly in her ear, "She's glad you came. Took her by surprise is all. Seeing Mike again, now you. Thinking of who our boy would be now."

He pulled open a desk drawer and removed a cream-colored sheet of paper, folded in half. The homemade funeral program, which looked like it could have been printed in the main office at Trinity Academy. Seven years later, and they still had copies on hand. He handed it to her and she gratefully accepted.

Andrew shut the door as soon as she'd crossed the threshold. She rolled down the car window. In an upstairs window, she caught the flutter of a yellow curtain. Molly. She appeared tall as a giant in the second-story window. Long auburn hair cascaded around her shoulders. A steady gaze, unafraid to be seen. Carey thought Molly was reaching out a hand. To wave, to touch the window. Carey's own hand instinctively raised. Molly, now twenty-five, grabbed the curtain and slowly drew it around her body like a shawl, never once breaking eye contact with her dead brother's lost girlfriend. The one who refused to read a piece of scripture at his memorial. Carey pulled the manila envelope from her purse and mouthed, "For you." Molly nodded and pointed to the mailbox, where Carey deposited it. She put the car in reverse and backed down the crumbling cement driveway.

She parked down the street and read and re-read the funeral program. A small slip of paper fluttered out: directions from Trinity Church to the cemetery in Fortville. On the cover, a picture of Ben in Mexico. The day he went hiking alone, bare-chested and skinny, in the baggy green shorts held up by a brown leather belt. It was just a black-and-white photocopy, but she knew the shorts were military green. She knew the belt was brown. His glistening lips red as a cherry Popsicle, curly hair glinting with shades of copper that came out in the sun. She knew his eyes, green behind the sun-squint.

Her sweaty palm smudged the program's ink. The paper in her hand wouldn't last. Eventually, even the thick black ink of the picture would fade, the hilly shadows of Ben's hike growing indistinct. Her few photographs would disintegrate. Maybe in her lifetime, maybe not.

How she remembered Ben would not fit inside a backpack or on a cream-colored page. He became bigger the longer he was gone.

Facts and conjecture trickled into her mind like water seeping into a basement, soaking cardboard boxes, blackening documents with mold. Passports, newspapers, a journal held in two hands.

Her memories would continue to alter and fade. But not the way ink lightens with years, not the way pitch black night turns to gray, irreconcilable morning.

She knew all this and for once it didn't matter. She had lived alongside Ben, in color.

Later that night, she returned to the Williamson's house.

No moon, just the motion-sensor lights spotlighting her crouched form in the backyard, against the vinyl siding. The lights faded with her stillness. She considered pushing her way through the basement window, then knocked on the foggy glass. She waited. She knew Mike would be there. A disembodied hand parted the curtains, then he cranked open the window, disturbing a spider web.

"You again," he said, failing to keep the pleasure from his voice. "Hang on."

A moment later the basement door opened, setting off the lights. Mike stood in the dark, open doorway, moving aside for her. He wore only boxer shorts, and his bare white chest seemed to glow in the dark. She hesitated, ears buzzing.

"Come in," he said. "Otherwise the security lights will stay on."

The cool basement air held a concentrated musk, not unpleasant. In the old playroom, stacks of dusty board games occupied the shelves—Risk, Stratego, Trivial Pursuit. The pull-out sofa took up most of the small room. "So you get my email or what?"

"I didn't come here because of that," she said.

This was not entirely true, but she had to establish a wall, a perimeter, in the cramped room. The email had pulled her back in, as Mike surely hoped.

Mike nodded quickly. "Okay," he said. "Okay." He waited for her to say something more. At the marina she had told him their night together was a fluke, never would have happened under other circumstances, though the truth was less clear. A part of her had wanted it to happen. She'd wanted to know how he would be with her, the ways he would be like and unlike Ben. The ways he would be like and unlike himself.

"My mother might be cheating on my father," she announced.

He scratched one ear. "More common than you think."

She said nothing, remembering that his parents were divorced. And on some unforeseen date, Mike would be married.

"I'm sorry," Mike said, and she knew he meant it. About her parents, about other things.

"Are the Williamsons light sleepers?"

He shook his head. "Molly is, but she's out with her boyfriend."

They watched each other, waiting.

"You here for a game of Chutes & Ladders?" Mike finally asked. She appreciated his sarcasm, his normalcy.

"I wanted to see his room."

She feared he might argue or protest, but he stood. His face drooped, mainly from being woken, though there was a sadness there too, in the set of his mouth, the pillow marks on his cheek, like scars, even his lips a scar slashed into the bottom of his face. She avoided looking at his chest, not wanting to be reminded of his skin and muscle, curly hair in tiny rings, his smell, antiseptic and clean as mouthwash. She looked away, ashamed of her thoughts. He grabbed a t-shirt and threw it over his head, as if reading her mind. Maybe just her face. Same difference.

He silently led her upstairs, pointing out the creaky steps to avoid. In Ben's room he closed the door behind them. She'd expected walls filled with rock-star posters, piles of dirty laundry, reeking soccer cleats. Perhaps that had been Ben's room as a boy. This room belonged to adult Ben, or it had, and he'd gone away to college and to Mexico. This room belonged to a loose kind of monk. There was a stereo and speakers set up on the floor by the window, and crates of tapes, CDs, and records. Unadorned walls, and a single twin bed with a scuffed oak headboard. Worn-out avocado green carpet beneath their feet. A plain wooden dresser, and bookshelves crammed with paperbacks and piles of magazines. On the desk was a cardboard box, with Ben's straight, all-caps handwriting on top, a package addressed to himself, Brandywine Drive, Indianapolis. She turned to Mike.

"You're one step away from sniffing the pillow, aren't you," Mike said. "Please don't sniff the pillow."

She didn't expect to laugh, but it felt good. After a long moment, Mike braved a smile. "I really can leave you alone, if you want."

His generosity prompted her own. "No. Stay." She motioned to the box. "Have you looked?"

"Yeah. Crap he didn't want to lug home."

Mike sat on the bed and began rummaging through the nightstand's drawer. "I found some weed," he announced.

Carey ignored him and opened the box, and Ben's cologne drifted out faintly, attached to the clothes he'd shipped home. There was a battered Walkman, a few books and cassettes. A thick manila envelope rested at the bottom, filled with snapshots. She opened it.

The stack's topmost picture showed a runner mid-stride, and it took her a moment to realize it was herself. A candid shot, running along a crowded sidewalk in Guanajuato. She was the only thing in focus, her muscles visible even beneath her baggy shorts and shirt. She was caught at an angle; blurred in the background was the imitation Rivera mural painted on the cement wall, and the parked quesadilla cart. As if the wall and the cart were moving, and she, in hard focus, was still.

Ben had photographed her after all.

The picture showed her as she'd never seen herself, all those times posing in the mirror, or rearranging her features in front of a store window, or in front of a man. The photo showed sweat dripping, a distorted, unaware face, not ugly or pretty but determined. Her jaw clamped shut, her nostrils flaring like a horse's, wide eyes a little wild. It made her lose her breath. The image belied her idea of who she'd been in Mexico; here was another version, a missing person, someone she wanted to meet. Her expression indicated a belief that the coordinated action of her feet and legs and arms kept the world spinning along its axis. Kept her world spinning. How lucky to have had that faith:

the unquestionable importance of one individual, a fancy hamster on a wheel.

"Did you see this?" She motioned to the picture, and he looked over her shoulder.

"I remember that one."

Her heart seized; maybe Ben had not taken the photo. Maybe Mike's memory came from behind the camera. He seemed to sense her unease.

"I've been through the box," Mike said.

She sank onto the bed and the mattress springs creaked.

"It's been so long," she said. "Why hasn't it gotten better?"

Mike touched her shoulder, briefly, the way a softball coach might remind the next batter of her turn.

"It will," he said.

"Tell me how," she said.

He still held the small plastic bag of crumbling pot in one hand, rolling it back and forth. "If you tell yourself a lie often enough, you start to believe it."

"It will get better," she said out loud.

He smiled and held out the bag. "We could smoke this."

"No," she said. "I haven't forgiven you. I'm still angry."

"It will get better," he mocked himself, solemnly. His blue eyes turned alert. "Can I ask you something?"

She waited.

"How bad was your life, because of me?" he asked. "I never wanted anyone to get hurt. You know that, right?"

She blinked. "I do now," she said, trying to sound neutral.

"Right," he said, his face hollow and gaunt. How healthy he had looked, how satiated, with a little extra weight. She kept hurting him, intentionally and unintentionally.

"Did I ever tell you I knew Ben before Mexico?" she asked, knowing she'd never breathed a word. Mike shook his head. This was her gift: to show him he was not alone in his covert ways, to help him understand why she couldn't—or wouldn't—see him back then, not the way he wanted to be seen.

"I was infatuated," she said. "I followed him around."

"Did he know?" Mike asked.

"No," she said. She touched the pillow briefly, lightly, before removing her hand. Carey wore shorts and a sweatshirt, and was aware of Mike's proximity, of the stubbled hair on her legs that he might brush against.

"What about all those times he cancelled plans?" she asked.

"Mostly me," Mike said. "Sometimes him."

She couldn't look away; Mike's glance might reveal whatever went unspoken.

"I know there were probably other girls," she said. "But I need to know if he ever talked about me. I mean did ever tell you about me."

Mike hesitated, careful with her request. He might tell her what she wanted to hear. It might coincide with the truth. Either would be a gift.

He exhaled slowly out his nose. "All the time, dummy," he said. "All the time. I wanted him to shut up, and I wanted him to go on. Glutton for punishment, I guess."

She returned the photograph to the top of the stack and the stack to the envelope and the envelope to the box. She didn't look at the rest of the pictures. They were either all of her or none of her. It couldn't matter anymore.

Then Mike was standing behind her, hugging her, and she faced him. She let herself be hugged. He kissed the part in her hair, twice, and her forehead, her eyes and cheeks, and it comforted her, like a blessing. Before reaching her lips, he stopped. His eyes were closed. In that pause, she knew he was giving her time. There was nothing left in her to make a decision, though now she knew: even passivity is a choice.

She laid a palm flat against his chest, pressure against his heartbeat. Pushing off him like a boat from a dock, turning, propelled from the room, down the creaking stairs, out into the yard. The motion detector set off the backyard light, so she stayed in the shadows on her way to the street, moving along a row of bushes. Seconds later, the motion-detector light went off next door, illuminating Mike in his t-shirt and shorts. He jogged to catch up, setting off the next house's lights as well.

"I'm still here," he yelled. She could tell by his voice that he was crying. "Carey!"

She could still smell—or remember the smell—the spicy pine scent, cologne and deodorant trapped in Ben's clothes, wafting from the cardboard box in his room. He was not the person she created in her mind, or the one Mike conjured with keystrokes. For years she'd tried to reconcile Ben's duplicity, using it to justify her own— the spying, the chat rooms, the space between who she was and how she presented herself. Ben had been covert, but not in the way she'd imagined. Her rationalizations dwindled to nothing, a piece of ash pushed along an alleyway, a speck of dust glimpsed in a shaft of light. Carey had indebted herself to Ben, and debts to the dead are binding. They're all that's left. Even regret is better than forgetting.

She was almost to the car. Mike had stopped beneath a sycamore tree, waiting.

"Carey? Can you see me? I'm still here."

"I know," she hissed across the dewy lawns. "So is he."

CHAPTER 20

HER MEMORY PLAYED AND PLAYED, but the picture always remained partial. How to account for what was forgotten, for all the things she had not given herself the room to remember? There were days and weeks in Mexico that, free of turmoil, had merged into nothingness.

That bright October morning when she watched Alicia's soccer game. After scoring a goal, Alicia immediately sought her out on the sidelines.

Carey had brought a bag of chocolate chips from home and made cookies, a novelty. The Alarcóns ate three dozen in one day. Hector grinned, chocolate on his teeth, and smiled wider as a joke when Lupe pointed it out.

The one day in class when she'd impressed the teacher with her pronunciation.

And something she'd scarcely thought of since: an afternoon at the private swimming club, possibly the one place in Guanajuato that didn't teeter on a cliff or sink into the valley. The pool provided the American students one free pass, and Carey took Alicia as her guest one warm Sunday in September.

Alicia sunbathed. Carey swam freestyle with long, slow strokes. Sometimes she porpoised underwater, her body moving like a tilde. Diving down to the pool's textured floor, resurfacing for air. Calm, suspended, weightless.

It wasn't long before she caught the flash of Alicia's magenta bathing suit from the corner of her eye. Carey stopped and raised her head, her feet finding the shallow end's floor. Alicia paddled around her in circles, trying to mimic Carey's movement.

Carey held her under the stomach with one forearm. Alicia splashed and giggled, still paddling, as Carey led her around the pool. "Use your arms," Carey instructed. "Los abrazos."

Alicia laughed harder, sputtering in the water. "Los *brazos*," Alicia cried. "No *ah*-brazos."

And Carey laughed, too. Use your hugs, she'd been telling Alicia, who embraced the water in great armfuls, shrieking with laughter. She was fifteen, Carey twenty-one; the water turned them into children. They hung on the pool edge and scissored their legs. A band of a half-dozen loud young boys entered through the gate. They were shirtless in baggy trunks, towels around their thin necks. Their chaperone, a teenage girl, settled into a webbed chair with a book.

"Hola Alicia, qué tal?" one boy asked.

"Alicia! Mira!" another commanded as he jumped into the pool.

Alicia waved to them. "They go to my old school," she told Carey. "They are only fifth graders."

They cannonballed into the water, splashing Carey and Alicia, who splashed them back. A blue rubber ball made the rounds as they played a game of keep-away. Carey couldn't keep track of her teammates, and relegated herself to the center.

"Not again!" she mocked herself in Spanish. The boys shouted over and over, Watch me! Watch me! And they would perform flips and handstands and other impressive aquatic feats. The sun glinted off their dark shining heads, their slippery young arms and legs.

Waterlogged, Alicia returned to sunbathing. Carey headed to the garden paths. She had changed into dry clothes, always a strange sensation after swimming, like growing a coat of fur. She tightened her shoelaces and set off. For as long as she'd been running, she would exercise through rain or illness. She felt fine that day, and her body could have gone for miles. But she stopped.

The garden air was heavy and quiet. She found a wrought-iron bench and sat down.

She wanted nothing. To look at a tree and think about a tree. To track a monarch butterfly's looping path for no greater purpose than the beauty of its movement. Something was growing in her, something without a name or an image. All she needed to do was be still. She welcomed the foreign feeling, which she did not know would disappear as soon as she returned to the Alarcón house, to classes, to the twisting paths Ben and Mike led her down. The paths she followed, running blind.

Maybe an hour later, Alicia hustled down the walk in her flip-flops, towel wrapped tightly around her small body. Her dried hair clung to her head like a cap. I was worried about you, she told Carey, who smiled, surprised. They'd go home for dinner, the chlorine still tart on their skin and hair. Any messages? Carey would ask Lupe, then settle into the couch to watch reruns on television. Carey's jiggling leg caused Alicia to place a hardback book on her knee to weigh her down. Alicia, collapsing with giggles, repeated, "Use your hugs." After everyone had gone to bed, Carey checked her email, disappointed by the empty inbox.

But first, that hour of stillness. She sat peacefully without thinking. The butterfly performed aerial tricks, loop-de-loops, smooth landings and take-offs on branches and flowers. Inside, a sensation in her chest mimicked that flight. She felt no loneliness. She settled into the comfortable exhaustion of swimming. This moment marked by a welcome absence: lack of want. She had what she needed. She was what she needed.

On the bush across from her, the butterfly alighted. The black and amber wings, like perfectly symmetrical modern art, opened and closed. Clapping.

CHAPTER 21

THE MAZDA'S WARM STEERING wheel felt pliant as taffy beneath Carey's hands. The cloth car seats rubbed against her legs, bare in running shorts. Perfect driving weather, flawless spring, the world cast in greens and blues. Soon she passed the giant pink plaster elephant with the martini glass in its curled trunk. On the county exchange route, her tires kicked up gravel.

Squares of soybean fields on one side, and perfectly aligned rows of young corn on the other. About a mile down the road stood an unassuming white house next to a brick church, both abutting a working farm.

The Williamson family plot took up a small square of earth. Thirty-some headstones lined end to end. A freshly-painted white picket fence around a country cemetery seemed like something out of a John Mellencamp video. An idea of Indiana rather than reality. No. A reality she had not seen.

Today was Ben's birthday.

Earlier that day at Oakview Mall, she had purchased a poster at the shop filled with preteens, which sold black lights and itching powder. She walked by Prisanti's. Glanced briefly at the young dough-tosser contained behind the glass, maybe somebody's Ben. A framed photo of Ben wearing a white apron still hung on the wall, next to a laminated copy of his obituary.

Mexico had its altars, its Day of the Dead in November, when relatives of the deceased brought food and liquor and flowers to the graves. Ben's grave bore no decoration aside from the mottled pink and gray headstone.

BENJAMIN CURTIS WILLIAMSON
April 28, 1972 - February 25, 1996
Beloved Son and Brother
Nunca Olvidado

Nunca Olvidado: Never Forgotten. Sun on smooth granite, winking off bits of rock glitter. Pockmarks like one or both dimples, depending on the smile.

Back in high school, a classmate Carey barely knew had died junior year in a car accident. The newspaper ran pictures of the crash site, where the girl's friends had left stuffed animals, necklaces, lip gloss tubes. Wasteful, Carey had thought, misunderstanding.

The living need to exhume the dead in memory. To bring them back to life with props. From her black shoulder bag, she removed a can of mango juice with its blue and orange Spanish-language label, which she'd purchased from the market near Casa Colmo. She unrolled the poster. In the tacky gift shop, she'd looked for one of Jim Morrison. They only had The Doors, and she picked a shot of the lead singer standing in front, bare-chested. She'd brought Scotch tape, which now seemed ludicrous: a Doors poster taped to a tombstone in a quiet country cemetery where Ben lay among his ancestors. She placed the cardboard tube on the ledge.

Next, the mix tape she made. Her father's computer had a CD burner she did not try to understand. She'd tried to replicate the song list Ben had created in his journal that day on the roof, improvising the music she lacked. Her father's jazz discs, tracks from Ben's CDs as well as her old ones—Indigo Girls, 1980s Madonna, The Beatles. Mexican pop, including some Cristian Castro. That little soccer player, the girl in a jersey, had compared Ben to the Mexican heartthrob. Ben wouldn't have listened to him. Carey still wished he could hear.

The gravel crunched as another vehicle approached. The black car, reflected in Ben's highly polished tombstone, drove on. She and Mike had not seen each other since the week before at the Williamson's house. They'd exchanged a few emails about the nonexistent progress in Ben's case, but that was all. Her fingers unclenched, and she popped the tape she made for Ben into her own Walkman.

Stretching out, the sweet damp grass pricked her bare legs. She lay slightly to the left of Ben's grave, on the grass. Not exactly on top. Pillowing her hands beneath her head. "Penny Lane" piped into her ears.

Ben's body was buried beneath her and to the right. There was no avoiding it. A coffin, human remains in a box, soil, worms. What happened to his eyeballs? His lips? She'd imagined and reimagined what death had done to Ben's body. Now, lying in the cemetery, she focused on the pink stone. The smell of earth and grass, soybean, the faint hint of manure. Blue sky with flat-bottomed white clouds. She saw whatever she wanted. The time Ben stole the tequila shot at the disco, jealous of Luis. She could imagine it was night, Ben flat on his back next to her, tracing a VW Beetle as if it were a constellation. Or the time on the rooftop, late afternoon, when he hovered over her and smiled. He'd said, God, I love...this.

This. The green grass wiggling beneath her legs as if alive. Eyes closed against the sun, regal music in her ears. She could be anyone, anywhere. She just happened to be here now. The movie in her mind jumped ahead accordingly. Somewhere on the other side of town, Juan and Elena were preparing a package for their parents in Dolores Hidalgo: an envelope of cash, Oreo cookies, Polaroids of the shiny bar top Roberto was installing in the restaurant. Carey had made no promises. But the Morales siblings, ever optimistic, said in unison, Just in case.

Yesterday, the travel agent had offered Carey two days to decide; after that, he couldn't guarantee the fare. She thought of the picture Ben had taken surreptitiously while she ran along the streets of Guanajuato, a girl she barely recognized. She thought of the Alarcóns, and their walled-in house opened wide for her. And she thought, of course, of Ben. Unceasingly and without censor. Carey didn't need two days to decide. She was buying time, making room on her credit cards. Rearranging the debt.

Carey slept. She dreamt of a rickety bus, a driver named Cesár. She couldn't see his face. He drove along flat roads instead of hills and mountains. The bus was full of students. Everyone faced forward in his or her seat. Ben and Mike sat silently in front of her, though they hadn't been on the bus from Mexico City to Guanajuato. She asked Cesár to show her the Sleeping Woman, the purple-shaded volcano, and he shook his head. Instead he drove them down an Indiana two-lane highway that bisected farm fields: on the right, beans tied to tall poles; on the left, thousands of metallic pinwheels blowing in the breeze, filling a field.

When she woke, the cassette had ended. She returned the tape to its plastic case and set it on the tombstone ledge.

Back in the car, driving along the county extension, she felt empty and light. She had gone to the cemetery to honor Ben. It had taken her too long to visit Ben's parents, and then his grave, but she thought Ben would've appreciated her visit. That he was somewhere in the universe, "Penny Lane" jangling in his head, posing like the shirtless Jim Morrison while he ogled her bare legs. The thought made her laugh, though her stomach muscles' contracting was more like a spasm. Ben, in the poses of a young man; Ben, who forever would be a young man. Carey would turn twenty-nine in two weeks. By the day, she grew too old for Ben. The gap would only widen. She hunched over the wheel, tears clouding her vision, and soon she sobbed. The car as claustrophobic as she imagined a coffin would be. He could be sitting in her passenger seat if not for timing, if not for their mistakes, hers and the ones he owned.

She pulled over by a dry cleaner's on the main drag. Left the Mazda unlocked and the keys in the ignition. She would carry nothing.

She was unprepared. Her hair pulled back messily in a tortoiseshell clip, no sports bra, sockless in running shoes. The same shoes the vendor had tried to buy from her at Mercado Hidalgo years ago, dusty with age. But her feet cared nothing of blisters. They wanted to run.

Down the few short blocks of storefronts, parked across the street in front of the drugstore, was a black sedan with Wisconsin plates. Of course it had been Mike at the cemetery. For a brief moment, she loved him. For finding her. For leaving her alone. They needed each other without knowing why. Mike sat inside on a lunch counter stool and waved. She held up one palm. She meant to tell him hello, back off, wait. She'd learn his response, or she wouldn't.

She jogged along the residential section, muscles complaining. But her body remembered. A mile, three miles, once seemed like nothing. Now she wondered how far she could go. She turned down street after street, racking up blocks. Long, paint-peeling ranch homes crouched next to old Victorians in garish reds and purples. Her feet pounded on wide cement sidewalks. She ran down the middle of empty neighborhood streets. The wind dried her eyes. She used the sweat on her forehead to slick back her hair, strands falling freely from the clip.

She moved surely despite her long rest. She was slower. Her hips felt unoiled, inflexible. Hers was still a familiar body, just changed. Running meant no curtain, no stage, no film projector on endless playback. Just a body and its path. No equipment besides shoes, not even a ball to chase, that elusive bit of leather rolling out of reach. Running left her alone with herself, a place she'd avoided for too long.

She exited the neighborhood and picked up speed along the open stretch of road between fields. The two-lane highway had no shoulder, so she ran on the edge of the white line, steady as a gymnast on a balance beam. A blue Ford pickup, the only car for miles, slowed to pass her. The elderly driver, a man in a green mesh baseball cap, nodded hello. Then the truck vanished behind her. The asphalt stretched out, a flat black ribbon dotted with fresh yellow paint. Perhaps more cars or houses or barns popped up down the line. Pastures filled with dairy cows, a field growing nothing but metallic pinwheels glinting in the sun. Perhaps not.

This was where the world disappeared: right in front of her. She kept going.

ACKNOWLEDGMENTS

Thank you:

Victoria Barrett and Engine Books believed in this novel and labored to get it out in the world. My thanks seem somehow not enough, but I offer them anyway, many times over.

To my parents, John and Terri Layden, for their unflagging faith and encouragement, and my sister, Katie Layden Robbins, first friend, ally and copy editor extraordinaire. I thank my in-laws, Eileen and Sam LaMarca and Patricia Murphy, for their constant caring and support.

I owe a great deal to the faculty of Purdue University's English department, where I first worked on this novel as an MFA thesis: Porter Shreve, Patricia Henley, Sharon Solwitz, Charles Wyatt, and Emily Allen. Brilliant, kind, and witty professors all.

Gratitude abounds for my MFA classmates, in particular Barney Haney, Sarah White, and Cassander Smith. Your thoughtfulness and honesty are ingrained in me.

To Michael Martone and Cathy Day, Hoosier ambassadors to the world.

Thanks to the Indiana University Honors Program in Foreign Languages, which gives high school students the chance to study abroad for a summer. The families and friends I met in San Luis Potosí, Mexico were warm, welcoming people; the experience remains rich in my memory. My English and Spanish teachers in high school and college fueled my love of language and culture, and any translation errors in the text are a failing on my part, not theirs.

My journalism professors at Syracuse University and my former newspaper colleagues at *The Post-Standard* provided daily opportunities to observe, report, write, and edit. Each day we got the chance to try again, and if that's not a life lesson, what is?

To friends who became readers and offered great feedback: Katie and Doug King, Charlotte Shoulders, Jennifer Murphy, and Danielle Bethke. The true believers.

Special thanks for the editorial guidance of Barb Shoup, Mark Latta, Bryan Furuness, B.J. Hollars, Margaret McMullan, Linda Oblack, and Sarah Jacobi.

Andrew Scott and Victoria Barrett motivated me when they published an excerpt from this novel in *Freight Stories* many years ago. Thanks, too, to Angela Craig, editor of the *Dia de los Muertos* anthology, and the editors of *Cantaraville*, where chapters of the book appear in slightly different form.

The students and faculty at IUPUI energize, challenge, and inspire me. Each day I am glad for the opportunity to learn, converse, and write in the English Department community.

To the Miller family: Bert, Don, Braden, and Adrianne. Readers, adventurers, dear friends, beautiful souls. I am lucky to know you.

Finally, my immense thanks and love to Tom Murphy, who never gave up, and our sons, Trevor and Brendan. You are my home.

ABOUT THE AUTHOR

SARAH LAYDEN is the winner of the Allen and Nirelle Galson Prize for fiction and an AWP Intro Award. Her short fiction can be found in *Stone Canoe, Blackbird, Artful Dodge, The Evansville Review, Booth, PANK,* the anthology *Sudden Flash Youth,* and elsewhere. A two-time Society of Professional Journalists award winner, her recent essays, interviews and articles have appeared in *Ladies' Home Journal, The Writer's Chronicle, NUVO,* and *The Humanist.* She is a lecturer in the Writing Program at Indiana University-Purdue University Indianapolis, and also teaches at the Indiana Writers Center.

author photo by Eric Learned